THE CIRCLE EIGHT

MATTHEW

THE CIRCLE EIGHT

MATTHEW

EMMA LANG

BRAVA

KENSINGTON PUBLISHING CORP.

www.kensingtonbooks.com

BRAVA BOOKS are published by

Kensington Publishing Corp.
119 West 40th Street
New York, NY 10018

All Kensington titles, imprints and distributed lines are available at special quantity discounts for bulk purchases for sales promotion, premiums, fund-raising, educational or institutional use.

Special book excerpts or customized printings can also be created to fit specific needs. For details, write or phone the office of the Kensington Special Sales Manager: Kensington Publishing Corp., 119 West 40th Street, New York, NY 10018. Attn. Special Sales Department. Phone: 1-800-221-2647.

Brava and the B logo are Reg. U.S. Pat. & TM Off.

ISBN-13:978-0-7582-6904-1
ISBN-10: 0-7582-6904-8

First Kensington Trade Paperback Printing: February 2012

10 9 8 7 6 5 4 3 2 1

Printed in the United States of America

PROLOGUE

March 1836

The back of Matthew Graham's neck prickled, the little hairs standing up like tiny soldiers. He turned his head slowly to look around without appearing as though he was. His instincts told him something wasn't right and he had learned to trust those instincts.

"Matt, what's wrong?" His brother Caleb stepped up beside him on the wood-planked sidewalk. The gentle early spring breeze ruffled his chocolate brown hair under his battered hat.

"Dunno." Matthew didn't notice anything out of the ordinary in town. It looked as it always did—like a small town in eastern Texas. Nothing seemed out of place, yet he knew something was.

His other brothers and sisters were gathered around the front of the mercantile. Two of his sisters, Olivia and Elizabeth, played checkers while the youngest, Catherine, sat on Livy's lap. Rebecca and Nicholas played marbles in the dirt.

Matthew had performed a supply trip every Saturday for the last four years, always bringing the brood with him to give his parents time alone. Today had been no different, until now.

"Go see what's keeping Joseph with the nails. We need

to get home." Matthew didn't wait to see if Caleb did as he was bade. The Graham children fought and competed daily, but when they needed to, they closed ranks and became a formidable force.

"Livy." He caught his sister's attention. She glanced up at him, her blue eyes alert. "Get 'em ready."

Again, she didn't question his order, she just acted. If only that could happen daily instead of once in a blue moon. They were all in the wagon within ten minutes, which at any other time would have been an incredible feat. Today it was nine minutes too long.

All of them seemed to sense Matthew's urgency because their usual banter, bickering, and general noise were tucked away. The two-hour ride back to the ranch grew tenser with each passing minute.

His parents were home alone with five-year-old Benjamin, the youngest of the Grahams' eight siblings. Even their cook Eva Vasquez, and her two sons, Javier and Lorenzo, were gone until tomorrow. Matthew could not have explained his urgency if anyone had asked him.

He just knew he had to get home.

The first sign something was wrong was the smoke. It curled into the bright blue sky like a black snake. Matthew's heart ceased beating for a second, then it pounded harder than the horses' hooves.

He snapped the reins, standing up in the wagon to shout at the team. "Hiya, boys, hiya!" Sweat ran into his eyes and his arm muscles ached as he controlled the two racing bays. Dirt and rocks kicked up by their hooves stung his skin, but he didn't pay them any attention.

The younger children started crying and clung to Olivia. Caleb held on to the seat beside him with a tight jaw and panic in his gaze.

No one spoke even as Matthew drove the team at breakneck speed. The clouds of smoke billowed higher and his throat grew tighter. He could see the fire was near his mother's garden.

Their ranch was only six hundred acres, enough to make a living raising cattle, but just barely. Any loss would be devastating, and a fire could be catastrophic. He prayed it was just a small fire.

But then he saw the front porch of the house.

And his mother's body lying in the dirt beside it.

CHAPTER ONE

May 1836

Matthew rose before the sun, finding his way outside into the gray pre-dawn light. He walked as silently as the air around him, his early morning sojourn a habit born of necessity.

It was the only time of the day he could find quiet.

The noise of his brothers and sisters constantly rang in his ears. There was no way to escape all of them except when they were sleeping. Matt had taken to getting up at four-thirty each day to go for a ride. At first he was so sleepy he nearly fell out of the saddle, but now it had become a pleasure he never missed, even during bad weather.

As he entered the barn, he picked up a bridle from a nail on the wall. The tinkle of the metal was met with a soft whinny from the last stall. His gelding, Winston, was a quarter horse with a crooked blaze down his nose. His parents had given the animal to Matt for his twelfth birthday. Although Winston was at least fifteen years old, he was a good, solid ranch horse.

Matt stepped into Winston's stall and the horse immediately pushed his head toward him, sniffing at his coat pockets.

"Easy, boy. I've got something for you, just don't tell Olivia or she'll have my hide." He spoke low and soft, careful not to disturb any of the other horses or livestock. Matt pulled a cloth from his pocket and poured a half cup of sugar into his hand. Winston lapped at the sweet treat until every last morsel was gone. Matt had to push his mouth away. "That's it, boy."

The quarter horse seemed reluctant to stop, but smacked his lips as Matt saddled him quickly. Their routine was as familiar as breathing, and within ten minutes, Matt walked the gelding outside into the cool early morning air.

He took a deep breath and then another. They rode their standard route, stopping only for Winston to take a drink in a nearby creek. Matt found that he needed this time alone more and more. Each passing day reminded him of their difficult situation, how much responsibility he'd had to take on, and how heavily it weighed on his shoulders.

Their ranch wasn't as big as others, but was large enough to get lost in for an hour each morning. The sun was turning the sky pink when he started back toward home.

When he returned, the lights in the house were on, and he knew the rest of the Grahams were stirring. Life on a ranch started early every day. Although their lives had taken a hard right turn two months ago, chores still needed to be done. After he took care of Winston, he walked toward the house with slower steps than when he'd left. As he reached the door, Matt took a deep breath and stepped in.

"You have to go claim it." Olivia crossed her arms and glared at Matt, her blue gaze cold as an icicle. "Pa would have wanted us to get those acres. He wanted this ranch to be something."

Sometimes Matt wished he didn't have siblings. Like today. The seven of them were in the kitchen sitting at the enormous table their father had built after Matthew was born. It was their standard meeting place when they discussed family business. Unfortunately, this wasn't a discussion. It was a flat out argument.

Lately all they seemed to do was bicker, fight, and argue everything to death. Matthew wanted to *do* something, not just talk about it until his ears bled.

Pa had intended to claim four thousand acres offered by the Republic of Texas to residents. It was going to make their little six hundred acre ranch six times bigger. He knew it had been Pa's dream to create a legacy for his children, but his murder had turned that dream to ashes.

Now the burden fell on Matt to decide what to do. Of course, the rest of the Graham children thought they had to tell him exactly how they felt about the decision. For days, even weeks on end. As much as he loved them, his siblings were driving him loco. His father had usually taken his side, but circumstances had taken his father instead.

"Elizabeth, take Catherine and Rebecca outside to play." Matthew didn't need the younger girls clouding the issue. They didn't understand and were still recovering from the loss of their parents.

"I don't want to go outside." At nine Rebecca could be incredibly stubborn. She pouted her lip and flung her caramel colored braids back over her shoulders.

"That's too bad because you're going anyway." He gave them his best big brother glare and Rebecca sniffled dramatically.

Little Catherine rose and took her sister's hands. She was a peacemaker like Mama had been, although Benjamin's disappearance had affected her deeply. Sometimes he heard her at night talking to Benjamin although their five-year-old brother had not been found in the two months since their parents' deaths.

"Let's go play." She was the only blonde girl in the family, the others having varying shades of brown hair. Rebecca and Elizabeth both walked out haughtily, but they went outside as he ordered.

"You know, they have every right to be here." Nicholas was fifteen and had an opinion about everything. He and Olivia were his biggest problems in that regard.

"Right now I don't need the little ones here. They're not going to help." Matthew sipped at his coffee which was now cold.

"They're Grahams, too." Olivia sat beside her brother, staring him down.

"Right now we don't need to fight. We need to agree on something." Matthew's heart still ached at the way he'd been thrust into the role of parent. At twenty-five, he was too young to be responsible for his entire family and their ranch, but he accepted the role. He loved his family and the Circle Eight.

"Matt's right." Caleb was seventeen, the third oldest in the family. He had wavy dark brown hair and his father's brown eyes. "Let's stop fighting and start talking."

"I've been trying to do that all morning," Olivia said harshly. She had been bitter ever since she'd spurned her young man. Just when she needed his understanding most, the fool had tried to make her leave the ranch and forget about the unsolved murders of her parents.

Matthew was secretly glad the man had been tossed out on his ass, literally, by him and his brothers. He thought perhaps her bruised heart had closed in on itself after that. She was harder than she'd ever been, rarely giving an inch, and her smile had become a rarity.

"We have the papers Pa had ready to claim the acres. Now you just need to go to Houston and file them. You're the oldest Graham now and you're an adult." She pointed at him. "I don't see what there is to argue about."

"Four thousand acres is six times the size of what we have now. Lorenzo and Javier are crack hands, but even so we don't have enough men to handle that much land." Matthew's fingers tightened on his cup. He wanted to roar at the unfairness of their situation, to run screaming into the field and let loose the grief he had locked away inside.

"Then we claim it and add cattle as we can. If we ride the line to check on the land every week, we can do it." Caleb shrugged. "I think Pa wouldn't want us to miss our chance to take it because we were scared."

"I'm not scared. I'm practical." Matthew felt stung by his brother's reversal.

"Practical is okay, but we need to do what's right." Nicholas fiddled with the rest of his biscuit, the crumbs littering his plate.

This decision would affect all the siblings and their families for generations. It wasn't to be made lightly and the weight of it forced almost all the air out of Matthew. He considered everything his brothers and sister had said, and realized they were right. He was scared. But he had to get past that. This family was everything to him, and if he made the wrong decision, they'd all suffer. He was practical enough to know that he, his brothers and their two ranch hands could take care of four thousand acres. Caleb's idea to build slowly was a good one.

Thoughts whirled around in Matthew's head until he slammed his fist on the table, startling everyone. He closed his eyes and took a deep breath. The only thought left in his head was, *what would Pa do?*

"I'm going to Houston."

Caleb and Nicholas smiled while Olivia nodded at him. The Grahams were going to take a chance.

Houston was so much larger than he had expected. Matthew felt like an ant on a hill. There were so many people he could hardly walk down the street without bumping into someone. Olivia had stayed behind to take care of the ranch, but Nicholas accompanied Matthew. They were both goggle-eyed at the big city.

They had found the land grant office after a few wrong turns, then waited for nearly two hours before the name "Graham" was called. Matthew wouldn't admit it to Nicholas, but a passel of frogs were currently jumping in his stomach.

The man behind the desk was bald with round spectacles. He was also plump, and if Matthew had to venture a guess, the fellow hadn't done a lick of hard labor in his life. His pasty white hands thumbed through their papers. With each passing moment, Matthew thought he might lose his breakfast. To his surprise, Nicholas appeared calm, even studying the stranger with curiosity.

"Your father died then, did he?" The man peered at them through his thick spectacles.

"Yes, sir, Mr. Prentiss. He died in March. I'm twenty-five and control the ranch and property now." Matthew managed to swallow the lump in his throat. He was not comfortable in a place like this, in a situation like this. Put him on a horse and he was unstoppable, but here he felt useless.

"Of course you do. I'm sure you're doing a fine job, too." He picked up his pen and dipped it in the inkwell. "Just tell me the name of your wife and we can finalize the land claim."

Time seemed to stand still as the dust particles floated in midair in the small office. Matthew managed not to sound like a complete idiot although he had to choke back the word that immediately danced on his tongue. *Wife?*

"You need my wife's name?" His voice sounded far away to his ears.

"Yes, we do, Mr. Graham. This land grant is for a family. That includes a husband and wife, current and future children. Now I realize the children are your brothers and sisters, so we'll overlook that particular. All we need is your wife's name for the deed." His pen was poised atop the paper.

Matthew knew if he lied, he would be putting his family and the ranch in jeopardy. If he didn't lie, they would lose the land grant they were entitled to. It was an untenable position, and he only had seconds to decide what to do.

"Hannah. Her name is Hannah." He managed a weak smile.

Nicholas started in the chair next to him, but blessedly kept his mouth quiet. Thank God Matt hadn't brought Livy or Caleb. They'd likely have called him on the lie— he couldn't lie worth a damn.

"Fine then. I'll just write her name down here." Mr. Prentiss fussed a bit more with the papers, then looked up at Matt again. "Is your wife here in Houston with you?"

"Uh, no, she stayed home to help take care of the children." The lies were just rolling off his tongue now. His mother would have taken a switch to him.

"I see. Well, because you seem like honest boys and have had such a tragedy in your lives, I will grant you a thirty-day extension." He stacked the papers neatly. "Until then I will hold your land for you."

Matt had no idea what the man was talking about. "What is an extension?"

"It means that within the next thirty days, you must bring your wife with you to Houston to sign the papers. It doesn't matter if she doesn't know how to write; an X will do just fine. I can't turn over the grant until then." Mr. Prentiss pushed up his glasses with one pudgy finger. "I hope you understand, Mr. Graham."

Oh, he understood all right. He had just lied to a Texas

official, to the *law,* and now he had thirty days to find a wife named Hannah or they would lose their land grant.

His family would tan his hide.

"What do you mean, you lied?" Caleb looked more shocked than anyone. "You never lie."

Matthew continued taking the saddle off his horse as his brother hopped around like grease on a hot griddle. It was time to be calm because if anyone knew how many knots his stomach was in, there'd be no end to the dramatics.

"I had to." Matthew stopped and stared at the three of them, Olivia, Caleb, and Nicholas. "Nick was there. He'll tell you I'm right. If I wasn't married, then we wouldn't get the land."

"All right, you lied to them. What happens now?" Olivia got the words out through gritted teeth. Matthew noted she had started to put her hair in a bun like Mama used to, making her look forty instead of nineteen.

"He has to find a wife in thirty days and her name has to be Hannah." The words jumped out of Nicholas's mouth so fast and loud, Matt actually winced.

"What?" Olivia's hands clenched into fists. "Are you plumb loco, Matt? How are you going to find a wife in thirty days and one named Hannah to boot? There is no one in this county who would marry you. You're ornery, a liar, and bad company." Her cheeks flushed as red as the sunset behind her. "You've just cost us that land."

Matt endured his sister's insults even though he wanted to yell right back at her. She was plenty ornery herself.

"Matt did what he had to." Nicholas took the blanket off his own horse. "I almost believed him when he told the man he had a wife named Hannah."

"Yes, but he doesn't." Caleb slapped his hat on his leg, a cloud of dust rising from the worn trousers.

"What if you buy a wife? I heard tell of folks getting a

mail-order woman to marry 'em." Nicholas started currying the horse as the bay placidly munched on feed.

"No time. I have to be there in thirty days and no woman in her right mind would move to Texas to live on a small ranch with the six of you. I sure as hell wouldn't." Matthew couldn't count on finding a wife in a newspaper advertisement, much less one willing to take on an entire family.

"I wouldn't either, but unfortunately we don't have a choice, do we?" Olivia stomped out of the barn. He could almost see the waves of fury coming off her body.

"Livy sure likes to be mad at me. It helps keep things normal for her." Matt took off his hat and wiped his brow. "I am in a pickle though, and it's of my own making."

"What are you going to do?" Caleb frowned at him.

Matthew leaned against the stable door. "I don't have much of a choice. I'm going to find a wife named Hannah in thirty days."

CHAPTER TWO

Hannah Foley hated doing dishes. There was no worse chore, in her opinion, than scrubbing greasy food off plates and forks. She hated the feel of it, the way her fingers pruned up, and especially the way her back ached after standing at the sink for an hour. There were more dishes to wash at a boardinghouse than a regular household, which made it even worse.

She wiped her forehead on her sleeve and tried to focus on one dish at a time, rather than the mound still waiting for her attention. It would be nice if there was someone to help her, but with Granny's arthritis, and no money to pay any help, it was up to Hannah alone.

Sometimes while she washed dishes, she imagined being somewhere and someone else. It was a little game of "what if" she played with herself. Of course she never told Granny about it—she didn't want her to think she wasn't grateful for the place to live and food to eat. Orphans couldn't exactly be choosy.

She had one particular daydream that recurred each time she allowed her mind to drift. She was at a picnic by the river in town, and she was dressed in a lovely new blue dress and pretty new shoes. Her hair was braided and the sun shone on its hidden red and gold strands. Her large family surrounded her, but she was also with a beau, a handsome man with a big smile and a booming laugh. Around them she heard the sounds of the water gurgling in a nearby stream, her family laughing and chatting, but most of all, she heard the beating of her heart. And she felt peace and happiness.

A silly daydream of course. At twenty-three, she wasn't the youngest or even remotely the prettiest girl in town. There weren't likely going to be any beaus, since there hadn't been any yet. No, she would live at the boarding-house with Granny and that would be that.

Her silly heart, however, could not help but keep bring-ing the daydream back at every opportunity. Some days she didn't like being a woman at all. Truthfully, she knew she wasn't very attractive. Hannah was what her granny called "sturdy." The word made her wince, but she couldn't deny it described her.

She had thick brown hair that she could barely wrangle into a braid, mud brown eyes, big breasts, and a plumpness to her behind she was unsuccessful at wishing away. Plain as toast for sure. There were many other pretty girls in town worthy of a beau or even multiple beaus, but not Hannah.

She wasn't bitter about it, just wishful. That darned heart of hers had a mind of its own. Perhaps one day she could ignore those daydreams about a family, a man, a future other than chapped hands and serving strangers.

A realization hit her with the force of a mule kick. Han-nah stopped so suddenly, she splashed water all over her chest. She had been wallowing in self-pity, like some crazy old spinster. That was not what she wanted, ever.

She had a good life, and she was grateful for it. This silly behavior had to stop. There were things she could change and things she couldn't. Her looks and her family were set in stone; her attitude was not.

Hannah knew she'd given herself a brain slap and was glad for it. Somebody had to, might as well be her.

After tamping down on her mental meanderings, she finished the dishes and moved on to the task of making a stew for dinner.

"Hannah?" her grandmother called from the parlor.

"Yes, Granny?" Hannah's hands were covered with the flour she was currently rolling the stew meat in. She hoped her grandmother didn't need anything immediately.

"I need you."

Hannah blew out a breath so hard her hair moved off her forehead. "Can it wait about ten minutes? I'm fixing the stew."

There was a brief pause. "I s'pose."

Hannah's chin fell to her chest and she counted to ten. Twice. "I'll be right there."

She cleaned her hands as best she could on the rag and headed into the parlor. Granny had bad pain in her joints and sometimes needed help getting up from bed and chairs. She was a tough old bird though, insisted on making the beds and tidying every day. Hannah worried Granny was doing too much, but there was no one else to do it, and there was only so much Hannah could do with the time she had.

Within a year, Granny might not be able to do anything, which would leave all the work to Hannah. They'd have to close off half of the eight rooms they rented to folks in the huge house her great-grandfather had built. It would mean their income would be cut in half, and they barely made ends meet as it was. Hannah dismissed the thought for now. There was nothing she could do and fussing about it would do her no good.

Hannah walked into the parlor and found Granny on her knees beside the settee. Panic coursed through her as she raced toward her grandmother.

"What happened? Are you all right?" She crouched down

and peered at Granny's face. "Did you break anything? How did you fall?"

"For pity's sake, child, stop your caterwauling." Granny flapped her hand in the air as if Hannah were a pesky fly. "I dropped my needle while I was doing some darning. I picked it up but couldn't quite make it back onto my seat. Now you can help me."

Granny wasn't a small woman, but she was smaller than Hannah. In fact, when she lifted her grandmother up by the armpits, she was shocked to find just how light the older woman had become. It was as if old age was stealing her body inch by inch, turning her into a shell of the robust woman she had been.

"Have you been eating?"

"Not as much as I should." Granny let out a sigh of relief when her behind connected with the settee cushion. "My stomach's been feeling poorly for a while now. I eat enough to get by and it ain't like I'm gonna starve to death. We Foleys are bred to survive and built to have babies." She turned a frown on Hannah. "Speaking of which . . ."

"Do we have to talk about this again?" Hannah wanted to run from the house, heck from the entire town, rather than talk about her lack of a husband *again*. It had become a nearly daily conversation with Granny, and she was tired of it. Bad enough her own heart kept returning again and again to a fantasy it could never have.

"Don't sass me, child. I raised you better than that." Sometimes Granny still treated her as a seven-year-old orphan.

"I'm not a child, Granny. I am a grown woman and if I don't want to talk about my obvious lack of a husband, then I damn well won't." Hannah almost slapped her hand across her mouth for not only backtalking but cussing, too.

Yet she didn't. It was time she stopped hiding behind a sink full of dirty dishes.

Granny smiled at her and wagged her finger. "Now you sound like me."

They both broke out laughing and Hannah sat down beside her, pulling her grandmother into a hug.

A surge of love and concern for Granny flooded through Hannah. Her grandmother was getting old—heck, she *was* old at sixty-two, which meant she would be getting sick more often. They couldn't afford a doctor and that meant Granny wouldn't even tell Hannah if she felt sick.

Shaking off her disturbing thoughts, Hannah got to her feet. "Everything okay now?"

"Pshaw. On with you now, young'un. You'd better get to making that stew or we won't eat dinner until supper."

Hannah went back to the kitchen, shaking her head and hoping she was that much of a curmudgeon at sixty-two.

Making the stew brought some order back into her scattered thoughts. She cut up the carrots and onions, then pulled out the sack of turnips from the pantry.

"Damn." The curse was under her breath so she wouldn't have to endure any reprimand.

There were only three turnips to feed twelve people. Hannah vaguely remembered telling herself to get more at the store, but she had forgotten to add it to her list. And now she didn't have enough to make dinner for everyone. She had a little bit of time, perhaps a half hour, to get to the store and then get back.

Hannah dried her hands quickly, then took off her apron. "I'm going to the store, Granny. Be right back." Luckily she had a dollar in her reticule, which she grabbed from beneath the sink.

As she headed out the door, she tripped and fell down the two steps, landing squarely on her knees in a mud puddle. She cursed again, this time a bit more loudly, then got to her feet and looked down at her mud-spattered skirt.

It wasn't her best garment, but it had been clean. Until now. She would change later. For now she'd just have to endure people staring and possibly pointing at her. It wasn't the ideal situation but there was no help for it.

She hurried down the street, nodding at folks who glanced her way. Who cared if she had flour on her blouse, mud on her skirt, and a grimace on her face? It had already been a bit of an unlucky day for her. Things couldn't possibly get any worse.

Matthew stared at the collection of rifles for sale. He had his father's to use, and had given his old one to Nicholas, but Caleb needed a gun. They were so doggone expensive though. He didn't want to choose between food and a weapon, although with a rifle he could get food.

It was Saturday again, and he'd had three days to mull over the pickle he was in. So far, he hadn't come up with any solution other than finding a wife named Hannah in the next twenty-seven days. Easier said than done. Most of the women in town were married, and the ones who weren't were either too young or too old. And he didn't know of one named Hannah who wasn't married.

The bell over the door to the store tinkled and he heard a muffled curse, then a slam. Matthew peered around the display to see Caleb sprawled on the floor while a woman bent over with her hand outstretched to help him up.

"I don't need no help," his little brother snapped.

"I'm sorry about that, mister. I'm in a bit of a hurry." Her voice was like whiskey, husky and rich. The sound of it intrigued him.

He must have made a noise because she straightened up and his gaze locked with hers. His first thought was that she was plain as prairie wheat; brown hair, brown mud on her skirt, with a round bosom to match her round behind.

Yet she had that voice. He still felt a tingle from it.

With a nod, she stepped around Caleb, who was just getting to his feet. "Stupid cow."

"Caleb. Apologize to the lady."

"I don't see no lady." Caleb stuck out his lip like a five-year-old.

"What you will see is my fist when you get knocked on your ass again." Matt towered over him. "Now apologize."

"Sorry." The word was flung without grace or sincerity.

Matt met the woman's gaze again. She shrugged and turned away, but not before he saw a glimmer of pain in the depths of her eyes.

He should just go about his business and not worry about a woman he didn't know. Yet something told him to make peace with her. It was what his mother would have wanted. That thought alone made his feet move.

Matt found her by the turnips, empty sack in hand.

"Excuse me, ma'am?" He was surprised to see her start. "I didn't mean to scare you."

"You didn't. I'm just, well, never mind. It's been a bad day." She didn't even look up from examining the vegetables.

It gave him the opportunity to study her. She smelled of flour and fresh bread, with just a hint of onions. Her hands were long-fingered and although she obviously worked with them, they were elegant. Her skirt had mud on it and was as plain as the potato sack in her hand.

Her hair, which looked like light brown from far away, had bits of gold and red in it. Curls were stuffed into a fat braid that swung with each movement. He wondered what that hair would feel like in his hands.

Matt almost choked on his own spit. First her voice woke up his body into imaginings, and now his imagination was getting into the act. What he needed to do was stop thinking about this stranger and focus on his more immediate problem with the land grant.

"I just wanted to apologize for my brother."

"Don't fuss over it. He's a boy." She had the sack half full by then, picking turnips faster with each word out of his mouth.

Matt reached out and took her wrist to stop her, wanting to explain why Caleb acted so foolish. He never got the chance. A jolt of something like lightning raced through him, hitting him square in the stomach. He dropped her arm and jumped back a foot, much to his embarrassment.

She stared at him, her brown gaze wide. "What was that?"

"I have no idea."

"Why did you touch me?" She clutched the potato sack to her chest and inched her way toward the counter.

"I don't know. I was trying to apologize."

"You already did that." She bumped into the counter, never taking her gaze off him.

"I know. I'm sorry." He was tripping over his own tongue, trying to figure out what the hell was wrong with him.

She put a dollar on the counter. "I only got half a sack, Frank. I'll be back tomorrow for the other half."

With that, she almost flew out the window, like a muddy brown bird running from an eagle who had threatened her.

Matt wanted to slap his forehead. He didn't have a huge amount of experience with women, but he had some. Enough to know he had just acted like a bigger jackass than Caleb.

Frank, the mercantile owner with eyebrows that had a life of their own, eyeballed him with a frown. "What did you say to Hannah to make her run like that?"

A second jolt of lightning smashed into him. "Did you say her name was Hannah?"

"Yes, you young fool. Hannah Foley is one of my best customers. Doesn't usually come in on Saturday and you done run her off." Frank wagged his finger at Matt. "You had no call to be rude to her."

"I wasn't rude. Jesus, did you say her name was Hannah?" He surely sounded like a young fool.

"Are you deaf, boy? I done told you that already." Frank leaned forward. "Are you teched in the head or somethin'?"

Matt shook his head. "No, just a huge fool. Is she new in town?"

"She's lived here all her life at the boardinghouse with her granny. You and your kin are the new ones in town." Frank humphed.

"I really didn't mean to scare her. I was just trying to apologize." Matt knew he might have just made another big mistake by letting Hannah leave the store. Not only did she have the right name, but there was a bizarre connection between them.

He turned and glared at Caleb, who was back to staring at the rifles. "I ought to kick your ass six ways to Sunday."

Caleb's eyes widened at the ferocity in Matt's tone. "What did I do?"

"You just insulted my future wife."

CHAPTER THREE

Hannah walked as fast as she could with the sack of turnips clutched in her hands. Something had happened at the mercantile and she had no idea what. There was a man there and *something had happened*.

Her stomach jumped as if a dozen frogs had taken up residence in it. If she wasn't walking so fast, her knees would be knocking. Her experience with handsome men could fit into a thimble, and she had just met the most beautiful man she'd ever seen.

Nothing about him was ordinary, including his incredible blue-green eyes, strong jaw, and wide shoulders. She'd never forget his hands. When he'd touched her wrist, it was as if something had traveled between them, making every small hair on her body stand up. She was sure he'd felt it, too.

It was extraordinary.

Hannah refused to let her imagination loose, but it was damn hard. For the first time in her life, something romantic had happened to her. Muddy, disheveled, and so very plain, she had caught his attention. What did it mean? She should talk to Granny about it, but first she wanted to relive every moment as she cut up the turnips.

This time, her fantasy wasn't something she made up. Hannah had a real man to daydream about. Hannah wanted to chide herself for dwelling on the handsome blue-eyed man. Perhaps if there hadn't been an instant spark between them it would have been easy to dismiss him, but there had been and so she couldn't.

"Hannah, what are you doing?" Granny's voice yanked her out of her reverie like a bucket of cold water.

"What?" She looked down and realized she was standing in the kitchen clutching the potato sack while the stew bubbled merrily on the stove.

"It looks like you're touched in the head, child." Granny's cane thumped on the wooden floor as she walked toward the small table and chairs. "I've been calling you the last five minutes."

Hannah's cheeks heated. "I'm sorry. I had to go buy turnips at the general store and I, uh, was wool-gathering a bit."

With more fervor than necessary, she got busy washing more turnips for the stew. She cut them into smaller pieces since they should have been in the pot thirty minutes ago. Granny sat there, staring a hole in Hannah's back until she was about ready to scream.

"Why are you staring at me?" she finally asked, keeping her voice as steady as she could.

"I'm trying to puzzle out what is wrong with you." Granny was too observant.

"There's nothing wrong with *me*. But lots of other things have gone wrong today." Just then the knife slipped and she sliced open her thumb. "Dammit to hell."

"Hannah Josephine Foley! Who taught you how to cuss?" Granny had shot to her feet, her face flushed, her jowels swinging with each word, her finger wagging. "I ought to wash your mouth out with soap."

"I'm not a little girl. I can cuss if I want to." Hannah was embarrassed to have cursed in front of her grandmother, but her thumb pulsed with pain. She wrapped a towel around it and held her arm up. For a time about five years ago, the town doctor had lived at the boardinghouse and he taught Hannah a lot about taking care of wounds and sickness. She'd had dreams of marrying him, but he was thirty and a widower. Within six months there were more young women buzzing around the boardinghouse than flies. He'd been married by the end of the year, leaving Hannah with nothing but some medical knowledge. It did prove useful though. She knew the bleeding would stop faster if she applied pressure to the cut.

"Not in this house you won't." Granny had moved on to true anger.

Hannah moved right along with her. "Then maybe I won't live here anymore."

"Where do you think you're going?" Granny thumped her cane hard this time. "You have a beau I don't know about?"

Granny was too close to the mark for Hannah's comfort. She had met a man, or sort of met a man, this morning, and perhaps he was the beau she had been dreaming of. Granny's tone assured her the older woman was being as sarcastic as she could be.

"Now you're just being mean, Granny. I don't need a feeble old widow like you cutting me down." With that, she stomped out the back door.

The air outside felt good on her skin, which was sweaty from the heat of the stew and her own emotions. She plopped down on an upended log and tried to calm herself. Her heart raced with the events of the day, culminating in yelling at her grandmother. The woman who'd raised her and loved her. The woman who was probably too hurt to follow Hannah out the door to demand an apology.

They had both been unkind to each other, but Hannah was definitely meaner. She had actually called her granny old and feeble. Completely true, but remarks more fitting to a harridan than a granddaughter. Hannah sighed and pressed her forehead against her arm. What a mess she'd made of things.

"I'm sorry, child." Granny appeared on the steps. "I didn't know."

Hannah stared at the ground. "Know what?"

"That you had met a beau. I didn't mean nothing by what I said. Just an old woman mouthing off like an old fool." She shook her head, one gray curl bouncing in the breeze.

Hannah's laugh was more like a strangled chuckle. "I didn't meet a beau. I met a man who made me act like a fool. I could hardly speak to the fellow." She finally met her grandmother's gaze, and saw understanding clearly shining in her wise eyes.

"That's what we do. Act like fools around them until they get up the nerve to come courting." Granny waved at her. "Come on back in and let's take a look at your thumb. And we can talk about your young man."

"He's not my young man." Hannah got to her feet and almost dragged herself toward the back door. Granny would ask so many questions she didn't want to answer, or perhaps couldn't answer. It would be awkward, but it was also exactly what she'd been hoping for. Someone to talk to who would understand and maybe give her the advice she needed.

One thing she did know. Something had happened and she owed it to herself to find out what.

After wrapping her thumb in a strip of cloth, she got all the turnips in the stew. Within twenty minutes, she'd started the gravy with some fat from the meat. The work gave her time to stop thinking about everything. Granny hummed as she snapped peas from her perch at the table. Things felt normal again.

Matthew had paced outside the boardinghouse for a good thirty minutes before Olivia found him. She put her hands on her hips and narrowed her gaze. The afternoon sun cast a shadow beneath the rim of her bonnet so he couldn't see just how annoyed she was. Good thing, too.

"What are you doing? We've been looking for you." She tapped her foot, raising a cloud of dust with each movement of her boot.

The last thing he needed was Livy sticking her nose into his business again. She needed to let him be head of the household without following him around like an angry hen. He wanted to talk to this Hannah Foley.

And he needed to do it on his own or not at all.

"Go back and make sure the young'uns are all doing what they're supposed to."

"You cannot talk to me like that, Matthew Bodine Graham." She pinched her lips together so tight, they were nearly bloodless.

"Yes, I can, Olivia Mae Graham. I run this family and make the decisions that best suit everyone." He gave her a hard stare. "Now go back to the store and make sure everyone does what they're told."

"But—"

"No, I'm done talking, Livy. This is important." He pointed. "Go."

She glared at him, letting him know he would hear all about how unhappy she was later. She was strong like Mama, but unlike their mother, Livy did not want to listen to what anyone else had to say. After she turned and stomped away, he turned and strode up the steps of the boardinghouse.

The paint on the door was peeling, but the porch was

well-swept and tidy with four rocking chairs, which were also showing wear. He swallowed and knocked on the door.

Voices sounded from within, two females if he wasn't mistaken, and they were getting louder by the second. The door was flung open and Hannah stood there with a surprised expression.

And a big glob of gravy on her cheek.

"Good morning, Miss Foley, my name is Matthew Graham. I, uh, hope you don't mind me dropping by like this." He tried not to sound like a stuttering fool, but his tongue had other ideas. "I, uh, did I interrupt something, Miss Foley?"

"No. I was making—oh never mind." She flapped her hand, which reminded him of a small bird. "Why are you here?" Her cheeks colored and she slapped her hand across her mouth. When her fingers came in contact with the gravy, she pulled her hand away to look. Her eyes widened.

"Oh shit."

With that, she disappeared into the house and slammed the door behind her.

He stared at the door, blinking and trying to figure out what had just happened. When he heard a wail from inside, he knew he needed to follow her in. This was a boardinghouse so it wasn't as if he was walking into someone's private home. Strangers walked in all the time. Besides he had introduced himself so he wasn't a stranger anymore.

"Miss Foley?" He opened the door and poked his head in. Voices echoed from deeper in the house, but no one answered him. Matt stepped in and left the door open behind him.

The house was neat as a pin, but everything he could see was very worn. The upholstery on the chairs was a bit tattered, the wood floors dull and scuffed by years of use.

However it was the smell of cooking food that hit him the hardest. It was the most heavenly scent he'd smelled for quite some time. If he wasn't mistaken, it was stew or pot roast.

"Miss Foley?"

He walked deeper into the house, following a hallway toward the voices. And the smell.

"I can't believe that just happened, Granny. Not only am I perspiring, but I have grease, flour, and gravy on me. On my face!" It was Miss Foley, talking to her grandmother obviously. "Never in my life have I been so embarrassed."

"Ain't no never mind, Hannah. Done is done." The older woman's voice was gravelly and rough.

"Yes, I know. Done." Miss Foley sounded so defeated, it pinched at his conscience. After all, he'd been the one to show up on her doorstep without being invited. He owed her an apology.

Matt cleared his throat and shuffled his feet as he approached the open door to what he assumed was the kitchen. "Miss Foley?" Complete silence met his words. When he finally stepped into the kitchen, both women were staring at him.

Miss Foley's face was even redder and the older woman, a gray-haired version of her granddaughter, chuckled when she saw him.

"Well, ain't that a hoot." She slapped her knee, spilling a bowl of snap peas across the table.

"Granny!" Miss Foley exclaimed, but kept her gaze on him. He realized in the bright sunlight of the kitchen that her brown eyes weren't a singular color. They had shades of amber and whiskey in them.

He shook himself mentally to stop forgetting why he was there. Miss Foley didn't have to be pretty or smart or a good cook, she just had to be willing to marry him. If she happened to be any of those things, too, well, so much the better.

Matt took off his hat and nodded at the older woman. "Ma'am my name is Matthew Graham. I'm pleased to make your acquaintance."

"Just call me Granny Foley, Matthew. Everybody does." She snorted another laugh, while her granddaughter shot her daggers from her eyes.

"Why are you in my kitchen? I mean, I'm sorry, Mr. Graham. I don't understand why you're here, and I really don't know why you came into the house." Her voice sounded all breathy and even huskier than before. It sent a line of chill bumps down his back.

"If we can sit down, I will explain." Of course, he didn't know how he would explain what he was doing. It was a fool's errand but he was fast running out of time.

"Sit down, child." Granny pulled out one of the mismatched chairs. "Let the man speak." She gestured to the other chair and winked at him.

Winked! Oh boy, now he really had to contend with something. Granny Foley obviously thought he was there as a beau. This situation just kept getting stickier.

After they all sat, Matt realized just how difficult it would be to explain his proposal.

"I don't know if you knew my parents, Granny, but we own a ranch about an hour outside town. Stuart and Meredith Graham?"

Granny nodded. "I remember them a bit. Nice folks, lots of young'uns."

"Yes, ma'am, there are eight of us."

She leaned forward and peered at him, and the sharpness of her gaze was not lost on him. "Something bad happened back a piece, didn't it?"

This time he had to swallow the lump in his throat. Twice. "My parents were murdered and my youngest brother, Benjamin, disappeared."

"Cryin' shame that is. Why would anyone kill good folks like that? And steal a boy? Sounds like Injuns to me." Granny shook her head. "You young'uns are running the ranch then?"

"Yes, ma'am. We have a couple of ranch hands too and our housekeeper, Eva. I'm the oldest, so I take care of the business end of things." He glanced at Miss Foley, who was staring at him with her hands clasped in her lap. "We, uh, that is, my father had applied for the land grant from Texas. It's six thousand acres to every resident."

"Six thousand? I can't even imagine how big that is." The younger woman finally spoke again.

"Miss Foley, it's as far as the eye can see, and then some. It's going to make our ranch ten times its original size."

"Hannah." Her voice had slid down into a near whisper.

"Pardon?" He leaned toward her and got a whiff of her scent again.

"My name is Hannah." She caught her lip with her teeth. They were straight and white, contrasting sharply with the dark pink of her lips.

Matt told himself to stop acting stupid.

"Hannah." The name fit her perfectly, slightly feminine but strong. "My Pa didn't have a chance to claim the land grant before he died. I went to Houston to claim it, but it seems there's a requirement I don't meet."

"Spit it out, boy." Granny was obviously not shy.

"I, uh, need to be married. The wording on the land grant means the Graham who claims it must be married." He let that piece of information sink in before speaking again. "While I was in the land grant office, I did something I shouldn't have and now I'm, well, truly stuck between a rock and a hard place."

"What did you do?" Hannah leaned forward, her whiskey eyes wide.

"I told them I was already married." He paused and couldn't even muster up enough spit to swallow. "And that my wife's name was Hannah."

The only sound in the room was the burbling of whatever smelled so good on the stove. Granny's gaze narrowed while Hannah's eyes just kept growing wider.

"And you're here because my Hannah isn't married and you need a wife named Hannah to get your land." The older woman's tone was not very warm.

"I didn't want there to be any misunderstanding about my intentions." He turned to Hannah. "I can offer you a good home, a faithful marriage, and a promise that I'll always take care of you the best I can." There, he'd finally gotten it all out. Funny thing was, he didn't feel any better.

"A-are you asking me to *marry* you?" Hannah's mouth was slightly open.

"Yes, yes I am." He slid off the chair and onto one knee. "I know you don't know me from the next person. Please don't say no right away. Take a week to get to know me before you make a decision." He took her hand, ignoring the rush of lightning that again hit him as soon as they touched. "Please."

She stared at him, her hand trembling in his. "I, uh . . ." Hannah glanced at her grandmother while he waited, his stomach somewhere near his throat. "Okay."

"Okay, you'll take a week to get to know me?" Now his voice sounded almost as breathy as hers.

She shook her head. "No, okay, I'll marry you."

There was a rushing sound in his ears as he realized he'd found a woman named Hannah, one he was already attracted to, *and* she was a good cook. Best of all, she'd agreed to marry him. A surge of joy hit him and he leaned forward and kissed her hard.

He didn't know who was more surprised, he or Hannah.

She put her fingers to her lips while he sat back in his chair. The silence hung between them, low and heavy.

"I guess we're having a weddin'," Granny cackled merrily from her perch.

Matthew managed to make it back to the store without making a fool of himself, but his knees were still knocking an hour later. He'd actually asked a stranger to marry him, invited her into his home, to share his name and likely have children with him.

His stomach turned over once, then twice, leaving a coating of bile in the back of his throat.

Olivia waited by the wagon, fussing over the younger ones like baby chicks, as was her way. She didn't bother to look at Matt, but started to shoo the Graham brood onto the wagon. He knew she'd seen him and that she was still fuming about his dismissal thirty minutes earlier.

Now he would have to deal with her wrath. He had a moment to wonder what it would be like when Hannah moved in and had to fight for control of the house with his sister. No doubt it would be more than interesting. Hannah seemed a bit shy, but she also appeared to be strong. All she had to do was stand up to Livy and she'd be all right.

Matt nodded to Caleb, who stood next to the wagon smoking a cheroot. "Let's go."

The ride back to the ranch was quiet except for the melodic voice of Rebecca reading a story in the back of the wagon. Livy rode between him and Caleb, speaking not a word, her ramrod straight back never bending even a smidge.

Her silence was okay by Matt since it gave him time to think about what he had done and what was in store for him in a week's time. He'd first have to tell everyone about Hannah, and that included Eva and her sons. It gave them only one week to ready the house for a wedding and a new mistress.

It also meant he would have to move into his parents' bedroom. He'd avoided it since their deaths, but he couldn't expect Hannah to sleep on a narrow bed in the same room with Nick and Caleb. That left the biggest bedroom, which stood empty, full of ghosts and memories.

It was a chore he had put off as long as possible. Who wanted to go through the things that had belonged to their parents? It was a weakness he'd tried to overcome but hadn't been able to. Neither had Livy or Caleb for that matter. The room had become a sanctuary of sorts, an area they didn't go into for fear they'd lose something, or perhaps destroy the memories of their parents.

It was silly to think or feel that way, but there it was. He didn't know how to deal with losing his parents so abruptly and violently. So he avoided thinking about it at all. There were so many other things to occupy his mind, after all. Excuses, of course.

Perhaps marrying Hannah would let him confront the painful task of letting his parents go.

Hannah was not a small girl, thank God, so perhaps his mother's things would fit her. Most of the Graham children had taken after their father in height and slenderness, except Rebecca and Catherine. Matt knew his mother would approve of someone like Hannah wearing her clothes. She'd always altered clothes for the next sibling down, eeking out every last possible use from a garment before it was cut up into rags to be used for cleaning. Very rarely was anything thrown away.

They were within ten minutes of the house when Livy finally decided to speak.

"Are you going to tell me why you acted like such a jackass?" Olivia demanded.

"I wasn't acting like a jackass." Matt kept his temper under control. He wouldn't give her the satisfaction of seeing that she had riled him. "I was acting like the head of the family."

"Humph. That'll be the day."

He turned to look at her. "Whether or not you like it, I am head of this family. Ma and Pa are gone and I'm the oldest. Sometimes you might not like what I have to say or do, but that's just too bad."

Her brows drew together as he spoke, forming a brown caterpillar of annoyance. "I won't accept that."

"Find yourself a husband then."

Caleb snickered while Nicholas sucked in a breath. Livy punched him in the arm. Hard.

"Now don't start something you can't finish, sis." His arm smarted from her knuckles.

"I'll finish it, all right. You can't tell me what to do, and that's that."

Matt's sleeping temper rose and he pulled on the reins, stopping the wagon in the middle of the road. He turned to her. "No, you are wrong, Livy. I do have the right. I have to make hard decisions and our family can't turn into an ant hill of insanity every time I do. I just asked a perfect stranger to marry me for this family. Don't think for a second you have the right to do whatever you want. I certainly don't have that right and neither do you."

The only sounds were the drone of bees nearby and the occasional chirp of a bird. Olivia's mouth had fallen open. Everyone else stared at him with wide eyes.

"What did you say?" Livy whispered.

"You heard me. I found myself a wife." He leveled a fierce stare at all of them. "Now shut up until we get home and I'll tell you about her."

To his surprise, they did just that. He sat back to enjoy the minutes of peace before they reached home. The next week, hell, the next month, would be a whirlwind of chaos.

★   ★   ★

Hannah's hands shook so hard, she burned herself three times just trying to get the biscuits out of the oven. The day had started so badly, and now it seemed as though she had stepped into a dream, or perhaps a nightmare.

A man she barely knew had asked to marry her. He was handsome, had a ranch and nice teeth. Yet the only reason he wanted to marry her was to make his ranch bigger and to hide his own lie.

It wasn't an especially good start to a marriage, by any stretch of the imagination. She should have said no, for that matter, she shouldn't have even listened to what he had to say. He'd had the audacity to walk into the boardinghouse without being invited. But she hadn't said no; instead, she had agreed to marry him.

What was wrong with her? Was she that desperate for a husband she'd accept a total stranger? *Something* had compelled her to accept his sideways proposal and she didn't know what.

Granny had gone upstairs to take a nap, so Hannah was left alone with her whirling thoughts. Hours later, she poured herself a cup of coffee and sat down heavily in the chair to watch the setting sun paint the back of the kitchen shades of orange and pink.

He'd kissed her. That was what was running through her mind over and over, even more than the impending marriage. It was her first kiss, such as it was, though of course he couldn't know that. His lips were soft but firm, and she tasted a bit of sweetness like he'd been eating a peppermint.

She had stopped breathing for a moment afterward, dumbstruck by not only the kiss, but the idea that she would be married in one week's time.

Married!

Aside from changing the course of her life irrevocably, the agreement meant Hannah would be leaving the boardinghouse and Granny. That didn't sit too well with her. It was a dark cloud on what could be a bright horizon. She couldn't leave her grandmother alone to run the boardinghouse, which left her two choices. One, they must hire someone to cook and clean, which they couldn't afford. Two, Granny must close the boardinghouse, which would leave her with no income. Either option would be tough.

She sipped the bitter brew and thought about how selfish she had been not to have considered how her leaving would affect Granny. For the last ten years, Hannah had been the one running the boardinghouse. Her grandmother socialized with the boarders, kept them happy and collected their rent. Hannah did everything else.

As the reality of her decision hit her, Hannah knew she'd made the wrong choice. No matter how handsome or appealing Matthew was, he was not more important than Granny. She would have to tell him she couldn't marry him. The thought made her heart pinch, but it had to be done.

"Don't you think about changing your mind, child." Granny's voice made her jump a country mile.

"How did you—" She stared at her grandmother, amazed by the woman's perceptiveness.

"Now that you've had time to think about it, you remembered the boardinghouse." Granny pointed at her with one bony finger. "Don't you dare be giving up this chance for a husband and family because of it."

Hannah opened her mouth to refute the accusation, but closed it, knowing Granny was absolutely right. This was her chance and obviously she was meant to have it, but that didn't make it any easier to contemplate Granny's fate. She refused to put her own happiness in front of her grandmother's entirely.

"What will you do?"

Granny shrugged. "I'm too old to run this place anyway.

Have been for some time. You been running it, child. It's high time I sell it and live out my days watching sunsets and sunrises. Been thinking about doing that for a while now but I didn't know what you would do. Now God saw fit to solve both problems."

Hannah had never considered that her grandmother wanted to sell the boardinghouse. What a strange twist of fate to have Matthew Graham need a wife named Hannah, and Hannah needing a way to fulfill her fondest wish for a family of her own.

"Then I guess I'm getting married."

Granny grinned and pulled her into a robust hug. "Then we'd best get busy selling this house and making you a weddin' dress."

Hannah was scared to death.

CHAPTER FOUR

The day of the wedding dawned full of clouds with a misty rain in the air. The steel gray of the sky loomed overhead as Hannah and her grandmother walked toward the church. She wore Granny's old shoes, the ones she'd worn at her own wedding fifty years earlier. They were old, dusty, and a little too small, but they were better than clumpy boots, the only footwear Hannah had.

Hannah had thought she wouldn't be nervous, but she was. With each footstep, her stomach twisted tighter. She was about to be married! For the last few years, that had seemed like an impossible dream. The unreality of the situation was not lost on her.

She felt like a different person, and she wore a pretty dress for the occasion. It was light blue, made from Granny's own wedding dress as well. Fitting because it was borrowed, old, and blue, if they were to follow the rhyme. Granny was a genius with a sewing needle and, within four days, had altered the dress to fit Hannah's rounder, shorter figure.

For the first time in her life, Hannah felt pretty. Too bad she also felt like she wanted to vomit.

They were to meet the groom at ten o'clock at the small church and although it was only nine thirty, they headed over. Sometimes the cold weather made it difficult for

Granny to walk and Hannah didn't want her grandmother to have to rush. That could lead to an injury, the very last thing they needed.

Hannah had actually spent time fixing her hair that morning, another unusual occurrence. She normally put it in a braid or in a knot and never thought twice about it. Of course, she had wasted her time attempting to look pretty, for the rain had already turned her hair into a mass of kinky curls. It had been the first time she'd tried ironing it, too. She hoped her new husband didn't notice the burn mark on her neck.

The door to the church was slightly ajar. Perhaps the preacher was already there, waiting or preparing for the ceremony. Matthew had told her he would make the arrangements. She hadn't heard anything from him except a cryptic note three days earlier to meet him at the church at ten.

That time had almost arrived.

"Stop pinching my arm, child." Granny pulled her to a stop. "There's no need to be scared. He's a good man."

"I'm not scared, Granny. I'm, um, well, I'm not scared." Her stomach told another story, but she wasn't about to admit it. "I'm just worried is all. Nobody's bought the boardinghouse yet."

"That fella from Eagle Creek might. He came back twice already. Said he was gonna bring his missus next week." Granny waved her free hand in dismissal. "I ain't worried, so you don't need to be."

"But I—"

"We're done jawing about it." The older woman started walking again and Hannah had no choice but to keep up. "You are trying to slow down time and it won't work."

Was that what she was doing? Trying to hold onto her maiden status just a few minutes longer? Granny was probably right. Hannah held her head high and straightened her shoulders. At least she could maintain her dignity and show her new husband just how much of a lady she was.

She pulled the church door open and held it for Granny. When they stepped inside the gloom of the foyer, the church was totally silent. Then as Hannah walked into the light, she realized that although it was quiet, the church was not empty by any means.

There were seven of them, all standing together at the altar. The tallest was Matthew, but there were two other young men beside him, and four girls. Hannah recognized the oldest girl from long ago when she had attended school, but couldn't remember her name. They were all of varying sizes, some with brown straight hair, some with brown wavy hair, even one with blond hair. Their eyes, however, were very similar, all shades of the same bluish green, all blinking at her like a family of owls.

Hannah's heart slammed into her throat and she couldn't have made a sound if she'd tried. Granny must have sensed Hannah's panic and the old woman saved her again.

"Well, howdy. I didn't know we'd have a passel of folks here." Granny stepped forward, peering at each of them in turn. "I'm Martha Dolan. You can call me Granny. This here is my granddaughter, Hannah Foley."

Hannah was able to catch her breath and murmur a hello. Not a great first impression to make with her new family, but there it was.

"She's tall." The smallest of the bunch, a blond-haired girl, peered up at Hannah. "Almost as tall as Matt."

Matt. It suited him better than Matthew. One was formal while the other matched him, at least what she knew of him. She felt as if she'd stepped back in time and had an arranged marriage. But instead of the marriage being arranged by their parents, they'd done it themselves. Many marriages still started out that way, where the bride and groom barely knew each other.

"Hush now, Catherine. Let me introduce you proper." Matt nodded at Hannah. "Miss Foley, Mrs. Dolan, may I present Olivia, Caleb, Nicholas, Elizabeth, Rebecca, and Catherine Graham." Each sibling in turn either nodded or curtseyed toward them. They were obviously a well mannered family.

"It's very nice to meet you all." Hannah winced to hear how breathy she sounded. "I knew you had a big family but didn't realize how big." She smiled shakily at Olivia. "I remember you from Miss Green's classroom when I was seven."

Olivia's brows drew together. "Now that you mention it, yes, I do remember you. You left after that year, didn't you?"

The memory of not going back to school hit Hannah. Her parents had died of a fever within two days of each other, leaving Hannah an orphan, and in her grandmother's care. It was the darkest time of her life, one she was sorry she had brought up.

"I did, that's right." Hannah turned her attention to Matthew, trying to close the door on her ancient pain. "Is the preacher here?"

"Uh, not yet. We got here early."

"We had to get up before the sun," the young girl said. "That was really eeeearly. I had to eat in the wagon, and I dropped a piece of my biscuit." She looked very unhappy about that biscuit.

"Catherine, hush up," Olivia snapped. "Miss Foley doesn't need to hear any of that from you."

"Don't tell her to hush up." Another sister, possibly Rebecca, stuck her chin up in the air.

"Don't think you can just do whatever you please." Olivia put her hands on her hips. "I am still—"

"Enough." Matt's hand cut through the air. "Now is not the time for bickering." He turned his gaze to Hannah and in the depths of his pretty eyes, she saw exhaustion and stress. "Can I talk to you?"

Hannah's heart did a little flip. She wondered if he'd changed his mind before they even saw the preacher. It wasn't as if she would blame him for changing his mind, but oh, how it would hurt.

He took her elbow lightly, leading her toward the back of the small church and away from the big ears of his family. Granny started talking to the Grahams, distracting them so Hannah and Matt could speak privately.

He stopped in the shadowy corner by the door. After blowing out a breath, he took off his hat and met her gaze. "I just want to make sure you still want to marry me. I wouldn't blame you if you didn't. I surprised you and now that you've had a week to think about it, I thought you might have changed your mind."

She looked at him in astonishment. He thought *she* might change her mind? The very idea almost made her laugh but she kept it inside through sheer force of will.

"No, I haven't changed my mind." She clasped her hands together so he wouldn't see them shaking.

"What about your grandmother?"

Hannah blinked. "What about her?"

"Will she want to live with us at the ranch?"

"Um, I'm not sure. All the boarders moved out this week, but we need to sell the boardinghouse. There is no way she can run it without me. Then she has to decide what she wants to do." She and Granny had talked about it each night, speculating what she might want to do.

"We have a housekeeper and cook, Eva, but she's lonely, always talking about visiting in town with other women." He spun his hat on his hand. "I just wanted to tell you your granny is welcome to live with us. We can find room for her."

At that very moment, Hannah fell a little in love with

Matt. He had worried about her grandmother, which told her a lot about his character. She smiled at him, the first genuine smile she'd felt since meeting him.

"That's very kind of you. I think she might accept." She glanced at her grandmother, knee deep in little girls. "Granny loves to tell stories and be around young'uns."

"There's plenty of those around the ranch." He put his hat back on his head and held out his arm.

Matt might be a cowboy but he was a gentleman. Hannah nestled her arm in his and took the first step toward her new life.

Matt had never felt so out of control in his life. Hannah and her grandmother weren't making him nervous; his stomach was. He was about to marry someone and spend the rest of his life with her, and he didn't even know her middle name. It was loco and the stupidest thing he'd ever done, yet he wasn't going to stop now. He'd made sure she was still going to go through with it and that reassurance was all he needed. It was too important to his family that he go through with this quick marriage.

Too bad nobody had told his stomach. He hoped he didn't embarrass himself and vomit all over his intended.

The preacher appeared through the back door, scowling at all of them. They were being loud, as always, but most of them were crowded around Mrs. Dolan as she spun a yarn about a chicken and a full moon.

"This is a house of God, children. You must show the proper respect." Reverend Beechum was not his favorite person. In fact, Matt had never liked him, and neither had his father. They didn't go to church much because of the gray-haired bible-thumper. He made children feel like sinners if they lied about sneaking a cookie, but he was the only preacher in town. That left Matt with no choice.

The children hushed up, frightened by the preacher's

surly visage. Matt felt Hannah tighten up beside him and he didn't blame her a whit. This church was not a happy place.

"Mr. Graham, do you have my fee?" Another reason Matt didn't want to be here. They were paying the man *five* dollars to perform a marriage ceremony. It stuck in Matt's craw to even give the man the time of day, much less a chunk of their money. However, he handed it over, albeit grudgingly.

"Excellent." The money disappeared into the voluminous trousers the preacher wore. "Now, are we ready to begin?"

Matt swallowed the huge lump in his throat. "Yes, we are."

He stepped forward with Hannah at his side and knew the course of his life had just taken a sharp right turn. He was stepping into his future.

The preacher spoke his words quickly, a simple ceremony that could have been done by a judge. The only time the man showed a glimmer of emotion was when Matt told him he didn't have a ring.

"No ring?" His disapproval was almost palpable.

"No, sir. I didn't have money for one." He turned to Hannah. "I promise I'll get you one someday."

She shook her head. "I don't mind waiting. It's okay."

Matt was lying to both his new wife and the obnoxious minister marrying them. He had a ring—his mother's. She'd hardly worn it because she did so much work with her hands that she was always afraid of losing it. The ring sat in a small pouch in the chest of drawers her husband had made for her, beneath the clothes she'd never wear again. Matt had found it when he had cleaned their room.

He had stared at the ring in his palm, knowing he should give it to Hannah. It was what his mother would have wanted, but he couldn't do it. The ring was now safely tucked away beneath his own clothes in the chest of drawers in his parents' room, the room that was now his.

"It's not proper, but I understand the need to conserve funds with so many children in the family." The preacher made it sound as if having children was a bad idea. Didn't the church promote being fruitful?

"Ain't nothing wrong with lots of young'uns," Granny piped up. Matt decided he really liked Martha. If she were a man, he'd say she had brass balls.

With a disapproving look at the older woman, the preacher finished the ceremony within a minute or two. "I now pronounce you man and wife."

Without preamble, he led them to a table in the corner to sign the marriage certificate. Matt had forgotten to ask Hannah if she could write, and was glad to see her sign her name, even if it was with a shaking hand.

"Congratulations, Mr. Graham. Mrs. Graham. Now if you'll excuse me, I have other duties to attend to."

Reverend Beechum herded all of them out of the church and they found themselves outside in the rain, the door firmly shut behind them.

"He didn't do the kiss the bride part." Catherine always had something to say. "Does that mean you're not married?"

Matt looked at his new wife and saw a glint of amusement in her gaze. "No, we're married, sprite. True and proper."

He was about to ask Hannah if she wanted to head back to the ranch after dinner when the heavens opened up and the mist turned into a downpour. The young ones squealed while the older ones scrambled to cover everyone up.

"Let's head to the boardinghouse. We can get dry there." Hannah took Catherine's and Rebecca's hands and started running, heedless of the rain or the mud.

He scooped up Granny, who squealed in his ear, and ran after his new wife.

"Jehoshaphat, boy! What in tarnation are you doing?"

Matt didn't bother to see if the rest of his siblings followed. Either they did or they would spend the afternoon in the rain without shelter. It took only minutes to reach the boardinghouse but he was soaking wet by the time he arrived.

Hannah had left the door open, and he skimmed in sideways with the older woman still hooting in his arms. Giggling echoed from the kitchen so he followed the sound. He found the girls sitting at the table and Hannah handing them each a towel.

She glanced up at him, then at her grandmother. A smile spread across her face and a laugh burst from her. It wasn't a little tinkling laugh, but a full-fledged belly laugh. Matt was so surprised by the way she looked and sounded, he stopped in his tracks.

Hannah was lovely.

"Well, put me down then, young man. I need a towel, too."

Matt broke out of his momentary stupor and managed to get Mrs. Dolan into a chair without dropping her. It really had been the strangest day and it still wasn't over yet. In fact, it had only just begun.

The rest of his family tromped in, dripping and complaining. Hannah handled the situation with a quiet grace, handing out dry towels and rags, even arranging the shoes by the stove to dry. After stoking up the fire, she put on a pot of coffee. She obviously worked hard at the boardinghouse—not a big surprise—but he was amazed by how well she did it all.

"You don't have to serve us." Matt stood by the back door, watching her flit around like a bumblebee in a field of flowers.

"I'm used to it," was her only response.

The young ones took to her right away. Catherine in

particular seemed to be attached to Hannah's hip. She missed Mama the most and her new sister-in-law represented a mother figure. Besides, Hannah was obviously comfortable in the kitchen and accommodating of big groups of people. Even if she wasn't being as social as his mother had been, she made everyone feel at ease by taking care of them.

He noted she hadn't taken care of herself. She still wore her wet clothes and shoes. Her hair hung in kinky curls, framing her face, making the paleness of her skin that much more prominent.

During all the hubbub, Livy was the only one who stood apart. She didn't take off her shoes and only accepted a small rag to wipe her face. Matt's sister was not happy about the marriage and he would try to find out why later. For now he'd have to ignore her unfriendly behavior and hope Hannah didn't take it personally.

They were, after all, family now, for better or for worse.

Hannah had gotten everyone comfortable and warm. The kitchen was cozy with so many folks gathered around. It was different from the boarders, these folks weren't there for ten minutes of food only to run off again. Her relationships with the former residents of the building had always been cordial, but a little impersonal. She was almost glad of the rain since it gave her a chance to meet the Grahams in the comfort of her home.

She'd spent countless hours in the last week wondering what Matt's family would be like. They'd surprised her and scared her. Olivia was seething with dislike or annoyance, she couldn't tell which. The younger three girls, however, were charming children. So bright and full of life. Hannah thought perhaps she would feel better about moving to the Graham ranch now that she'd met them.

Matt's brothers eyed her with curiosity, but kept their

distance. They accepted coffee and spent their time mur-
muring to each other. She didn't sense bad intentions from
them, more curiosity than anything.

She tried not to pay attention to Matt though. He
watched her as she worked, making her more nervous than
she already was. Hannah knew if she looked at him, it
would only make her nervousness worse.

Thunder rumbled in the distance, bringing all conversation to a stop.

"Damn." Matt's soft curse sounded loud in the quiet
room.

"Does that mean we're stuck here?" Elizabeth appeared
to be about twelve, and she seemed to take care of Catherine and Rebecca well.

"Yes, at least until the storm passes. We can't be out in
the wagon if there's lightning." Matt snagged Hannah's
gaze. "I know we've already invaded your house."

Hannah gave a nervous chuckle. "It's Granny's house,
not mine. Besides we're used to feeding at least eight
boarders at a time." She shrugged. "You're welcome to stay
here as long as you like."

"We don't want to put you out." Matt's brows drew
together. "Besides, Eva was planning on a big feast for
supper."

She knew Eva was their housekeeper and cook. Another
person Hannah was nervous about meeting. No woman
liked another moving into her territory. It would be a relationship that would take time, of that she was certain.

"If it's thundering outside, she won't expect you."
Granny slurped her coffee noisily.

"Do you think?" Matt glanced outside. "She'd started
making bread this morning before we left."

"I met Eva a few times, knew your Mama, too. Eva can
put the bread up and keep the supper for tomorrow."
Granny belched more loudly than her slurp. The young

girls giggled. "Excuse me y'all. Things don't work right much anymore."

Hannah felt her cheeks heat. Granny kept on drinking her coffee. Next thing, she'd probably fart.

"We've got plenty of food and rooms for everyone." Hannah realized she could spend her wedding night here, in her own bed, rather than at the Graham ranch. Once she thought of the possibility, she couldn't get it out of her head.

"I don't think the storm will last that long." Olivia finally spoke. "I certainly don't plan on staying here all night."

Matt frowned in her direction, then turned to Hannah. "I appreciate the offer. Let's just wait and see what happens." He nodded at his brother, Caleb. "Stay here and make sure they behave."

Before Hannah knew it, he'd taken her by the elbow and led her to the front of the house with a lantern in hand from the kitchen. The parlor was empty now; the boarders had been gone for a couple days. Matt gestured to the settee and Hannah perched on the edge. When he sat across from her in a chair, she felt herself relax a little.

"I wanted to talk to you alone without our families stirring things up." He rested his elbows on his knees and captured her gaze.

Lord above, the man was handsome as sin.

The ghost of whiskers had started to appear on his cheeks and chin. His eyes looked very green in the meager light of the parlor. She found herself falling into their depths. His scent surrounded her, a combination of man and clean soap. Quite heady.

"I know this marriage isn't starting in the best circumstances. I just wanted to say thank you." He held her gaze while she digested what he'd just said.

Thank you? That's what he wanted to say?

It felt like a slap. She wanted to be insulted and tell him to go to hell, but she didn't. Hannah had no illusions this was a marriage of love. He had been honest with her when he'd proposed. She really had no right to react emotionally.

Yet her heart could not be convinced otherwise.

"You're welcome, Matthew. I, um, hope I won't disappoint you." She didn't want him to have illusions either. "Believe it or not, I don't have a lot of experience with men." She wanted to look away, but she didn't. If this marriage was going to have a chance, she had to be herself.

To her relief, he smiled. "Disappoint me? I don't think that will ever happen."

"I won't hold you to that."

He chuffed a laugh. "You have a sense of humor."

She gave him a small smile, but inside she was grinning widely. "I guess I do."

That's when a small kernel of hope blossomed within her. Perhaps her marriage would be more than she expected.

The rain continued as if it would never cease. The road turned into a river of mud while the trees swayed with each gust of wind. It was the storm of the season, and on Matt and Hannah's wedding day.

Hannah didn't know if she should take it as a bad omen or a sign of good things to come, a cleansing of the earth. Either way, they were well and truly stuck at the boardinghouse. Even if it stopped raining, by some small miracle, the mud would prohibit travel for a while. How long depended on when the sun came out.

Hannah was making beds for the Grahams, absurdly glad she had done the laundry the day before. The boarders had left something of a mess in each room so she was finishing up the cleaning as she went from room to room.

When Hannah finished, she ended up in her own room, staring at the narrow bed. There was no way a man Matt's size could share that bed with a woman of her size. That would make their wedding night more than awkward.

She had to put someone else in her room and take one of the two rooms with a larger bed. There was no help for it—she knew the consummation of the vows was important to start a marriage. Without a proper bed, it would be a disaster in the making. After the nearly hostile preacher and the rain, she couldn't allow the actual wedding night to go haywire as well.

"He only married you for the land you know."

Hannah jumped at the sound of her new sister-in-law's voice. Olivia stood in the doorway, arms crossed, lips pinched shut.

"I know that." Hannah was glad of the fact Matt had been completely honest with her. "Matthew told me everything."

"And you were so desperate for a husband you said yes?" Olivia's tone became knife sharp.

Hannah weighed her options. If she got into an argument with Olivia, it would set a precedent. But if she backed down, that would let her sister-in-law know Hannah could be intimidated. It was a narrow path to navigate.

"No, I was not desperate, but I recognized a good man and a good offer when I heard it." Hannah met the other woman's gaze. "You and I were friends when we were young'uns. I don't expect you to hug me or nothing, but I want a chance to fit in."

There, that sounded reasonable, and she wasn't shouting, although she was on the inside. Hannah had a bad habit of reacting to insults by biting the head off the insulter, but nobody liked a young woman with a temper.

"You won't get that chance from me." Olivia's eyes flashed. "My brother got us into this mess by lying and now we all have to live with the consequences. But that doesn't mean I have to like them."

"What put the bee in your bonnet?" Hannah sounded, now just as annoyed as her new sister-in-law. "You've no call to blame me for any of this."

Olivia's laugh was humorless. "Then who do I blame? The people who murdered my parents? The incompetent sheriff who couldn't catch them? Or maybe the bastard who took my little brother?" She straightened her shoulders. "All I know is you are a reminder of everything that went wrong in our lives and now my brother is saddled with a cow he never wanted."

Hannah felt every word as if she'd been punched in the gut. She pressed her hand to her stomach and leaned over. The Graham family had been through so much, but that didn't give Olivia a reason to be so dang vicious.

"You've no call to be like this to me."

"I have every right. This is my family." Olivia turned and disappeared from view.

"It's my family now, too." The walls were the only witness to Hannah's whisper.

It wasn't as if everything Olivia had said wasn't true, even though her words had a knife-sharp edge. Her new sister-in-law had just ripped her to shreds on her wedding day. Hannah realized words had more power to hurt than the biggest stick in the world.

It took her ten minutes before she felt in control again. She didn't check to see if the sheets were on sideways or were even tucked in. Completely unlike her, but so was the fact she was now married. Her world was topsy-turvy.

After she finished making the last bed, she sat down on the window seat in her room. She pressed her forehead against the cool glass and stared out into the nearly unrecognizable street.

The rain was coming down in sheets outside. Hannah

was trapped in her own home with her new family who didn't want her and a husband who'd married her because her name was Hannah.

The storm had definitely not been a good sign.

She didn't know how long she sat there before she noticed the rain had stopped and someone was calling her name. Getting to her feet, she realized she must have fallen asleep. Her feet and legs prickled as she stood up. Her hair was a mess of curls sticking every which way.

"Hannah?" A voice echoed down the hallway.

She rubbed her eyes and tried to remember what had happened and why she was asleep on her window seat. A yawn grabbed hold of her and wouldn't let go.

That's how her new husband found her. The day could get worse, but she couldn't possibly think how.

CHAPTER FIVE

The rain had turned the street into a lake. There was no chance the Grahams would be able to leave for home. Hell, Matt probably couldn't even make it to the livery for the wagon and horses without drowning.

After he had surprised Hannah, she'd disappeared into the kitchen, mumbling an excuse about preparing supper. Of course, that was hours before that particular meal was usually served, so he didn't know what she was doing except avoiding him.

Olivia had been upstairs, and he'd bet a nickel she'd said something to Hannah. Something not very nice. It was no secret Livy did not want Matt to marry Hannah, but she'd never given him any valid reasons why.

They were all in the parlor except for Catherine, who remained in the kitchen with Hannah and her grandmother. Livy sat in the corner, barely acknowledging anyone while the younger kids played checkers and jacks. The games must have been Hannah's when she was younger because they were well used, but well maintained. Like everything else in the house.

Matt watched the clouds break up just in time for the sun to set. Fortunately they could stay at the boardinghouse for the night and not have to pay for a hotel or a restaurant. With seven of them, that could get awfully expensive.

After paying Reverend Beechum five dollars, there wasn't any extra money to throw around.

"Mattie?" Catherine snuck up next to him, cuddling against his side as she'd done since she was a little girl.

"Hey there, sprite." He hugged her close, her blond curls tickling his chin.

"Don't squish me." She pushed at his arms. "I came to tell you it's time for supper."

Matt got to his feet and tossed Catherine on his shoulder. She squealed, as she always did, and he tickled her with each step. The rest of the Grahams followed him into the dining room. It had been set up for the boarders, so there were plenty of chairs, although mismatched, for everyone.

Hannah stood at the table with a bowl of steaming mashed turnips. Two thoughts flew through his mind.

Turnips were the reason they'd met; and her expression was so full of longing it made his breath catch. She was watching the play between him and Catherine. With Mrs. Dolan as her only family, he knew right then Hannah had never really known the affection of siblings as his brothers and sisters did.

He turned away, uncomfortable with the personal knowledge she'd given him and unsure of what to do with it. Catherine dropped to her feet and scrambled around to one of the chairs.

"This is my seat." She climbed onto the chair and pointed at the chair across from her. "That's your seat."

Matt sat down where she'd indicated while the others awkwardly found a place to perch. Hannah waited until everyone had found a spot before she put the food on the table. It was simple fare, but it smelled delicious.

With the Grahams filling the dining room, there was only one chair empty. Matt started to rise but Hannah shook her head.

"Don't worry about us. Granny and I always eat in the

kitchen. Eating in here would feel strange." She shrugged. "I don't mind, really."

He didn't know how to respond so he let her leave the room without saying a word. Caleb frowned at him and Catherine kicked him in the shin.

"Ow, why are you kicking me?" He rubbed his leg and scowled at his youngest sister.

"You let Granny and Hannah eat in the kitchen. That's not very nice." She crossed her little arms like a forty-year-old schoolteacher.

"Heck, Matt, we could have taken turns." Caleb joined the blame party.

"I didn't tell them to eat in the kitchen."

"She's your wife. You tell her where she eats." Nicholas wasn't prepared for the punch in his arm Olivia landed.

"I'm hitting you because that's a stupid thing to say. Men don't have the right to tell women where to eat." She reached for the food and started filling the younger children's plates.

"You'd best do something," Caleb added. "I think Nick is right. She's your wife."

Matt pondered what they'd said and realized this was one of the first tests of their marriage. He couldn't possibly let his wife eat in the kitchen on their wedding day. How was he going to stop her though? He didn't want to just tell her what to do, but he also didn't want her to think he wasn't the head of their new family.

He got to his feet and all six pairs of eyes watched him, some judgmental, others curious, and one downright hostile. Livy and he would have to have a talk when they got back to the ranch. He couldn't live with that kind of hostility from his sister.

Hannah and her grandmother sat at the kitchen table, talking quietly. When he walked in, they both looked up at him with identical expressions of surprise.

"Are you out of food already?" Hannah started to rise.

"No, nothing like that." Matt knew there wasn't room for both of them in the dining room, and he couldn't leave Mrs. Dolan in the kitchen by herself. Likely Hannah wouldn't let her eat alone either. He was in a tight situation again and this time it was over something as minor as a meal.

"I'll be right back." He went back into the dining room.

All six of them started talking at once but he ignored them and took the empty chair. Then the noise stopped and he allowed himself to snort at the fact that he'd shut them up.

When he returned to the kitchen with the chair, the two women were still watching him. Hannah stared at the chair, then returned her gaze to his.

"You don't have to eat in the kitchen with us." She shook her head. "It's not proper for a guest to be in here for a meal."

He chuckled. "I'm not a guest. I'm your husband."

Her eyes widened at the word, and sure enough it made him pause, too. Husband. It almost fell out of his mouth like a stone into a still pond.

"That you are." Mrs. Dolan pointed at the chair. "Then you'd best sit a spell and have some vittles."

Matt felt awkward, but he did just that. Hannah hopped up and fixed him a plate from the pots on the stove. She set his plate down on the narrow table and sat back down.

The silence remained as they ate. The only sounds were those of chewing. Mrs. Dolan mostly gummed her food, since apparently a good deal of her teeth were missing.

It was never quiet at meals at the Graham ranch, and he hadn't realized just how much noise people made when they chewed. He tried to think of something to say to break the silence but the longer it went on, the worse it got. He probably should have stayed in the dining room.

"You two need to sleep in the room at the top of the stairs tonight," Mrs. Dolan announced as she noisily smacked her lips on the last bite. "It's got the biggest bed." She winked at Matt.

His stomach flipped at the idea that she wanted them to use a big bed and flipped a second time when she winked at him. Matt was no fool—he knew Hannah and he needed to live as man and wife in all ways, but he sure as hell hadn't expected her grandmother to think about their having sex.

Matt made the mistake of meeting Hannah's gaze and saw all of what he was feeling, as well as something he'd hoped not to see, panic and fear.

It had been a long wedding day, and he knew it would be a very long wedding night.

Hannah wanted a hole to open up right there in the floor and swallow her. She knew she was blushing and looked like a complete fool, but she couldn't help it. Granny had no business talking about the bedroom or the size of the bed. She knew Hannah had next to no knowledge about men or bedding them.

It would be a disaster. What was she thinking? It already was a disaster. And she'd wondered how her wedding day could get worse.

After meeting Matt's gaze and seeing the same discomfort in his face, she wanted to weep. It would be bad enough to share a bed with the stranger who was now her husband, but to know he didn't want to be in the bed . . . that was ten times worse.

He obviously didn't want to share a bed with her. Yet he'd married her, for better or for worse. Apparently the worse would be arriving right around bedtime.

She didn't taste her food but mechanically chewed it anyway. Granny had taught her never to waste food so she did as she had always done—obeyed. Matthew ate heartily, finishing off what was left in the pots and peering around for more. She didn't want to tell him again to go back to the dining room, but any remaining food would be in there.

Actually, they were lucky to have the food supplies they did. Making two meals for the Grahams had practically used up all of the food stores they had left. Somehow Hannah would have to find a way to restock the food before she left for her new home, or convince her grandmother to come with them. Coffee, some dried jerky, and a few biscuits were not going to last long.

Hannah got to her feet, ready to do something where she didn't have to think so hard. She started to clear the dishes and Matthew stood up.

"Oh, no, you are not going to clean up after us." He took her by the elbow and walked into the dining room. His hand felt warm even through the material of the dress—it was an odd but very pleasant feeling. "Who's on dishes today?"

To Hannah's surprise, his brother Nicholas got up.

"Who's on water duty?"

Rebecca got to her feet.

"Good. Both of you will clean up just like if you were at home. Becca, they have a pump in the sink so you don't have to go outside, but you should get to heating the water now." He turned his attention to Nicholas. "Don't break anything."

It was astonishing to think all of these children, including the boys, took turns at chores such as dishes and fetching water. Hannah truly hated doing dishes and to have that particular chore done by someone else lifted her spirits entirely. The Grahams were a unique family, that was for certain.

"You have five minutes." Matthew shepherded Hannah

out into the hallway. "When they're ready, show them where everything is."

Hannah wasn't used to men who took charge. After all, she'd lived with her grandmother. There were no strong male figures in her life. She wasn't sure if she should enjoy someone else taking control so she didn't have to, or if she should wrestle it back from him. This was their wedding day, after all, and it would likely set the tone for the rest of their marriage.

"Matthew, I um, want to say something." She met his gaze, then immediately looked down. It was hard to believe she had a husband who was so tall and so doggone handsome. She couldn't be assertive with that gorgeous visage in front of her. "Um, I wanted to thank you for asking your, well, telling your family to help with chores."

Not exactly what she'd planned to say but Hannah was tripping over her own tongue.

"They're your family now, too." He continued to stare down at her. She could feel his gaze as if it were a physical touch.

"Yes, but I don't know how I fit in with all of them. I hope they won't think I'm lazy because I'm not doing the dishes." God knew her relationship with Olivia was off to a bad start.

He chuckled and put his finger under her chin until she met his gaze. "I don't think there's a person in the world who could say you were lazy. You've been working nonstop since we arrived."

She felt herself falling into his eyes. They were very green in the low light of the hall. It was as if they'd stepped into another place, without their entire noisy family only feet away. His thumb grazed her lips and a skitter of heat slid down her body. Her stomach felt funny and her woman place grew warm and tingly. Hannah could hardly catch her breath.

"Are you going to kiss me?" she blurted.

He smiled and leaned down, his lips slowly approaching hers. She didn't want to close her eyes and miss it, but the closer he got, the more she fell into a whirlpool of unfamiliar sensations. His lips were softer than anything she'd felt before. Just a brush against hers, and then the second pass was a true kiss.

A small moan sighed from her throat as the second kiss turned into a third. Her body was throbbing to the frantic beating of her heart. Hannah didn't want to even take a breath for fear of interrupting the most erotic moment of her life.

His arms closed around her and she was pressed up against him. Oh my. He was hard from head to foot, harder than she'd expected. Matthew was a man who worked for a living, covered in muscle, with callused hands and a firm grip.

"Oh, yuck. Kissing already?" Nicholas's voice broke the spell between them.

Hannah jumped back, her hand pressed to her lips, still wet from her new husband's kisses. Her heart was about to jump right out of her chest, and he appeared completely unruffled.

"What do you want, Nick?" Matthew's voice was as controlled as the rest of him.

"Don't know where the soap is."

"I'll show him." Hannah didn't run, but she walked as quickly as possible out of the hallway, away from an amazing experience she'd been completely unprepared for. No one had told her that a kiss could turn her into a quivering pile of foolish. No one said her entire body would catch fire just by touching his, with clothes on even!

She was beyond flustered, and needed a few minutes away from the man who obviously knew now how to control his wife. Hannah wanted a moment to catch her breath and figure out how she could survive being Mrs. Matthew Graham.

"Nice timing, squirt." Matt tugged on Nick's hair. "I was enjoying myself with my wife."

"Kissing doesn't look fun. Lots of swapping spit is what it is." At fifteen, he admitted that he liked girls, but also admitted he wasn't quite sure he wanted to touch them yet.

"Well, it is fun. Now get on in the kitchen and get the dishes done before Hannah does them instead. We've imposed on her hospitality enough for one day."

After Nick scurried into the kitchen, Matt took a deep breath. Then he had to lean over and put his hands on his knees. That kiss was nearly his undoing. He'd never expected to have such a strong physical reaction to kissing Hannah.

She was attractive in an unconventional way. Her lips were incredibly soft and plump. Hell's bells, he'd completely lost control because of them. He was still hard as a hammer in his trousers. He wondered if she understood exactly what went on between a man and a woman.

If she didn't, their wedding night would be disastrous. He wasn't as experienced as many men, but he had been with women before, mostly away from home on trips with his father.

Now he would have a permanent woman in his bed. Matt was going to have to find some measure of control around her or she could lead him around by the dumb stick between his legs. No man in his right mind wanted to be controlled by a woman or his urges for that woman.

On the other hand, his father had loved his mother so deeply, so completely, his world had revolved around her and, as the product of that love, their children. Matt had always wanted to ask his father why he let his mother control everything. He'd never had the courage though and now, of course, it was too late.

Matt knew how incredible a marriage could be, but he also knew how dangerous it could be. He couldn't let Hannah realize just how much she affected him.

Hannah sat on the edge of the bed wringing her hands. The lamp was turned down so low it was barely a flicker in the darkness of the room. She heard footfalls on the stairs and knew Matthew was nearly there. The rest of the family was settled in their beds, which left only one person who could be walking up the steps.

Her husband.

Oh, she'd thought she was ready for this but she'd been sorely mistaken. Perhaps if she hadn't kissed him before, she might not have been so nervous. Now that she'd had a taste of him, of what it felt like to be in his arms, just how soft his lips were, she was a mass of quivering nerves.

The door slid open with barely a whisper and Matthew's form filled the doorway. Hannah's heart lodged in her throat while every small hair on her body stood up at attention.

"Good evening, Hannah." His soft voice was probably meant to calm her, but it didn't. In fact it was as if he had whispered in her ear, heightening the tension within her.

"Matthew." Her voice was not her own, huskier and deeper than normal.

He shut the door and she started, nearly falling off the bed. She certainly didn't present an air of sophistication.

"Matt, please call me Matt. The only time someone calls me Matthew is if I'm in trouble." He smiled and she was again reminded just how handsome her husband was.

"Matt." This time she whispered and his smile disappeared.

"I want to thank you for—"

She held up her hand to stop him. "Please do not thank me for marrying you. I don't think I could stay in this room if you did that."

He sat down beside her, dwarfing the bed. Lord, the man really was big. When he took her hand in his, his warmth had a calming effect on her frazzled nerves.

"I wasn't going to thank you for that." He kissed her knuckles. "I was going to thank you for cooking. We're a big crew and it takes a lot to satisfy us."

Hannah's heart decided to pick that moment to start racing like a thoroughbred. She could barely hear him over the rushing sound of the blood passing her ears.

"Y-you're welcome."

He reached up and cupped her cheek, his callused thumb sliding lazily across it. "Don't be scared, Hannah. I promise to always take care of you and keep you safe."

In the semi-darkness of the room, hearing the soft tones of his deep voice, she fell a little bit more in love with her new husband.

"I promise to be the best wife I can be, although I haven't had any practice."

He smiled and pressed his forehead against hers. His warm breath mingled with hers. Although they were barely touching, it was an incredibly erotic moment. For the first time in her life, she was sharing part of herself, her very breath, with someone else. She'd never been that close to anyone before, not even Granny.

She felt she could not have picked a better husband and although she'd only known him a week, Hannah trusted Matt. He would keep his promise. When his mouth moved close to hers, she shut her eyes and let the moment take over.

His lips were almost hot on hers, moving slowly across from one side to the other, nibbling and kissing. She was lightheaded from the sensations bombarding her, but it didn't matter.

Before she realized what was happening, he laid her back on the bed and they were pressed together again. This time the sensation didn't frighten her—it excited her. He was as hard as he'd been before, a sharp contrast to the soft plumpness of her own form.

His hands moved down her neck to her chest. She should have been frightened but she wasn't. When his hand closed around her breast, her nipple immediately popped against his palm. She groaned and he echoed the sound. Her nightdress was nothing but a thin layer of cotton between them. He pinched the nipple right through the cloth and she felt an answering thrill between her thighs.

Matt made quick work of the buttons and soon the cool night air caressed her heated skin. He kissed his way down her neck, moving closer to her aching breasts. She didn't know what she wanted, just that she needed him to do something. And he did.

His mouth closed around one turgid peak. The hot wetness of his mouth made her back arch toward him. His tongue swirled around while his teeth nipped at her. She had never known the pleasure to be had from the plump breasts she had always wished away. What a fool she'd been.

As his mouth feasted on one breast, then the other, his hand crept down her body to the aching core between her legs. Although she was inexperienced, Hannah opened her legs, eager for some relief. He inched up the nightdress until the darkness caressed her bare flesh.

His fingers touched her gently. "You're already wet."

Hannah had no idea what that meant, but didn't much care either because he started touching her. Her nipples had proved to be an exciting place when she was in bed with her husband. The place he had his hand now proved to be ten times more intense. Bolts of pleasure shot through her entire body as his nimble fingers rubbed and teased her.

She couldn't get a breath in as sensations bombarded her. A coil wound tight within her. His thumb pressed against the magic spot as his fingers moved lower. When they entered her, she almost sighed with relief. That was what she wanted.

He moved in and out, inching deeper with each thrust of his fingers. She pushed against him, needing more.

"Hang on, darlin'." He stood up leaving her in the cold air alone. She could have wept for the loss of sensation, of the ecstasy found with just his hands and mouth. Hannah didn't even feel like herself anymore. She was someone else, a wanton woman aching, throbbing, and pulsing for more of what a man could give her.

It was probably only seconds, but it felt like hours before he joined her on the bed, and this time, he was nude. She wished she had been smart enough to leave the light on so she could see him. Yet alas, it was too dark to make out anything but his general shape. But oh, her hands found his warm skin, the crinkly hairs on his chest. She touched him because she had to.

He kissed her from above as he positioned himself between her legs. When his thumb found the hooded button of pleasure again and his mouth closed around her nipple, Hannah closed her eyes and leapt into the abyss.

His cock nudged her entrance and she opened her legs even wider. As he slid in, he felt enormous, but strangely good. The slow slide turned into a friction that sent sparks through her. She wanted to tell him to go faster, but thought he would wonder why. Perhaps she truly was a wanton.

When he was finally embedded deep within her, Hannah took a breath and realized this was the closest she'd been to anyone. It was amazing, it was life altering.

He kissed her. "Okay?"

She murmured a yes and tugged a bit on his back. Hannah needed him to move and joyfully, he did. At first his pace was slow, giving her time to adjust to the sheer size of him. Then she raised her knees and he groaned above her.

Hannah knew he was holding himself up with one arm as he pleasured her and thrust his cock within her. She wanted to kiss him but couldn't. She whimpered as the coil within her wound so tight, she couldn't even think.

Then something crashed over her, stealing her breath and stopping her heart. The wave spread out from her center and through her body, an ecstasy that was almost unbearable. She thought she shouted his name, but realized she couldn't tell for the ringing in her ears.

He leaned down and kissed her then, his body finally covering hers completely. She clenched around him as he thrust faster and faster, his breath coming in grunts against her cheek. She opened her mouth to his questing tongue, just as her body was open to his staff.

Matt's fingers bunched the coverlet beneath them as he thrust in so deep, she saw stars. The pleasure that had been ebbing within her began again. She held him close as he whispered her name in her ear, filling her with his seed.

Tears formed in her eyes so she shut them tightly. She had never known what it meant to be close to someone, to have a mate. *She'd never known.*

Hannah had become Mrs. Matthew Graham.

Matt stared at the ceiling, his mind a jumble of thoughts. What he'd intended as a simple introduction to the ways of men and women had turned into something completely different. He'd lost control.

Again.

Hannah wasn't anything special. She was an ordinary woman with plain features. He had never noticed her before even if they had been in town at the same time. It was only through sheer coincidence they'd met in the store a week ago.

Then why? Why did he fall into some kind of spell every time he touched her?

He sure as hell didn't understand it, and if he were honest with himself, he didn't like it. Matt was the oldest, the one who had to be in charge and in control at all times. Hannah threw him off kilter, made his body react in ways it never had. And he lost the ability to think when he was with her.

It was disconcerting and maddening. It was also frightening.

Matt knew his parents' marriage had been one based on love. They were affectionate and had always respected each other. That wasn't a bad thing, but his father had also kowtowed to his mother's wishes. Matt wanted his marriage to be based on mutual respect and not this loco physical reaction he was wholly unprepared for.

Of course, at this point they were well and truly married, and there was no way to reverse that particular event. He still didn't know exactly what had happened after that first kiss. It was as if his mind took a nap while his body thoroughly tasted, teased, and joined with hers.

Just thinking about what they'd done made his cock hard again. It twitched beneath the covers at the memory of being with Hannah. Hungry again for her only minutes after their first time together.

She couldn't know how much she affected him. Ever. Matt wanted to hold the reins in their marriage and if Hannah knew she could control him with her body, he'd never touch those reins again.

He finally closed his eyes, the grit in them uncomfortable. Perhaps he would sleep or perhaps not. His wedding day had not turned out as he'd expected, that was for sure. As Matt began to drift off, he was vaguely aware Hannah had snuggled up beside him, her touch giving him the extra comfort he needed to finally sleep.

CHAPTER SIX

Hannah was awake and out of bed long before the sunrise. She could hardly put two thoughts together but she managed to make coffee. The first mouthful of the strong hot brew helped make her feel a bit more grounded.

Yesterday morning she'd drank coffee from the same cup in the same room. Today she was a completely different person, wedded and bedded, a girl no more. She was a little sore, but ignored the discomfort. After all, it was probably normal. She had other things to worry about.

She had made a batch of biscuits and still had jerky. That and coffee would have to do for breakfast. Now she had to convince Granny to come with them to the Graham ranch. Hannah could not allow her to stay at the boardinghouse alone.

"Good morning." Matt appeared in the doorway, wearing the same clothes he'd worn the day before.

Memories of the night's activities flooded her thoughts. She was suddenly hotter than the coffee and distinctly tingly between her legs. Was this supposed to happen when she saw her husband?

"Morning." Hannah jumped up and poured him a cup of coffee. She couldn't sit still for more than a few moments. If she did, she might grab him and kiss him until neither one of them could see straight.

He sat at the table and reached for a biscuit. When she set the coffee down, he smiled up at her. "Thank you, Hannah."

Her tongue had ceased to function so she just nodded and stepped back. To her relief, the rest of the Grahams started filing into the room, each of them quiet and sleepy-looking.

"Caleb, you and Nick go get the team hitched up. The road is still muddy but it ain't a lake anymore." Matt took a bite of his biscuit. "Girls, make the beds upstairs and make sure everything is clean."

This time when Matt glanced at Hannah, the smiling seductiveness of last night was gone. He was as serious as she'd ever seen him.

"How soon can you have everything packed so we can leave?"

"Um, I'm already packed. I need to talk to Granny though." She had to do more than talk to her—she had to convince her.

"Then get to it. I want to be on our way in fifteen minutes." He finished his biscuit and rose with a piece of jerky in his hand. "I'll make sure the outside of the house is secure."

There it was again. That bossiness she'd noticed the night before. He had been in charge at the ranch only a few months so it must be something he'd always done. That didn't mean she had to like it though.

She left the Grahams to eat what they wanted of the humble meal. The hallway was deserted as she walked to her grandmother's room. She heard her talking aloud as Hannah knocked.

"Who is it?" her grandmother called from inside.

"It's me, Granny. It's time to go."

"So go." She sounded as grumpy as normal.

"I mean both of us need to leave with the Grahams," she said through the closed door.

"I ain't leaving until this place is sold. That's that."

Hannah waited a minute before speaking again. She needed to find a way for her grandmother to think it was her own idea to leave.

"I need your help, Granny. I . . . I can't go to the ranch with all of those strangers. At least one of them doesn't like me already." She pressed her forehead on the door, feeling every word for the truth it was. "I feel lost and I need you with me. Please."

The door opened so suddenly Hannah fell in the room. She landed on her hands and knees with a painful thud. At least she didn't land on her face.

"What are you doing, child?"

Hannah's wrists throbbed as she got back to her feet. "Trying to break my arms, apparently."

"Well, get up then. We've got to pack my things, I reckon." Granny grinned at her. "How much time did that handsome husband give you?"

"Fifteen minutes." Hannah knew her wrists would hurt like the dickens later, but for now she had no time to think about it.

"Best get crackin' then." Granny pointed at her traveling bag, open on the bed. "I already started."

Hannah hugged her grandmother so hard, she felt her own bones creak. "Thank you."

"Don't thank me yet. I may fight so much with Eva, you will send me back here on a mule."

They both laughed as they made quick work of packing Granny's belongings. There wasn't much, most of it sentimental pieces from her parents, husband, and daughter.

Hannah started when she saw Matt standing in the doorway, hat on his head and a scowl on his face.

"We were just, uh, finishing up in here." She took her grandmother's hand. "Granny is going to come with us."

"Fine then. We need to get back to the ranch. There's a lot of chores and animals that need tending to." He gestured to her traveling bag. "I took your things to the wagon already, Hannah. Is that everything you need, Mrs. Dolan?"

"Yep. I'm leaving everything else here for now. Maybe whoever buys the old place will want the furnishings." Granny tucked Hannah's elbow in her own.

Matt picked up the bag and led them out of the room. Hannah didn't know what to think of his brusque behavior other than that he was worried about the ranch. He hadn't acted like this with her before. Maybe now that they were married, he had dropped the kind and soft-spoken mask. She hoped not because that would make fifty years seem like an eternity.

As they walked toward the front door, Hannah found her steps slowing. This boardinghouse was the only home she knew. Her parents had died when she was young enough that she'd forgotten their small farmhouse almost completely. When they reached the front door, she stopped.

Granny patted her arm. "I know how you feel, child. It's time to go to your new home, though. No use looking back." She pointed at Matt, who was currently putting the bag in the back of the wagon. "Look instead at what's ahead."

Matt bent down, giving them an unobstructed view of his behind. It was a very nicely shaped rear end, something she hadn't noticed before. Staring at it made her cheeks flush and a hint of memory from last night whipped through her.

"Are you ready?"

The sound of Granny's voice cut through Hannah's distracted thoughts. "Um, yes, I'm ready now." No need to let her grandmother know exactly what she had been thinking about.

They walked outside, the sound of the door closing behind them a final thump on the first chapter of Hannah's life. She wouldn't dwell on what could be or she'd drive herself loco. The truth was, she had no idea what waited for them at the Graham ranch. There was only one way to find out.

The wagon was full of the Grahams, all staring at her and Granny. Hannah didn't know whether to be scared or excited.

"We made you a seat, Mrs. Dolan." Catherine jumped up and down beside them. "Matt said you can't ride like we do so we made you a special seat."

"Is that so? How thoughtful of him." Granny allowed Matt and Caleb to help her up into the wagon.

Catherine hopped up beside her and took her hand, leading her to the front. "Right here, Mrs. Granny."

Hannah smiled as her grandmother settled down on the seat made of what appeared to be blankets draped over something, perhaps a couple crates. Catherine perched beside her, her hand firmly clasped with Granny's.

"You want to ride up front with me?" Matt asked from behind her, his warm breath gusting past her cheek.

She closed her eyes for a moment at the unfamiliar sensation. "Do you want me to?" she blurted. "I mean, yes, I'd like to."

Matt took her elbow again. This was a familiar touch and she found herself enjoying it. A lot. In that moment, it was as if they were a regular married couple sharing casual touches, with no boundaries between them.

Hannah couldn't help the smile that spread across her face at the thought. Perhaps there was a future for the two of them, regardless of the challenges coming their way. If they were as compatible emotionally as they were physically, then it was going to be a good life.

Then she caught sight of Olivia in the corner of the wagon. Her gaze was full of dark emotions and anger, all directed at Hannah. She had no idea what would make her new sister-in-law treat her as if she had committed a crime. It destroyed her good mood, wiped the smile off her face, and made her lose her footing.

Matt grabbed her arm, his grip tight on her wrist. She winced at the pain, sucking in a breath.

He sighed. "Are you okay?"

"Oh, I'm fine. Sorry about that. I, uh, can be clumsy." Avoiding her new husband's gaze, Hannah put her foot on the wheel and hauled herself up into the wagon.

When she got herself settled, she realized Caleb was waiting for her to move to the center. It appeared she would ride between Matt and his brother. They were both big men and their shoulders and legs touched hers. Another new and decidedly strange sensation.

When the ranch came into view, her stomach quivered and her heart followed suit. She was about to arrive at her new home.

Matt squirmed in the wagon seat. He had woken up that morning expecting Hannah to be next to him, but she had left him alone in the bed. For a reason he could not understand, it had put him in a foul mood. He should be ecstatic. After all, he was married and could now claim the acreage from Texas.

He was far from being happy though, bordering on downright grumpy. The ride out to the ranch took twice as long as usual because of the muddy condition of the ground. The horses pulled them through, albeit slowly, and they arrived by late morning.

Everything looked fine, and he knew there was no reason to worry about the ranch. Yet as soon as the wagon stopped in front of the house, he tossed the reins to Caleb and jumped down.

"I'm going to check on things. Take care of the wagon." Without a word to Hannah or Mrs. Dolan, he walked to the barn.

"That wasn't very nice." Catherine's voice followed him across the still muddy ground. She was right, of course, but he wasn't about to change his mind.

Matt needed to be alone for a bit. He missed his morning rides, that peaceful time when he could be completely by himself. It would be harder to do that with a wife, he realized. Now was the time he truly could not stop himself from escaping. Later he would explain why if Hannah asked.

Obviously Javier or Lorenzo had already cleaned the stalls that morning. It was usually Nick's job, but the ranch hands did what they had to. They were good people as was their mother, Eva. Without her helping with the young'uns, Matt didn't think they would have survived after their parents' deaths and Ben's disappearance. The Vasquez family was linked with the Grahams, and he hoped when they did get the land, to give some of it to them. He knew it was the right thing to do, and his father would have approved wholeheartedly.

Matt walked farther into the barn and the familiar surroundings made him feel better immediately. Winston poked his head out of the stall and nickered when he caught sight of Matt. With a grin, Matt scratched the big gelding behind his ears and endured the snuffling of his pockets for treats he didn't have.

"Sorry, boy, I'm just back from town. Later I'll bring you something." He leaned his forehead against the horse's neck and tried to calm down.

Something was making him so tense, his teeth were beginning to ache from clenching them. He thought it might
have to do with bringing Hannah home and moving into
his parents' room. It was also a significant adjustment to
suddenly have someone who was legally bound to him,
and yet another person he was responsible for keeping safe.
It wasn't her fault, of course. He had to place all the
blame right where it belonged, on his own shoulders. Hannah was a good person. She'd accepted his loco proposal
although she should have kicked him out of the boardinghouse. Now she was not only married but bedded, and
there was no turning back.

His stomach did a funny flip at the thought of sleeping
with her every night for the rest of his life. He was not prepared for that kind of intimacy, especially sharing everything with her. Even though he was part of such a big
family, Matt knew he was something of a loner. He spent
time with his family, but most times he kept his thoughts
and feelings to himself. Maybe it was because he was the
oldest, but no matter the reason, he kept himself to himself. Hannah might put a kink in that whole approach to
life.

Matt wasn't looking forward to that. There was a reason
he was a loner, it kept him solid and focused. A wife would
be a completely new element in an already complex situation. Too many siblings, too much tragedy, and a ranch to
run. A ranch that was about to grow ten times bigger. He
would also never give up the quest to find his parents'
murderer and locate his youngest brother. There was a big
goddamn hole in his heart and it wouldn't be filled until he
accomplished both those tasks.

As he brooded over the significant changes in his life,
Matt saddled Winston and then led him out the back of the
barn. He mounted the horse, briefly considering the idea
of showing Hannah around the ranch, introducing her to

Eva, Lorenzo, and Javier, but then he dismissed it. His sisters and brothers could take care of that. Matt needed to think.

Hannah didn't let the hurt show on her face after Matt walked away from the wagon. He had dismissed her as if she were just another one of his siblings, no one of consequence or importance. Caleb didn't say anything as he helped her down. The rest of the Grahams dispersed like a swarm of bees, going every which way. Nicholas at least brought their bags inside the house before disappearing.

That left Granny and her standing on the doorstep of the Graham ranch house. Hannah felt like crying and screaming at the same time. Was this treatment what she must accept for the rest of her life? To be an afterthought, not even warranting the attention of a guest? It was heartbreaking to know she was so unimportant to every Graham, particularly the one she had pledged her life to.

"Are you ready to meet Eva?" Catherine appeared beside them, her gap-toothed grin wide on her pixie face.

Hannah could have cried for the sweetness of the child. Instead she hugged her and took her hand. As natural as could be, Catherine wrapped her hand around Hannah's.

"I'm ready," Hannah said.

"Okay, then let me show you everything." Catherine pointed at the house. "This is our home and our front porch. We live here."

With a lighter heart, Hannah took her grandmother's arm and they walked into the house with little Catherine. It had already been a long day, and the most difficult part still awaited them.

The interior of the house smelled of wood and bread. They were comfortable scents, almost welcoming. The front part of the house was a big room with furniture and a rag rug positioned in front of a large fireplace. There were nails in the wood to the left of the door with a few coats hanging on them. Several pairs of muddy boots sat beneath them. At least Eva had them trained to keep dirty shoes out of the house.

The room was obviously where they gathered as a family, with well-worn pillows and an afghan dotting the sofa. She liked this room and all it represented.

"This is the parlor. We have fires over yonder in the fireplace when it's cold and Matt reads to me at night on the sofa. At Christmas we even sing 'round the fire." Catherine's interpretation of everything was so refreshing. She didn't see the room's practical functions, but rather the memories of good times she'd had in it.

"It's lovely." Hannah smiled at her. "I like it a lot."

"Me, too." Catherine tugged at her hand. "Now let's go to the kitchen. That's where we eat."

Hannah heard Granny chuckle as they both walked through a large archway into the very spacious kitchen. Sitting in the middle of it was the biggest table she'd ever seen, a necessity no doubt with a big family like the Grahams.

"This is the table my Pa built." Catherine pointed to a diminutive woman Hannah hadn't noticed. "Eva, this is my new sister."

The woman turned, her dark chocolate eyes assessing and incredibly sharp. This was the person who ran the house. The one Hannah would have to win over or she would never be at home in the house.

Hannah managed to smile. "Hello, Mrs. Vasquez. I'm Hannah."

There was a pause before the other woman spoke. *"Buenos dias, señora."*

Hannah knew some Spanish but not enough. "It's wonderful to meet you."

Eva's gaze moved to beyond Hannah's shoulder and her expression changed to surprise. "Martha!"

"Eva Vasquez. How long has it been?" Granny pulled the other woman into a hug. "I can't believe I had to ride all the way out here to see you again."

Eva chuckled. "You are still a *mujer loca. ¿Es la señora su nieta?*"

"Yes, she is. Joanna's girl." Granny gave Hannah a wink. "She's been running the boardinghouse for the last five years. Lord knows I ain't worth a damn anymore."

"*Si, es la verdad.*" Eva turned to Hannah, and after a moment, took her hands. "Welcome to our home. *Bienvenidos.*"

Hannah couldn't have been happier to feel the small woman's callused palms against her own. She'd had no idea what to expect at the Graham ranch, and was doubly glad Granny had come with them. Without Granny's friendship with Eva, she sensed the greeting would have been very different.

Catherine must have grown bored with the adults' conversation. She stood in the doorway and did a little dance. "Let's go now. I need to show you the rest of the house."

"*Hija,* you need to be patient." Eva didn't raise her voice, but her tone made the little girl stop fidgeting.

"Yes, ma'am." The sigh was small but dramatic nonetheless. "May I please show Hannah the rest of the house now?" Catherine twirled her braids around her fingers. "Please?"

"*Uno momento, hija.*" Eva squeezed Hannah's hands. "Come back after your journey with Catarina. We will talk."

"I'm gonna stay here and chat a spell with Eva. You go on, child." Granny lowered herself into a chair.

"I look forward to it." Hannah smiled at Eva. The

housekeeper could definitely be a good source of information about her new husband. He certainly didn't appear to be very forthcoming and had acted as if he didn't even want her at the ranch. Perhaps his motives were as he said, simply to get a wife so he could secure the land for the ranch. She had hoped for more, much more, but no one could ever know that.

Hannah kissed her grandmother's forehead, then walked over to Catherine and took her hand.

"Oh good, now I can show you the room you will sleep in. My Mama and Papa used to sleep there, but they went to Heaven to be with Jesus." Catherine's tone spoke of much more than a simple seven-year-old's understanding. "Their bedroom is empty and it makes me sad when I see it."

She led Hannah to an open door down the hallway, one of five that must lead to other bedrooms. Bright sunshine spilled through a window with white lace curtains hanging on either side. Hannah knew that someone had decorated the room with love. She saw not only the intricate lace curtains, but a beautiful quilt on a bed with a headboard of carved wooden flowers. A chest of drawers sat in one corner, one drawer askew. There was a fresh smell in the air, as if it had been newly cleaned.

Hannah couldn't have explained it well, but the room made her feel safe. The Grahams had loved each other; she'd understood that right away. They had died together, violently from what she knew. Yet instead of their horrific end, Hannah sensed the good life they had lived.

"Do you like it? It's an awful big bed." Catherine climbed up and bounced on it.

"Yes, I like it very much. It's lovely." She ran her hand along the tight stitches on the quilt and wondered who had made it. Her first instinct was that Matt's mother had made

it while preparing for her own wedding. The romantic notion made her smile.

"Now let's see my room." Catherine jumped down and
pulled Hannah from the room.

As she followed the girl around the house, Hannah's
thoughts remained in her new room, and what the night
held in store.

CHAPTER SEVEN

Matt rode Winston until the horse was lathered and breathing hard. When he finally realized his horse was exhausted, he gentled his movements until he saw the creek up ahead. After he climbed down off the horse, he realized his knees were sore from gripping the saddle.

What the hell was he doing running away and almost killing his horse in the process? Stupid and foolhardy. Something a boy ten years younger would do, not a man who was responsible for almost a dozen people's lives. He had to remain strong and keep hold of his emotions. Outbursts would not help anything and certainly couldn't happen again.

He let his horse drink his fill and graze on the sweet grass on the bank. Matt looked east, toward where the house was, and his future. His wife. He needed to talk to someone about how to act around her. It was awkward and downright uncomfortable between them, mostly due to his own behavior.

Knowing he'd been a coward, and angry at himself, Matt threw himself up into Winston's saddle. He rode back toward the ranch, toward Hannah. He had to find a way to accept his new life and his new wife.

★ ★ ★

No matter how much he told himself to go into the house, Matt spent an inordinate amount of time rubbing down, then currying Winston. The gelding would have been smiling if he could have.

"Are you hiding?" Nicholas appeared with Javier in the stall doorway. The younger Vasquez was sixteen, the same age as Nick, but he was as big as his brother, Lorenzo. Both Vasquez men were natural horsemen and miracle workers with ornery cattle. Each of them was devoted to their mother, and had the same olive-toned skin, chocolate eyes, and thick black hair.

"Yes." Matt didn't think lying to his brother would work, so he just blurted the truth.

"She seems nice." Nick stepped in and leaned against the wall.

"Yeah, she's nice. I just . . . Hell, I don't know what to do with a wife." Even after watching his parents all his life, he found the relationship between them a mystery. He just didn't understand it.

Javier shook his head, a grin splitting his face. "You don't know what do with your new *esposa?*"

Matt realized what he'd said, and to his annoyance, felt his cheeks heat. "That's not what I meant. I don't know what else to do with her."

"You could start by talking to her. Maybe even have a meal with her." Nick snorted at his not-so-funny quips and Javier laughed out loud.

"Both of you get the hell out of here. Don't you have work to do? Some cattle to take care of?" Matt snapped.

"Nope, we're done for now. We came back for supper." Nick turned to leave, still chuckling under his breath.

"Supper?" Matt repeated. It couldn't possibly be that late, could it?

"It's five o'clock, Matt. You disappeared six hours ago. I

think Eva is ready to kick your ass." With that Nick and Javier left Matt alone.

It was five in the afternoon? He had been gone half the day, and not only had he left Hannah alone all that time, but he'd spent a second day doing no work around the ranch. Irresponsible didn't even begin to cover his behavior and no doubt Eva would tan his hide for it, not to mention what Mrs. Dolan would do. And dammit, he was hungry since he'd obviously missed dinner.

He finally left the barn, this time with a bit of speed in his step. Everything appeared to be normal as he walked into the house. Then he heard the laughter.

Hannah.

He'd heard her laugh once before, but nothing like this. The sound was full of joy that echoed around him and through him. Damned if it didn't make him smile. Whatever had happened while he'd been off on his own must have been better than he'd expected.

He took off his boots and hung up his hat, then headed into the kitchen. Not knowing what to expect, he tread lightly, peering around the corner so they wouldn't know he was there. Eva and Hannah stood beside each other at the counter. One tall and curvy, the other short and round. One dark, one light. They were a study in opposites, but they appeared to be in harmony.

The kitchen had an air of happiness he hadn't experienced in months. He wondered if it was Hannah's presence that had lifted the cloud of doom that had hung over the ranch for so long. When he'd met her in the store one week ago, Matt had had no idea how entwined their lives would become.

Perhaps he was foolish to stay away from her, to be afraid of being married. If Eva liked her, then he knew he'd made a good choice. He trusted the housekeeper implicitly— she'd been a second mother to him for the last fifteen years.

Maybe later he'd get some time with her. No doubt he'd have to endure a dressing down, but he'd also have a chance to talk to her about Hannah. That's what he should have done when he'd arrived instead of running away. He'd probably feel the repercussions of his behavior for a while.

Mrs. Dolan sat at the table with a cup. She was the first to spot him. "And the prodigal son returns. You'd best get on in here and get it over with. I'm thinking you have some groveling to do." Hannah's grandmother was definitely not one to keep a thought to herself.

Hannah and Eva turned to look at him as he walked into the kitchen. One woman was wary, the other most assuredly annoyed. They both had flour all over the aprons they wore and their hands.

"Eva is teaching me how to make tortillas," Hannah blurted before she turned back to the counter.

Eva shook her head at him, and he felt the force of that stare all the way to his toes. She could embarrass him further by scolding him right then and there. He sure as hell hoped she wouldn't.

"She is a fast learner." When Eva finally let her gaze move away from his, Matt took a deep breath. "Go ring the bell and wash up. Supper will be ready in fifteen minutes."

"Yes, ma'am."

Matt bolted out of the kitchen to ring the dinner bell. No need to tempt fate by giving Eva another opportunity to yell at him. He owed Hannah an apology but he couldn't seem to form the words. Maybe later when they went to bed, he'd feel more relaxed and be able to speak to her without tripping over his tongue.

Hannah hardly saw the tortilla in her hand for the pounding in her head and her heart. Matt had spent hours away from the house, and he didn't even say a word to her.

She managed to swallow the lump of hurt in her throat, but just barely. Eva must have sensed Hannah's discomfort because she took her hand.

"*No te preocupes, hija.* He does not know yet who he is."

Hannah didn't understand the Spanish but she recognized the message just the same. She nodded and managed to make some semblance of a tortilla.

"Why don't you stir the beans and then set the table. I will finish." Eva gently turned Hannah toward the stove.

After wiping her hands on a towel, she found the act of making dinner gave her back some normalcy on the strangest day of her life. She set the table for the twelve of them. Mr. Graham obviously knew what he'd been doing when he built a table with benches on either side. The two chairs had been for the parents and Hannah wondered who would sit there during this meal.

Within ten minutes, the Grahams started filing in and sat on the bench, including Matt. He did not meet her gaze, again, as she and Eva put the food on the table. A pot of beans with a bit of meat, tortillas, and pitchers of water comprised the simple fare.

Matt rose from the bench and went to the chair at one end of the table. He finally glanced up at her. His expression was unreadable, but he gestured her toward the chair at the other end. It was a small peace offering, and she was stupidly grateful for it.

"Sit, *hija,* sit." Eva pulled the chair out for her and helped Hannah sit. It was something a gentleman would do, but she had already realized her new husband wasn't necessarily trained to act as a gentleman should.

After they all sat, everyone dug in, filling fresh tortillas with beans. Hannah hadn't had such delicious food before and hoped Eva would show her the secrets of the spices. The flavorful beans danced on her tongue, while at the same time filling her belly quickly.

The family chatted throughout the meal, mostly about things to do with the ranch. Hannah was an observer, not really part of the conversation. No one spoke directly to her and Olivia continued to treat Hannah as a very unwelcome visitor. At least she was safe and warm, and accepted by two members of the family.

Catherine sat beside her, her legs swinging on the bench as she gobbled up her supper. With a bite still in her mouth, she looked at Eva. "May I be excused please?"

"Yes, *hija,* you go wash up and get your schooling books ready." Eva appeared to be the person who kept everyone on schedule.

"Can I read to Hannah tonight instead of you?" Catherine directed her question at Matt. It surprised both him and Hannah.

"You want to read with her?" Olivia snorted. "We don't even know if she can read."

Hannah flinched at the animosity in her sister-in-law's voice. "I can read. As you know, I went to school until I was seven. Afterward, Granny taught me at home."

"No need to be like that, Livy." Matt's tone was not very firm, even if he said the right words. "Are you sure, Catherine?"

Hannah didn't know whether he didn't trust her or whether he was jealous that Catherine had changed their routine. Either way it wasn't good for such emotions to be between them.

"It's okay. We can do it another time together, okay?" Hannah wanted to avoid the conflict and try to find a compromise with Matt.

"I don't want to do it another time." Catherine pouted her lip. "I want Hannah." She pointed at Matt. "Besides, you were mean to her today."

"I was not mean." Matt's brows slammed together. "I had chores to do after being away for more than a day."

"Is that why you went riding on Winston all afternoon?" Nicholas smirked at him.

"If you didn't want to marry her, you shouldn't have." Olivia apparently couldn't keep quiet any longer.

"Jesus please us, will you all just shut up?" Matt's face was flushed with anger.

"Don't use the Lord's name like that, Mateo." Eva sounded as mad as he was.

The supper that had started with the fun of making tortillas had turned into a family argument. And Hannah was squarely in the center of it.

"Listen, all of you, Hannah and I are married now, and you all have to accept that. You're embarrassing me and yourselves in front of her." He glared at each of them in turn. "This is hard enough without all of you acting like spoiled idiots."

Hannah could not bear one more second of the arguing. She got to her feet. "I'll start heating water for the dishes." The water could never be as hot as her cheeks felt.

Her departure seemed to defuse the situation, because the Grahams were suddenly quiet. All she heard as she pumped water into a bucket was chewing and breathing. Eva appeared at her elbow and touched her shoulder. It was a wordless gesture that meant a lot.

After the pail was nearly full, she picked up the handle and swung it over to the stove. She stoked up the fire and got the blaze glowing bright with a few pokes of a stick. When she turned to get another pail heated, she ran smack into Matt's chest. He felt as hard as he had the two times she'd touched him before, and her traitorous body reacted with a jolt of pure pleasure.

She stepped back and glanced around, eager to avoid his gaze and his touch. To her surprise, everyone else was gone, and he had apparently been left to clear the plates.

"They don't normally behave like that." He set a stack of plates in the sink.

"I don't know if I believe that." Hannah wanted to slap her hand across her mouth but it was the truth. "I mean, I think you are all painfully honest with each other."

He made a face but didn't disagree with her. "They feel things deeply and this year has been more than hard." He leaned against the sink. "Once we get the ranch expanded, solve some things and settle down a bit, things will be better."

She certainly hoped so or she would have a lot of trouble fitting in with them. "I didn't know Catherine would ask for me, I mean, for her reading."

"She misses Mama."

Hannah knew he didn't mean to say she was a substitute mother, but it sure felt that way. She pushed aside the silly notion that everything revolved around her. The Grahams had suffered a lot and she needed to stop thinking of herself.

"I won't ever be able to take your mother's place, but I hope I can be part of this family."

He looked surprised. "You already are."

She shook her head. "No, I'm not, but I'm trying." With that, she turned to the sink and busied herself filling another bucket. When she turned around a few minutes later, he was gone.

At least the day was nearly over.

Matt stood outside on the porch with Caleb at his side. The night air was cool on his skin, a much needed sensation after the supper that had turned into a fiasco.

"That could have gone better," Caleb said drily.

"Thanks for helping out there, brother."

"Livy has a bee in her bonnet about your wife, Catherine is stuck to her like a cocklebur, and Eva seems to like her." Caleb held up his hands. "I'm not getting in the middle of all that."

"I'm living in it. Knee deep in it." No matter what Matt did, it was the wrong thing. "I need to get to Houston with her to sign those papers. If it ain't raining, we'll go on Monday. I don't want to wait any longer."

"I don't blame you. You want me to come?"

"No, not this time. I need you here." Matt figured the trip alone with Hannah might help fix things between them, too.

The brothers went to the barn and checked the animals, making sure they were settled for the night. The darkness surrounded them as the night creatures began to sing. It was peaceful, at least temporarily. Caleb disappeared with Lorenzo, leaving Matt to return to the house alone.

It was time to go to his new bedroom and his new wife. He took a deep breath and headed back into the house.

The kitchen was empty, everything cleaned and put away. He walked down the hallway, feeling his heart thump with each step. The door was closed without any light shining beneath it. Matt took a deep breath and opened the door.

In a splash of moonlight coming through the curtains, he could see she was curled up in a corner of the bed, only her hair visible above the quilt. Since it was barely nine o'clock, he didn't know if she was truly sleeping or just avoiding him.

Either way, he didn't think he would be enjoying his marriage bed that night. As he began to undress, the reality of sleeping in this room hit him. The room wasn't his and neither was the bed. The only thing in the room he could claim was currently hiding or sleeping under the covers.

He closed his eyes and thought about how important it was to his family to expand the ranch, to do what his father had intended to do. Reminding himself this was just a room, and his parents were never going to use it again, didn't really help. Matt stood there with his shirt untucked and his fists clenched, unable to proceed or retreat.

What had started as a simple act of preparing for bed turned into a battle between his heart and his head. The unexpectedness of life shouldn't surprise him, but it always did.

"Matt?" Hannah's soft voice was like an angel's whisper.

He sucked in a breath and was finally able to move. "Sorry if I woke you, Hannah." Even his voice sounded odd.

"I was just dozing. Are you okay? You were just standing there like a statue." She must not be too angry with him; at least she was concerned about him and actually speaking to him.

"Yeah, I'm fine. It's just this room. I haven't slept in it before." He couldn't quite tell her how he'd been overcome with emotion and unable to take off his shirt. He'd been embarrassed enough for the day. He fumbled with the buttons on his shirt.

"You haven't?" There was a pause and then she spoke again. "Oh, Matt, I didn't realize."

The covers rustled and her hand pressed against the center of his back. Heat flowed from her into him and within seconds, he wasn't frozen any longer. In fact, he was too hot.

He turned around to face her and although she was only a shadow in the night, he could smell her, would have known it was Hannah even if he hadn't heard her voice. When he pulled her flush against him, her softness melded with his hardness. Matt knew he needed to talk to her, to find some peace between them after the crazy antics of supper, but at that moment, nothing could have stopped him from kissing her.

Her lips were as soft as the rest of her, pliant beneath his, moving with them as he explored her mouth. His cock turned into a hammer, pounding at her stomach, wanting to be let out and satisfied. Matt should have gone slower, he should have taken care of seducing her, but he didn't.

Within seconds, his clothes were on the floor along with her cotton nightdress and their skin was touching head to toe. It was incredible, indescribably wonderful.

"Oh my." Her breathy whisper skittered across his neck, raising goose flesh.

He scooped her up and set her on the bed, then climbed on top of her. If he thought standing naked near her felt good, lying on her was enough to make him come immediately. It was only through sheer force of will that he didn't.

Matt wanted to savor every second with Hannah in bed. It was the first time for them in their new room and he wanted this first memory to be a good one.

He kissed her jaw, making his way to her neck. She trembled as he nibbled and kissed a path down her neck to her collarbone. For some reason he found the hollow there interesting and spent time exploring the expanse of skin. She must've grown restless because she shifted beneath him and made a sighing noise.

Reminding himself to go back to that sweet spot later, he moved to her breasts. Ah, what a treasure they had been to discover. He'd had no idea what had been hidden behind her plain dress. They were the perfect size for his hand, and her nipples grew instantly hard when touched. She was obviously made for loving, so inherently passionate, he counted his lucky stars her name was Hannah and that she was his.

While he cupped her left breast, his mouth closed around the right. This time she moaned and then squeaked when he nipped at her. Hannah was a treasure and she didn't even know it. He switched breasts, pleasuring her and himself until he could wait no longer. His cock throbbed with each beat of his heart, wanting and needing more.

He raised himself up and kissed her, spreading her legs with his knees. She opened up to him like a flower waiting to be pollinated. As his cock touched those hidden petals, he groaned at the wetness and heat that greeted him. Hannah pulled at his shoulders when he paused. If he didn't think he'd explode, he might have laughed at how impatient she was.

He sank into her softness and shook with the raw pleasure coursing through him. She'd been made for him, the perfect size, the perfect fit, the perfect everything. She might not know it yet, but Matt did. He almost lost control once he was fully sheathed inside her.

After a moment's pause to regain his wits, Matt began to move, slowly at first. She picked up his rhythm and pushed up as he thrust down. As natural as could be, she was in tune with everything he did. It was astonishing, and if he had a thought in his head, he would have been frightened by the implications.

She tugged on his shoulders again and he picked up his pace. Her channel grew tighter with each thrust. His balls tingled as his release grew closer. He wanted her to experience pleasure too, so he lifted himself up in order to reach between them. Her clit was swollen, begging for his touch.

At the first flick of his fingers, she arched her back and gasped. He thrust faster and faster, pleasuring her clit as her tightness pleasured his cock. She was so slippery he couldn't hold back any longer.

"Come on, honey, come fly with me." The guttural voice didn't even sound like his.

She arched again, squeezing around him like a vise. "Matthew." Her whispered scream went straight to his balls and the world exploded around him.

Pure ecstasy flooded him as he pumped into her again and again. He held onto the bed for fear he'd truly fly away from the pleasure, the likes of which he'd never experienced.

His teeth buzzed in his head, every limb tingled and he was still hard, buried deep inside her. He pressed his forehead to hers and caught his breath.

When he could finally form a coherent thought, he rolled off her, almost groaning when he left the warmth of her body. Matt pulled her close until they were spooned together on the bed. He was asleep within minutes, his new wife's heart beating against his.

The best laid plans never come to fruition if Mother Nature has her way. Although Hannah knew the land grant deadline was approaching, they hadn't been able to get away from the ranch because of problems. First there were missing cattle, which took nearly half a day to find in a secluded valley on their neighbor's property. Then, two of the new calves got sick, and Matt seemed to have a magic touch with the tiny bovines.

Before Hannah knew it, four days had flown past and things were still unsaid between them. After their first night at the ranch, she had been asleep before Matt even came to bed; then he was up before the sun. They hadn't been close again, at least no closer than sleeping beside each other.

Thank God Eva had taken her under her wing. The things she'd learned in the kitchen, what people on a ranch ate, how to make things like tamales, filled her days. She helped to clean, do laundry, and tried to lend a hand with the children.

Yet she didn't feel at home yet. Perhaps it was Olivia's

ongoing hostility, the fact that Nicholas and Rebecca ignored her, or maybe it was that she couldn't find her place. No matter what she did or didn't do, nothing was quite right.

Granny was there to talk to but she'd taken to spending a great deal of time in the kitchen with Eva. They obviously had a lot in common and Hannah didn't begrudge them their friendship. Truthfully, without the boarders to take care of or Granny's company, Hannah was lonely.

She woke up Thursday morning without her husband. Again. She dragged her feet a bit washing up and getting dressed. Breakfast was likely just getting started, judging by the gray light of dawn coming through the window. Matt hadn't slept in their bed the night before, which just made her feel worse. Hannah knew he'd been taking care of a sick calf, but that didn't make the situation better. She couldn't help thinking he cared more for the animal than his wife.

Self-pity didn't become her and she tried to stop it from creeping into her thoughts. Hannah needed to find something to do, so she would feel useful.

When she arrived in the kitchen, Rebecca and Elizabeth were already there. Both of them murmured a greeting and then returned to their chores of making breakfast. Eva was nowhere to be seen, but the girls were busy making cornpone and some kind of hash.

"Anything I can do to help?" Hannah noted the shoulder on Elizabeth's dress was missing a few stitches.

"No." Rebecca looked at her sister. "Thank you anyway."

At least they weren't hostile like Olivia, but they were not nearly as friendly as Catherine. Hannah went over to the stove and checked the coffee pot. It was nearly ready so she replaced the top and turned to the sink to get some cold water to settle the grounds.

Elizabeth stood there, pinning her with those same greenish blue eyes Matt had. "Eva don't want you messing with the coffee."

"I was just taking a peek." Hannah managed a weak smile. "I'm good with a needle. I can fix your dress for you."

Elizabeth's expression softened with surprise and she fingered her shoulder. "Really? Eva can't sew worth a darn. Mama always—well, none of us learned how."

Rebecca stared at her. "You can sew?"

This time, Hannah genuinely smiled. "Yes, I can. Granny taught me from the time I was a little girl. I have my sewing box with me."

Rebecca disappeared down the hallway at a run. She reappeared moments later with a large basket in her hands. It was obviously well used but in good shape. When she grinned, Elizabeth did, too.

Rebecca set the basket on the big table. "She can sew!"

They danced around the table chanting a silly song about sewing. Hannah laughed along with them, her heart so much lighter than it had been five minutes earlier.

"*¿Que pasa, hijas?*" Eva walked into the kitchen, her brow furrowed.

"Hannah can sew." Rebecca pointed at the basket.

Eva's gaze snapped to hers. "Truly?"

"Yes, I'm right handy with a needle." Hannah almost wanted to do a dance herself.

"*Dios mio*, Hannah. I've got a pile almost as high as Catherine that needs fixing." Eva took her hand. "You stay right there. Girls, get back to cooking."

Elizabeth and Rebecca jumped to do their duties while Hannah took the large sewing basket and started looking through it. By the time breakfast was ready, Hannah had already fixed two shirts and darned a pair of socks.

The mood was high and the laughter abundant until Olivia walked in. She carried a basket of eggs and a scowl.

"Livy, Hannah can sew." Rebecca seemed to be the most pleased by the newfound knowledge.

"Does that call for a holiday?" Olivia set the basket on the counter.

Eva cracked the eggs into the readied pan, and a sizzling sound filled the room. "*Sí*, it does call for a holiday. We have much sewing with so many people."

Olivia shrugged. "I sew."

Elizabeth snorted. "Like a bull dances."

"Shut up." Olivia speared her younger sister with a fierce glare. "At least I tried. More than you did."

"I know I can't sew, but at least I can cook. All you can do is scrub floors and clothes." Elizabeth stuck her nose in the air.

Olivia nearly leapt across the room at her sister. Eva stopped her with one look. The rest of the Grahams came in, no doubt after hearing the commotion between the girls.

Nicholas and Caleb stood by the door while Catherine rushed in with her braids flying.

"What happened? You didn't yell at Hannah again, did you, Livy?" Catherine was her protector of sorts.

"No, she didn't." Hannah gestured to the basket. "I was getting some sewing done and everybody got excited." It sounded foolish to her ears, but her explanation seemed to appease everyone.

Then Matt stepped in, pushing his brothers aside. He surveyed the room quickly before his gaze settled on Hannah. With a nod, he came into the room and sat down at the other end of the table.

The tension dissipated and they all sat down to eat. Hannah finally had an appetite, after days of an upset stomach and an upset heart. The food was delicious, and she almost thought Olivia had softened just a smidge toward her. Hannah could have been imagining it, but she had a small bit of hope their relationship might be getting better.

"Hannah and I are going to Houston to sign the papers," Matt announced without any preamble, and without talking to Hannah about it first.

Everyone stopped eating and stared at him, then turned to look at Hannah. After finally finding a way to fit in at the ranch, Matt was taking her away.

"For how long?" She was surprised her voice didn't shake.

"Two days at the most." Matt glanced at her. "After breakfast, pack what we need, including food."

Just like that, her husband had taken that goodness away from her. She wanted to tell him no. She wanted to tell him to ask her to do things instead of ordering her. Anger mixed with hurt, churning in her stomach. She lost her appetite for the delicious breakfast.

Hannah got to her feet. "I'm going to go check on Granny."

Most mornings Granny had trouble getting up because of pain in her joints. She usually made it up after the sun rose, but today Hannah wasn't going to wait. Today she needed her grandmother.

CHAPTER EIGHT

Eva's stare nearly burned a hole in Matthew's head. She was obviously angry with him, but he wasn't about to invite her to tell him why. The rest of his siblings were a barrier he was glad was there.

He had handled delivering the news about the trip to Houston badly. Truth was he was tired and his thoughts were a bit jumbled. He'd rehearsed talking to Hannah about it in his head numerous times during the night while he was taking care of the calf. Then somehow he thought he had done it already. Judging by the look on Hannah's face, he sure as hell hadn't.

Damn.

After that first night in the bedroom, he thought they had started to understand each other. At least the sex had been incredible. Damn, he spent half his time thinking about going to bed with her now. Unfortunately his tiredness and his big mouth had put a dent in that possibility.

Matt knew he'd have to talk to her, he just wanted to avoid it until they were on the trail together. It was a long ride to Houston. Plenty of time to talk.

Now all he had to do was avoid Eva until they left.

"He's a man, child. That's all I can say." Granny slowly buttoned her dress with gnarled hands. Hannah knew if she offered to help the older woman would be insulted. "Men can bully you around if you let them."

"I don't want him to bully me around." Hannah frowned. "But it seems he only wants me for the land."

Granny snorted. "Well, he told you that the minute he proposed. Why is it a surprise to you?"

It wasn't a surprise; it was a disappointment. Hannah had let her romantic side wreak havoc with her practical side, and it had resulted in misery.

"It's not. I just, well, I wanted more." She sighed and sat on the bed beside her grandmother, whose familiar scent helped calm her.

"Then you gotta earn it." Granny held out her hand and Hannah helped her to her feet. "Ain't no call to sit around whining."

Hannah's mouth dropped open. "I'm not whining."

"Land sakes, you've done nothing but whine since we got here." Granny speared her with one of those looks that always made Hannah squirm.

"I didn't think I was whining." She thought back over the four days since her wedding and realized Granny was right. She had been just accepting what was given to her rather than asking for what she wanted. That caused resentment, and obviously, whining.

"It's only natural that you feel out of place, Hannah. They're a big family." Granny patted her knee. "What you need to do is stake your claim, let them know who you really are."

Hannah didn't want to admit she didn't know who she was, and couldn't tell anyone anything. "What if they don't like me then?" Her voice dropped to a whisper. "What if Matt doesn't?"

"Get a backbone, child. There ain't no guarantees in this world. You got to take what you want and fight for what you need." Granny pointed at the chest in the corner. "Fetch me my reticule from that chest."

After some searching, Hannah found the ancient looking reticule, oft-mended and tattered as it was. She handed it to her grandmother.

"Now when I first got married, your grandfather was a fool. He was a terrible husband. My mama saw that and told me the same thing I'm telling you. Stand up for yourself and don't let nobody step on you." Granny fished around in the reticule and pulled out a handkerchief yellowed with age. As she unfolded it, Hannah found herself leaning forward, trying to see. "This here was my mama's wedding band."

Granny held up a thin band of silver. "I don't know what it's made of, but it's worth something. She gave it to me and said to keep it hidden. It was mine to do with as I chose." She put it in Hannah's palm and closed her fingers around it. "It's now yours. If you need to, sell it for money, but only if it's for you. This whole ranch is your husband's, but now you have something of value, too."

The slight weight of the ring in her hand didn't compare to the significance of what her grandmother had given her. It might not be a treasure, but it was something she could keep and call her own. She hugged her grandmother, so happy to have her there, to have her support and her love.

"Thank you. I will keep it safe."

"A'course you will. That's a legacy, that is. Not much of one, but it's what I have to give you." Granny got to her feet.

She had given Hannah so much more than a ring. Without her grandmother's love and support, Hannah would have ended up in an orphanage or worse. Granny meant the world to Hannah.

"Now quit your whining. Go get what you want and

fight for what you need." Granny shuffled toward the door. "I need some vittles and you'd best get packing." She glanced back at Hannah. "I've got faith in you, child. Go get him."

With that, her cackling grandmother had left her alone with her thoughts whirling. Hannah didn't think she'd been whining, but what Granny said did make sense. Matt had told her up front exactly what he wanted from her, and she had turned their marriage into a fairy tale of epic proportions. Foolish girl.

It was time Hannah actually started building the foundation for her marriage instead of waiting for someone to open the door for her. She would find a way to earn Matt's love and respect, instead of simply being his roommate. Hannah got to her feet and marched to her bedroom, ready to do battle.

He arrived in the bedroom five minutes later. She had begun packing her own bag, not knowing where his was. Without turning, she knew he was in the doorway watching her.

"I packed what appeared to be your Sunday clothes, along with mine. I brought the boot polish and brush, and my hairbrush." She looked down at her outfit. "I have a split riding skirt that used to be my mother's. What will the temperature be like at night? Do I need to bring my wool cape?"

He stared at her, surprise clearly written in his expression. "You're packing my things?"

"Of course. Isn't it a wife's job?" She had no idea what a wife's job was, but maybe he didn't either.

"I guess." He nodded. "I reckon I'll say thank you." He glanced at the bag. "We ought to get moving soon."

Hannah went back to packing as if she'd had ample experience doing it, which was far from the truth. She'd only packed twice in her life, once to move to the boardinghouse after her parents' deaths, and once when she got married. There had been no trips anywhere for her. The one to Houston would be the first time she'd left their little town.

A glimmer of excitement tickled her chest. Perhaps she'd not only be able to get closer to her new husband but also have an adventure to one day tell her children. With an even lighter heart, she finished packing and changed into the butter soft leather riding skirt. It had been her mother's. Although Hannah remembered her as being tall, she must've been short. The skirt was at least six inches too short. It wasn't as if Hannah could make it longer now, so it would have to do.

As she carried the bag toward the kitchen, voices echoed down the hallway, two of them unfamiliar. Her feet faltered for a second, but she kept going. As soon as she stepped into the kitchen, she wanted to run back to the bedroom.

In front of her stood the most beautiful woman she'd ever seen. She had porcelain skin, auburn hair, cornflower blue eyes, and ruby red lips. The woman wore an elegant green dress in some fancy fabric with a matching hat. She was smiling at Matt, her pearly white teeth shining against her plump lips.

Holy Mary, the woman was simply stunning.

"That's right kind of you to stop by, Margaret, but I'm about to leave. You and Jeb are welcome to stay and visit, a'course." Matt hadn't even noticed Hannah.

Jeb was almost as good-looking as the woman, with the same auburn hair and blue eyes. No doubt the woman's brother. He spotted Hannah and smiled.

"Good morning, madam." He tipped his hat, his smile almost blinding. "Jeb Stinson. And you are?"

Matt swung around and his jaw tightened. "This is Hannah."

Margaret turned, smiling, with her hand outstretched. "My wife."

The other woman's smile disappeared and shock rippled across her perfect features. "Wife?"

"You got married?" Jeb smiled and clapped Matt on the back. "I didn't know you were even courting anyone."

"Wife?" Margaret whirled around to face Matt. "Matthew Graham. I cannot believe my ears. You, well I thought, I'd never considered you would marry and not tell me."

Hannah's heart dropped to her feet. Obviously the woman had set her cap for Matt, and Hannah had destroyed that particular dream. She couldn't possibly feel more awkward than she did at that moment. If only there was a hole in the ground in front of her to drop into.

Matt frowned at Margaret. "You and me, we never courted. I know Mama had hopes, but you're a thoroughbred and I'm a cow pony."

The redhead put her gloved hand on his chest. "Matthew, I don't consider you beneath me. Just because Daddy has the biggest ranch in eastern Texas does not mean I wouldn't marry for love." Her lip quivered and her eyes grew moist.

Hannah dropped the bag and left the house, running after she cleared the front door. It didn't matter what they thought of her. She could not stand by and watch a perfect, beautiful woman throw herself at Matt.

Nicholas, Caleb, and the Vasquez boys were in the corral looking at a horse when she ran past. They all stopped to stare at her, but no one spoke. She didn't stop until she reached the crest of the hill just beyond the barn. By then she was out of breath and shaking.

She bent over and put her hands on her knees. Hannah tried to calm her breathing and her heart, which was about to break a rib it was beating so hard. There had been no way she could have stayed in the house a second longer.

The last thing she'd expected was a woman who had obviously been waiting to marry Matt. Why had he married Hannah instead?

"Hannah." Matt walked up the hill toward her. "What are you doing?"

The laugh that burst from her throat was more like a pitiful cry. She straightened up and met his gaze, knowing her pain and confusion shone in her eyes. "Why? Why did you marry me?"

"Hannah, I told you why." Matt put his hands on his hips and scowled. "I had to marry to get the land from Texas."

"Why didn't you marry her? She's beautiful, obviously rich, and she was expecting it from what I can tell." Hannah felt as if her heart was just pouring out of her mouth in a steady stream. No matter what, she had to get everything out or she would choke on it.

"Margaret?" He looked back toward the house. "I meant what I told her, a cow pony doesn't belong with a thoroughbred. She flirted with me, but I never took it seriously. She flirts with every man."

"She obviously wanted you to ask her to marry you. Now you've painted yourself into a corner and had to marry someone named Hannah." Hannah's hurt had turned to rage and she let the angry words fly. "You've made me into a second choice and saddled yourself with an ugly cow instead of a beautiful butterfly. You settled for me, and worst of all, I settled for you."

"Hannah." Matt's mouth opened in surprise. "You are not my second choice. I never even thought of Margaret when I needed a wife."

"Ha. I don't believe that." Hannah's face was likely redder than a beet from shouting at him.

"It's true. We don't suit, never have." He reached for her hand but she backed away.

"She's exquisitely beautiful." Her voice began to fade, as

did her anger. Her pain began to seep back up, stealing her breath.

"On the outside." Matt moved closer until he backed her into a huge tree. The bark scratched at her back. "I didn't marry her because I didn't want to."

Hannah stared into his eyes, wanting so desperately to see honesty, but she didn't know him well enough to tell for sure. His tone conveyed the truth, but she couldn't believe him entirely. Her head overruled her heart again.

"I don't believe you."

For a split second, she saw hurt in his gaze, and some evil little part of her was glad of it. He'd hurt her enough already.

"I can understand that, but I don't like it." He took her hands and pressed his forehead to hers. His breath gusted across her mouth and she breathed him in, his anger and hurt mingled with hers.

"Maybe one day, I'll change my mind," she whispered. "But right now I can't."

"You're my wife, Hannah, for now and always." He kissed her lightly. "Now let's get back to the house so we can start out."

She nodded and took his proffered arm. Hannah was exhausted, as if she had run from one end of Texas to the other. Her knees shook as they made their way down the hill and across the ground to the house. Jeb stood outside with Caleb, smoking a cigar.

"There you are, Mrs. Graham. I was worried we'd offended you." His accent was as smooth as his sister's, but he didn't set off any warning bells in Hannah's heart. He appeared to be just who he was, a good-natured young man.

"I'm sorry. I felt a little sick to my stomach." She gave him a weak smile and tightened her grip on Matt's arm.

"Caleb, can you get Winston and Buttercup saddled?"

Matt spoke to his brother. "We're leaving in just a few minutes."

"Sure thing, Matt." He frowned at both of them, but the younger Graham set off on his chore.

"You're leaving?" Jeb looked between them. "Nothing we said, is it?"

"No, we were heading to Houston to sign some papers." Matt opened the front door. "We can plan a visit after we get back."

"Margaret is already hatching a gathering to celebrate your wedding. No need for you to plan anything." Jeb followed them into the house.

Hannah looked around and realized so many things made sense, she wondered why she hadn't seen it before. Olivia sat beside Margaret, smiling and laughing, thick as thieves with the woman who wanted to be Mrs. Graham. It explained why Olivia didn't like her, why she was so hostile. Her sister-in-law expected her best friend to be Matt's wife, not a plump stranger plainer than prairie grass.

Eva stood at the stove, arms crossed, watching the young women. Granny sat at the table, also watching them. If she hadn't felt so awful, Hannah might have laughed at them. The sheer annoyance on the older women's faces was clear as day. Hannah realized nobody but Olivia tolerated Margaret.

"There you are, *hija*." Eva spotted them and smiled at Hannah. That simple gesture helped her feel ten times better. "I made you some food to take with you."

There on the counter was a large basket with a handle that would fit nicely on a saddle horn.

"*Gracias, Eva.*"

"*Hija?* Your housekeeper is already speaking Spanish to her?" Margaret's voice was nowhere near a whisper.

Olivia glanced at Eva, a smidge of guilt in her gaze.

"She's not just a housekeeper, and she talks Spanish to everyone."

"Well, we are in Texas, and we speak English. She should learn the words she needs to know." Margaret finally looked at Matt and Hannah. "I see you found your wayward wife. She should be careful. Accidents happen on ranches all the time."

Matt held Hannah tight when she surged forward. She wanted to punch the woman and possibly chip one of those perfect teeth.

"Easy," he said under his breath. "Let's just get our things and go."

Hannah breathed through her nose until the urge to do harm passed. Margaret turned a sparkling smile on Matt.

"I want to plan the biggest party in the state to celebrate your wedding. Livy will help me." Margaret patted Livy's shoulder. "Although she's apparently not happy with your marriage. I've convinced her it's for the best."

What nonsense was this woman spouting? She didn't know Hannah well enough to know anything about her marriage or whether it was for the best. The woman had a motive that was yet to be determined. Hannah knew she'd just found a reason to be on her guard.

"Why thank you, Margaret. That's right kind of you." Matt grabbed the basket and the traveling bag. "If you'll excuse us, we'll be on our way. Eva, we'll be back in two days."

"*Vaya con dios, hijos. Buen viaje.*" She smiled at Hannah. "Take care of him, *hija.*"

Hannah wasn't sure what that meant exactly but she did know she already loved Eva. The older woman could see right through someone to their soul. She was a person to be trusted, and she'd proved to be Hannah's first friend at the Graham ranch.

"You come back now, y'hear?" Granny speared her with her gaze. "Do what you need to, child."

Hannah almost blushed at the reminder of her conversation earlier with Granny, but managed to keep the heat from her cheeks.

"We'll see you in two days."

Matt shook Jeb's hand and they walked out of the house. When she and Matt finally walked into the barn, she let out the breath she'd been holding. It had been such a long day, and it was only nine o'clock in the morning.

Caleb had the horses saddled and ready, handing the reins to his brother. He nodded at them and disappeared back into the barn. The gelding was incredibly tall and broad, a perfect match for Matt. The mare was a dainty buckskin almost the color of buttermilk. Hannah thought the horse looked nice but she wasn't sure. Her experience with horses was extremely limited.

"Can you ride?" Matt murmured to her.

"A little."

He groaned. "I should have asked."

"It's okay. I rode some when I was younger, mostly on ponies, but I remember how." She approached the mare slowly.

"Let her get to know you first." Matt took her hand. "Breathe into her nostrils so she can get your scent."

Hannah thought that was about the strangest thing she'd heard all day, but she did it just the same. The horse whickered and pressed her big snout into Hannah's chest.

"Now pet the side of her neck. Let her feel your touch." He took her hand and flattened it on the horse's warm flesh. The combination of his callused fingers and touching the mare made tears prick her eyes, this time for the right reason.

"She likes you."

Hannah let a bit of joy into her heart. "I like her, too."

"Are you ready?" He was close enough she could almost count the thick eyelashes gracing his eyelids. He was so beautiful she could hardly believe he was really her husband.

"I'm ready."

Chapter Nine

Matt did not know exactly what had happened at the ranch, but as they rode away, he was damn glad to be leaving. Margaret had arrived and thrown everyone into a snit, as she usually did. Damn woman knew just how to stir the pot and she did a good job. Made Hannah think they were supposed to be married.

That was so far from the truth, it was laughable. Oh, maybe when he was fifteen, he'd followed her around. But he learned his lesson when she humiliated him in front of her family at a barbecue. Matt might have dreamed about her ten years ago, but now she'd turned into something more like a nightmare.

Jeb was good folk and Matt liked him a lot. The rest of the Stinsons were more like snakes in the grass, eager to show everyone just how much they had. Margaret was a product of her mother's demanding nature and her father's pride. Jeb was somehow different from the rest. If he hadn't looked exactly like his sister, Matt would have guessed he'd been adopted.

Shaking off his thoughts of the Stinsons, he concentrated instead on Hannah's childish wonder at the horse she rode. He could see she had some amount of skill but wasn't at all confident in her abilities. That seemed to be the case with most everything she did, except for cooking and sewing. She was a puzzle he had yet to figure out.

Hannah bounced a bit in the saddle, but she had a natural seat. With some practice, she'd do fine. He'd tucked some horse liniment in his bag just in case the long ride caused her discomfort later. No reason to embarrass her, but he knew just how sore a hind end and thighs could get.

The bright blue sky above them was dotted with a few white, puffy clouds. The day was warm with only a gentle breeze. It was a perfect day for a trip, and although the purpose was enough to make him quake in his boots, he focused instead on the sheer pleasure of the ride.

"How do you feel?"

Hannah shifted in the saddle. "Good so far. Don't know about later."

"I've got liniment in case you're sore." The idea of rubbing it into her skin, of the soft downy skin between her thighs, made his entire body harden at once. Particularly his cock, which thumped against his trouser buttons.

"Oh, good. Granny usually has a good remedy but I haven't gotten the knack of making a good poultice yet." She glanced back at him, then her gaze fell between his legs. Like a bullet, her gaze snapped back to his. She obviously saw his state and was probably wondering exactly why riding a horse had made him hard.

"I, uh, started thinking about you." Maybe telling her the bare truth was the right thing to do.

"Me?" Her eyes widened. "Really?"

His grin felt more like a wolf's leer. "Yes, you, Mrs. Graham."

She giggled and the sound went straight to his throbbing staff. It was going to be a long ride.

With Margaret and the troubles at the ranch behind them, the rest of the morning passed by mostly in silence.

As if they were comfortable with each other, at ease with silence.

"I hear you're a real hand at sewing." Matt tripped over his own tongue with that one.

"Oh, I know how to do basic things. I, uh, enjoy it." She looked down, as he discovered she always did when talking about herself. He realized it was embarrassment.

"That's a good thing. I mean, enjoying something that most folks think of as a chore." Matt kept his gaze on hers, willing her to look up. "I like taking care of my horse."

She finally lifted her lashes and looked at him out of the corner of her eyes. "Taking care of your horse?"

"Currying him, picking rocks out of his shoes, even using the hoof knife to keep his hooves healthy. It might be a chore to my brothers, but I like it." He patted Winston's neck. "He's, well, my friend. Stupid I know." Now it was his turn to be embarrassed.

To his surprise, Hannah raised her head. "It's not stupid. I think it's sweet." She smiled at him, and he found himself smiling back.

"Don't tell anyone else that. I won't hear the end of it."

This time, she laughed, that amazingly rich sound that always surprised him. As he watched, her freckled face lit up brighter than the sun. Hannah laughed with her entire being, the most genuine thing he'd ever seen.

After that, the ride was not silent. He found himself talking to Hannah about things he hadn't told anyone else. Not even Caleb, who was closest to him.

The conversation continued as they feasted on Eva's ham and tortillas. They'd found a shaded spot to sit down, with a creek and sweet grass for the horses. The cool water in their canteens washed everything down. It was a simple meal, but the first one he'd truly enjoyed in six months, since his parents were taken from him.

She cleaned everything up efficiently while he retrieved

the horses from the tree they were tied to. Hannah might not think much of herself, but Matt already did. He'd not admit to her that he hadn't expected much from their marriage, but he was damn glad to be proven wrong.

"You never told me the story of the land grant." She hung the basket on her horse's saddle horn.

Her question hit Matt like a punch to the gut. It was true he'd only given her the barest information about the reason behind the land grant. The entire story was painful for him and he hadn't known her well enough to tell it when he'd married her.

"I am curious, but if you don't want to tell me, that's okay." She put her foot in the stirrup and tried to boost herself into the saddle.

Matt put his hands on her behind and pushed her up.

"Oh shit!" The curse popped out of her mouth fast and hard. Matt barely had time to react before she did it again as she landed on the saddle. "Son of a bitch."

She turned to look at him, this time not hiding her pinkened cheeks. "Oh my God."

Matt did the only thing he could think of. He threw back his head and laughed. "Hannah, I can't even begin to tell you how glad I am you married me."

"I, uh, do tend to cuss sometimes," she confessed.

"Me, too." He patted her thigh. "We're going to be just fine Hannah Graham."

Matt meant every word of it. He'd found a hidden treasure in his wife and he intended to hang onto her, come hell or high water.

They spent the night in a sheltered area just outside Houston, surrounded by rocks and the protection of the horses. Although it wasn't an ideal place to make love, they did spoon together all night. Hannah felt safe in his arms, comfortable sleeping with him for the first time since they'd married.

In the morning, he rolled over and kissed her. The heat from his lips traveled down her body, leaving tingles in its wake. He kissed her again, this time slowly, nibbling her lips until she opened them.

She moaned in her throat and he swallowed the sound into his own. His kiss deepened and grew more demanding. His body became hard as an oak against hers and she found herself wishing they weren't on the ground, lying between two blankets. She wanted to touch him, feel his skin, and make love.

Hannah scooted closer, pressing her aching breasts into his chest. He reached between them and squeezed one nipple, drawing a gasp from deep within her. A throb of pure desire echoed through her and she knew she was already wet, again. She didn't want to admit to herself that she was falling in love with her husband, but she knew she was. Whether he would return her love had yet to be determined.

"Ah, excuse me, folks." A stranger's voice sounded from nearby. "I'm just passing through."

Hannah tucked her head into Matt's shoulder and tried not to die of embarrassment. Matt kissed her forehead and chuckled, a painful sound.

"I guess it's time to get going." He extricated himself from the blankets and held out his hand for her.

She glanced around and saw the stranger who had spoken walking down the road. The last thing she wanted to do was leave the cocoon she'd shared with Matt, but he was right. It was time to get going.

After a cold breakfast, they rode into the city. When they arrived in Houston proper, Hannah was goggle-eyed at the number of people, horses, carriages, wagons, and buildings.

She could hardly take it all in without hurting her neck craning it this way and that. Good thing he knew where he was going. She would never have been able to find her way without him.

He stabled the horses and led her out of the livery. Hannah hung onto his arm as they navigated the streets. Two people bumped into her and one wagon nearly ran her down. It truly made her miss home and the quiet pace of the life she didn't realize she loved so much.

Matt took them straight to the land grant office. An officious looking man in a navy suit made them sit down in the most uncomfortable chairs she'd ever had the misfortune of sitting in. Matt stared straight ahead, stoic-faced and silent. Hannah wondered if he was nervous. Judging by the way he fidgeted as they waited, he definitely was.

"What's wrong?" she whispered.

"Nothing. Just don't like being in places like this." He glanced down at his callused hands. "I'm a rancher, not a banker or an office man."

Hannah understood what he meant and felt the same level of discomfort being there, but it was important to the ranch. She had married Matt so he could get this land grant. There was no reason to be a coward now, even if her stomach was twittering as if a bird was trapped inside.

"Mr. and Mrs. Graham?" A short, round bald man with thick spectacles peered at them. He wore a dark gray suit and vest, which looked as if it would bust a button if he breathed too hard.

"Mr. Prentiss." Matt stood and held out his hand to help Hannah to her feet. It was a gentlemanly gesture, one she could get used to.

"I'm glad to see you back to finalize the paperwork." He turned his gaze to Hannah. "This must be your wife, Hannah."

"Yes, sir, this is my Hannah."

My Hannah. Oh, her stupid heart did a pittypat at the reference.

She nodded at him. "Pleased to meet you, sir."

"And you as well, Mrs. Graham. Why don't you both come into my office?" He led them through a frosted glass door and into a room with a large wooden desk and two of the same uncomfortable chairs in front of it. Were there no comfortable places to sit?

Hannah perched on the chair and tried to look the way she thought a respectable wife should. Her back was straight, her hands folded in her lap.

"I have papers for Mrs. Graham to sign, since you've already signed them, Mr. Graham." He pulled out a sheaf of papers and presented them to her with a fountain pen.

She'd worn her best white gloves, really the only good pair she had. As she took them off, she noted Mr. Prentiss glance at her bare ring finger. Her stomach dropped and panic danced on her neck. She forced herself to smile at Mr. Prentiss.

"My ring always gets caught on my glove." Hiding her shaking hands, she reached into her reticule and pulled out the ancient handkerchief with her great-grandmother's silver ring. She had no time to hope that it would fit. If it didn't, it would make the situation worse.

Her Grandma Peters must've been smiling down on her like a guardian angel. The ring slid onto her finger as if it were made for her, and not another woman seventy-five years earlier. Matt made a noise in his throat, which she assumed was surprise.

Mr. Prentiss gave her a small smile. "Very nice. Now if you'll sign these papers, we can complete the land grant process."

The next thirty minutes were a blur of papers, legal

terms she couldn't possibly follow, and a great deal of ink. Her signature was shaky on a few of the papers, but it didn't seem to matter to the clerk.

Mr. Prentiss pulled out a large map and spread it on his desk. "Now let me show you the property lines so you are well aware of where your new property lies."

Matt and Hannah leaned forward. It was the first time she'd seen a land map, and it had lots of squiggles and symbols on it she didn't understand.

"This is your current ranch here. To the east and south is the Stinson ranch, and to the west is the McRae ranch." He pointed to a pie shaped squiggle. "This is your new acreage. Note there is approximately two miles of land between the old property and the new."

Matt traced the property lines with one blunt-edged fingernail. "Who owns this?"

"Frederick Stinson."

Matt's jaw tightened as he continued to study the map. "Two miles hmm? And how long does it take to get through this two miles?"

"You'd have to go around the McRae's through this canyon. Rough estimate is thirty-five or forty miles." Mr. Stinson pushed his glasses up his nose.

Matt traced the swath of land with his finger. "How is it possible that he owns just this piece?"

"Oh, he doesn't own just this piece. His land grant was rather unusual. You see his property extended out to here." Mr. Stinson pointed to another line. "He requested the additional ten thousand acres directly adjoining his, but that wasn't possible given your father's claim. Instead he took the ragged land between."

"So what you're saying is that he deliberately took the land that separated our current property from the new property?" Matt sounded so calm, but she heard the steel in his voice.

"It appears so." Mr. Stinson pushed up his glasses again. "Why would the Republic do that? Stinson obviously wanted to prevent my father from using both tracts of land." Matt's hand curled into a fist. "How is that fair?"

"Mr. Graham, if a legal resident of Texas has a claim to land, we grant it to them. It's not up to the Republic to determine what's fair." Mr. Stinson spoke the words, but not very convincingly. He probably hadn't realized what had been done, but now that he did, he was in the unenviable position of explaining it to her and Matt.

Hannah was flabbergasted by the implications of what they'd discovered. She didn't know much about cattle, but making a forty-mile loop around a two-mile piece of land was ludicrous. It couldn't possibly be good for the animals to walk that far on a regular basis.

"That's a load of horse shit, pardon my language." Matt sat back in the chair. "I either move my entire ranch forty miles, including my house, or I deal with Stinson for easement rights."

"Well, I'm sorry about that, Mr. Graham, but it's out of my hands." Mr. Stinson folded his hands in front of him on the desk and gave Matt and Hannah an apologetic, weak look.

"Just give me my papers and we'll be on our way." Matt snatched the papers the other man held out to him. "Good day, sir."

He took Hannah's elbow with force, not enough to hurt her, but enough that she hurried along to leave the land grant office. She'd seen him annoyed but never so angry. However, she didn't blame him one bit. Hannah was angry, too. The very idea that someone had deliberately put himself between the two tracts of land was horrible.

"Why did he do it?" Hannah asked when they were out on the street.

"Stinson? He's a jackass with a big mouth and an even

bigger ego. My father never liked him, for good reason apparently." Matt almost marched down the street, his boots slamming into the hard-packed dirt.

"What will we do?" She was glad she had long legs to keep with him.

"Go home."

"And after that?"

He stopped and turned to meet her gaze. "I don't know, Hannah. I just don't know."

The ride back to the ranch was considerably less enjoyable than the trip to Houston. Matt pushed them and the horses until deep into the night. He didn't want to stop until he reached home. Hannah tried talking to him, but he wasn't in any mood to hold a conversation.

He was furious, more so than he'd ever been in his life. The legacy left by his father was now in jeopardy because of one man's greed. His family would join him in the anger, but the burden to find a solution to the situation was on his shoulders.

Hannah was strong, he knew that, but that long fifteen hours in the saddle proved to him she was stronger than he'd thought. A lesser woman would have complained or insisted they stop, yet she didn't. He was used to being in the saddle for long days, but she wasn't even much of a rider.

Now she'd spent the better part of two days on a horse. For him. It was humbling.

By the time they rode into the ranch, he was about to fall out of the saddle. Matt stopped at the barn and slid to the ground, his legs barely able to straighten. He made it to Hannah's horse and saw the lines cut into her face by sheer exhaustion.

"Come here, honey." He plucked her off the saddle and into his arms. The horses' heads hung down as they waited patiently for him to take care of them. First he had to take care of his wife.

Matt carried her toward the house and she shifted in his arms.

"What are you doing? Put me down. I'm too heavy for you." She sounded so weak he could have mistaken her for a kitten.

"Hush now. We're home." He laid her on the bed gently. Then he took off her shoes and pulled up the quilt to cover her. He kissed her forehead, then returned to take care of the horses.

By the time he made it back to Hannah, she was snoring softly. After he removed his own boots, he crawled in beside her, never so glad to be home.

In the morning, he would talk to his family about what he'd learned. For now, he snuggled up beside Hannah and closed his eyes.

Chapter Ten

Hannah's thighs and behind were on fire. The burning sensation yanked her out of a deep sleep. She gasped as she came into full consciousness and the soreness slammed into her. The two days spent riding had taken their toll on her unprepared hindquarters. She opened her eyes and recognized their bedroom at the ranch. A hazy memory of Matt carrying her flitted through her mind. It must have really happened because she certainly hadn't walked in there on her own. Heck, she wasn't sure if she could walk.

She groaned and turned on her side. Her husband was there, fast asleep, with dark smudges of exhaustion beneath his eyes. It was the first time she'd been able to study him without his knowing. He looked so much younger asleep, as though slumber had washed away all the stresses of the ranch.

He had dark lashes, not overly long but thick. A bump on the bridge of his nose spoke of an injury earlier in his life. Another scar marred his skin just above his left eyebrow, perhaps an inch long and whitened with age. The stubble that graced his chin and cheeks was darker than the hair on his head. Unable to resist she reached out and touched one fingertip to his chin. He was a beautiful man, even in sleep.

His eyes popped open and she froze in place. Her heart thumped hard as she waited for him to do something.

"Hannah." The rasp of his voice sent a skitter across her skin.

"Matthew."

Their gazes were locked and the air between them crackled. She wanted so badly to kiss him, but hesitated. They'd only been married a few short days, and although they'd been intimate, she was absolutely shy around him. Now she'd been caught ogling and fondling him. Perhaps what she'd done might not be considered fondling, she had been touching him.

"Where did you get the ring?"

She wasn't expecting the question. "The ring?" She held up her left hand, just now noticing she still wore it. "Granny gave it to me. It belonged to her mother."

"It fits you." He touched the ring with one finger.

"Like I was supposed to wear it."

His gaze snapped to hers and the moment stretched out. She leaned toward him and her muscles reminded her of just how much pain she was in. Hannah hissed in a breath and moved back to her side of the bed.

"Are you sore?" He shifted to a sitting position and the tension between them broke.

Hannah cursed her own foolishness and wondered if she would ever be strong enough to be a normal wife.

"Yes, a bit. Mostly on my, ah, the parts that rest on the saddle." Those parts were currently throbbing with more than soreness from the ride.

"I've got some liniment. Thought we'd use it when we were on our trip, but I didn't think we'd ride straight back either." He rose from bed and Hannah was startled to see his erection clearly evident in his drawers. Was it like that every morning?

He fished around in the saddlebags on the floor before pulling out a tin. "Found it."

She didn't know what would happen when he rubbed the liniment on her, but she was filled with anticipation.

"Roll over and pull up your nightdress, Hannah."

It didn't sound sexy, but it sure made her feel naughty as she managed to do what he asked. Her muscles were in sorry shape, but it was the idea that his bare hands would be rubbing her that was foremost in her mind.

"My hands are a little rough." He opened the tin and put some liniment on his hands.

"I don't mind," she confessed into the pillow. "I like your hands."

He chuckled softly. "I'm glad to hear it. Just try to relax."

Now that would be quite a challenge. She wanted to enjoy the experience, but her anxiety was warring with her need.

Matt touched her behind her knees, making circles as he worked his way up to her thighs. Although his fingers were strong, his touch wasn't rough. She closed her eyes and focused on how good it felt.

Her sore muscles slowly unknotted under his hands. Matt's thumbs swiped her inner thighs, so close to her pussy that she clenched her muscles. A jolt of pain slammed up her body at the sudden movement.

He stopped, his hands still touching her. "Easy, Hannah. I'm not going to hurt you. I promise."

"I know. I, um, I'm not used to people touching me there." She sounded foolish to her own ears.

"I'm not people. I'm your husband."

Hannah was glad he couldn't see her blushing. "Please keep going."

After a moment, he started again. She wanted to show

him how much she trusted him, truly she did, so she spread her legs wider.

He made a funny noise and his hands momentarily stopped. "You, ah, surprise me."

"I hope so." She spoke into her pillow but she hoped he heard her.

His thumbs traveled upward again, nearing her pulsing core, then slid past to her behind. He spread her cheeks with each circle, allowing cold air to land on her heated center. Cold. Hot. Cold. Hot.

When he kissed the nape of her neck, a moan popped out of her mouth. The massage had turned into something much more. His hardened staff brushed against her thigh.

"Hannah, I need you."

"I need you, too. Please, Matt." She pushed up against him until he was cradled right where she needed him most.

He jumped off the bed and shucked his drawers so quickly, her skin didn't even cool in the time he was gone. His now naked cock brushed her thighs, raising goose bumps in its wake.

The head teased her opening. She pushed up against him again, and he slid in further. She raised her behind up even further until he was fully sheathed inside her. Hannah gasped at the feeling of rightness. This was where she belonged, where he belonged.

His arms shook beside her as he began to thrust in and out. With each movement, their joining made a soft, wet noise that was strangely exciting.

Hannah didn't know people could make love back to front. The sensation was different, more intense. He slid deeper within her, joining them together in a profound way.

Her stomach fluttered as the pleasure burned low and deep in her belly. She gripped the bed, the scent of their lovemaking filling her nose. Her body recognized his, reached for the ultimate peak it would find only with Matt.

"Now, Hannah, now." His arms shook harder as his pace grew faster. He slammed into her, tugging her into a whirl of sensations.

She gave herself over, falling into blinding ecstasy that raced through her. A thousand points of light echoed through her, bringing her to another realm. Matt whispered her name as he found his own peak.

They both shook with the power of their joining. Hannah didn't know he had the power to bring her to such a place. She couldn't imagine a more beautiful experience and knew she would eagerly await the next time.

He kissed her neck again, then rolled off her with a groan. "Remind me to rub liniment on you more often."

Hannah giggled. In the privacy of their bedroom, Matt softened and became the man she had always dreamed of marrying. Outside the bedroom, he was the head of the ranch, bossy, and not at all the same person. She wouldn't admit this to him, but her heart was becoming Matthew's and she was helpless to stop it.

The silence in the kitchen was broken only by Catherine's slurping of her milk. The rest of the Grahams and Eva stared at Matt with expressions of disbelief, anger, and confusion.

Matt's anger had not truly dissipated. It had smoldered deep within him all the way back to the ranch. Making love to Hannah had allowed him to escape while they had been together. Yet reality came crashing down the moment he spread the map on the table and explained their problem.

"What does this all mean?" Olivia's face was pale. "We have to move?"

"It means we have a two-mile gap between this ranch

and our new land. We have a choice to make." He looked at all of them in turn. "We can negotiate with Stinson to run our herd back and forth across his two-mile tract. We can try to buy it from him, or we can move everything we have to the new property and abandon this one."

"That bastard." Caleb slammed his fist into the table. "He did this on purpose."

"I think so too, but that doesn't change the fact we have to make a decision." Matt wanted to tear the map to pieces and make Stinson eat every piece. "We probably have a fight on our hands."

"Damn right we have a fight on our hands." Nicholas's expression matched Caleb's. "If Pa were alive, he would fight that son of a bitch."

"Nicholas, *hijo,* your language," Eva scolded.

"He is a son of a bitch," Nicholas mumbled under his breath.

Matt stared at the map, at the two miles standing between their dream and reality. Stinson had done it deliberately, there wasn't a doubt about that, or the fact he was a bastard. Nick had that right.

"First thing we need to do is talk to him." Olivia was still pale but calm. "Mr. Stinson is a reasonable man, and I'm sure Margaret can convince him to work with us." Olivia cast a sideways glance at Hannah. "Too bad she didn't marry you when you asked."

Perhaps no one else saw it, but Matt did. Hannah flinched at Olivia's nastiness.

"That's enough, Livy. I was five years old. Ancient history. We don't have money to buy the land straight out obviously. I want to offer Stinson a share of profits our first year to buy the land." Matt had considered a great many possibilities on their return from Houston. The first one he discarded, since murder would only garner him a noose, not a ranch.

"Give him our profit?" Caleb shook his head.

"It's logical."

"It's *loco.*"

"Papa would whoop his behind."

"I'll whoop yours if you don't stop pushing me off the bench."

"We can't give him our hard-earned money."

"That's our blood, sweat, and tears, Matt."

"I don't sweat. I'm a lady."

"You sweat and you stink."

"Shut up."

"Enough, all of you!" Matt had no patience for their bickering today. "Sometimes life doesn't give you a good choice, but it does give you choices. We have to decide if it's the best one."

They all stopped yelling but there were glares around the table.

"What does Hannah think?" Catherine looked up at them, a milk mustache on her lip.

Everyone turned to look at Hannah. She'd been sipping her coffee quietly and paused with the cup halfway to her mouth.

"Me? I don't have a say in this."

"Yes, you do," Rebecca piped up. "You're a Graham now."

Matt caught her gaze and held it, telling her with his eyes the girls were right. Regardless of Livy's attitude, the rest of the family had accepted her. She was a Graham.

Hannah glanced at her grandmother, sitting in the corner on what was now "her stool." The older woman nodded.

"The best way to catch flies is with honey, not vinegar. If you sweeten the pot, he just might accept the offer." Hannah was a born diplomat if he ever met one.

"Hannah is right. We have to approach him as a neighbor with an offer." He stared hard at Olivia. "Hannah and I will head over there in the morning."

Matt walked out of the house because he didn't want to listen to the yelling as it began again. He knew Olivia would be angry and likely Caleb would want to be part of the trip to the Stinsons' ranch. Yet another family discussion stuck in the mire of too many opinions. He had too much on his mind to take grief from his siblings.

Winston was waiting in his stall for Matt. It was too late in the day for a ride, but he could spend time spoiling the gelding. After all, he'd been ridden hard on the trip to Houston. The least he could do was give the horse something back.

He didn't admit to himself he was hiding. After all, he was a rancher, a man, and a landowner. He had no reason to hide.

Hannah checked her reflection in the tiny mirror for the tenth time, trying to smooth down the wayward curls that would not behave. They were leaving for the Stinsons', riding over together as an old married couple would.

She didn't have any fancy outfit, but her clothes were clean and pressed. Perhaps one day she'd get some fabric and make herself something new. Today she had to make do with what she had.

"Are you ready yet?" Matt's voice sounded from the hallway, impatience evident in his tone.

"Yes, I'm ready." She smoothed her blouse one more time, then opened the bedroom door.

He was dressed as he normally would on any other day, in a shirt and trousers, but at least his boots were clean. She suddenly felt overdressed.

"Should I change?"

"For God's sake, no. Let's just go. You've wasted enough time already." He turned away to walk down the hall.

Something inside her snapped and a surge of pure anger hit her square between the eyes. "This is my first visit with the neighbors. I wanted to make a good impression."

He stopped and turned to look at her. "What are you talking about?"

"I'm new to this whole marriage, rancher's wife thing. And ignoring me or talking to me as if I'm an annoyance is not helping." Her cheeks grew warm but this time it wasn't with embarrassment. "I need your respect outside the bedroom."

Hannah wanted to slap her hand over her mouth but she held herself firm and didn't drop her gaze. He'd been the one to ask her opinion on what to do. Now he was back to snapping at her, but she wanted, needed, to be treated as his wife and not as an unwanted guest.

"Hannah. I, uh, was . . . I'm sorry." He ran his hands down his face. "Can you please come with me to the Stinsons now?"

Hannah nodded and walked down the hallway, her head held high. She'd taken Granny's advice for the first time. Although she was mortified by some of the things she'd said, for the first time, she was proud of herself. Hannah had stood on her own two feet.

It took them about half an hour to ride over to the Stinsons' ranch. A silent ride, much different from their previous trip to Houston. Matt was either angry with her or didn't know what to say.

Neither did Hannah.

Matt was the first man she'd spent significant time with, and obviously the first man she'd lain with. He was teaching her how to be a woman in more ways than one, even if he didn't want to.

The Stinsons' house was larger than anything she'd ever seen. It was so wide, there were at least ten rocking chairs on the front porch, and room for ten more. A barn two stories high towered over the trees. Everything was simply enormous.

They dismounted at the hitching post to the right of the front porch. Matt helped her down, silently of course, then held her elbow as they walked toward the front door. Surprisingly no one came out to greet them. The large house seemed to be deserted. Most ranch hands were likely out working, but she'd thought there would always be at least a few folks around. Someone to take care of such a big house.

Their boots echoed on the very well swept porch. There didn't seem to be a speck of dirt anywhere on the Stinson ranch. Perhaps dirt was as intimidated by the place as Hannah was.

Matt knocked on the door. Within seconds it was opened by a plump Mexican woman wearing a fancy black maid's outfit and a spotless white apron. She nodded at Matt.

"*Buenos dias, Señor Graham.*"

"*Buenos dias, Carmen. ¿Donde esta Señor Stinson?*"

"*Esta en la jardin alla.*" The woman opened the door wider and gestured them in.

"*Gracias.*" Matt took Hannah's arm again as they walked through the ranch house.

Hannah tried not to stare, but it was hard. Everywhere, she saw fancy furniture, paintings on the walls, elaborate vases, shiny crystals on an enormous chandelier, and rugs softer than anything she'd ever felt under her feet. It was a palace fit for a king.

That king was currently sitting on a bench in a beautiful garden, filled with blossoms and the drone of bees. He was as big as she'd expected, with broad shoulders and chest, black hair liberally sprinkled with silver, and gray eyes. He watched them approach but did not rise until they had nearly reached him.

"Graham." He rose to his full height, just a smidge shorter than Matt. "Didn't expect to see you today."

His gray gaze flickered to her, then back to Matt. She'd thought Matt treated her impolitely but this man just ignored her as if she didn't exist.

Their visit hadn't started well at all. Hannah didn't want to ruin their chances of getting the land they needed, but she had to do something. Hannah's newfound courage reared its head again.

"Good morning, Mr. Stinson." She smiled broadly. "I'm Hannah Graham. I'm so pleased to meet you."

"Good day, madam." He turned his head slightly in her direction. "What brings you by, Matthew?"

"We are planning a barbecue to celebrate our marriage," Hannah blurted, surprising herself. "Matt wanted to come by to invite you and your family personally."

"That so?" Stinson rocked back on his heels and studied Matt.

"Sure is. Hannah and Eva are planning it. I just need to slaughter the steer." Matt's smile was tight.

"When is this grand event taking place?" Unbelievably, Stinson seemed to relax a little at the invitation.

"Saturday." Hannah squeezed Matt's arm. "I thought perhaps you might have someone at the ranch who plays music, too." The words were pouring out of her mouth as if someone else were controlling her voice.

"I'll see what I can do." He studied Hannah with a stare as sharp as any knife. "You got gumption, girl. I like that."

Matt cleared his throat, but she didn't know if it was because of surprise or dismay.

"Thank you, sir." Hannah managed to smile again. "Will you be able to come to the barbecue?"

"I wouldn't miss it for the world." Mr. Stinson didn't smile but she saw the amusement in his gaze. He was a formidable man.

"It was a pleasure to meet you, sir. We'll see you on Saturday then." She sketched an awkward curtsy, then turned to Matt.

He was likely wrestling with whether or not to ask about the land tract. Hannah had given him the opportunity to get Mr. Stinson on the Graham ranch. Perhaps that was a better place to talk about an offer. She had taken a chance and hoped like mad it was the right one to take.

"Of course. I'll bring Margaret and Jeb." He tipped his hat to Matt. "You've got an interesting wife there, Graham. I look forward to the barbecue."

With that, he turned and left them alone in the garden. She was afraid Matt would be angry at her, but honestly she had done it for him, for the Grahams' future.

Matt wanted to throttle his wife at the same time he wanted to kiss her. Hannah had suddenly found her voice, along with a healthy dose of sass, and she seemed to be out of control. Not only had she told him exactly how she felt, but she'd told Stinson they were having a barbecue.

Even if they had been planning a barbecue, he sure as hell wouldn't have invited the Stinsons to it. Yet Hannah had thrown out the invitation as if they were all friends. His father had had nothing but disrespect for his neighbor. The rancher had been a pain in the ass ever since his father had settled on the property. To invite the man to a gathering at Circle Eight was almost an insult to his father's memory.

Hannah hadn't known the history between the Grahams and Stinsons. He could have told her but he hadn't. She could have asked him about the barbecue but she hadn't. Matt realized he shouldn't be too angry with her because they were both to blame.

He was still annoyed though.

As they walked out of the house and onto the porch,

they were both quiet. Hannah marched to Buttercup and got herself up in the saddle with very little grace. She looked down at him, her jaw set and her gaze calm. He didn't know her well enough to know what her demeanor meant.

He untied her reins from the hitching rail and handed them to her. She looked sheepish for a moment, then took them. Matt mounted Winston and they started back toward home.

After they rode for ten minutes, out of range of the house, Matt couldn't keep quiet any longer.

"Did you plan on asking my permission for the barbecue before the neighbors arrived?"

She frowned at him. "I know it came as a surprise to you, but I didn't think I had to ask permission to celebrate our wedding. I didn't want Margaret to plan it."

Matt felt the sting of her tone and her words. Though it was true they hadn't done anything to celebrate their wedding, he wasn't sure he liked being taken to task by his wife.

"A barbecue costs money, Hannah. Did you think of that?"

She huffed out a breath. "Folks bring a covered dish; the only cost is the steer for you to cook. Everything else will come from the garden. Maybe we can even do some hunting for hares and small game."

He had to admit, silently, she was right. He had no argument that would stand against her logic. However, it stuck in his craw that she'd made the decision and he had to live with it.

"There's not enough time to get ready."

She didn't respond, which irked him even further. Matt stewed for a while as they rode. If he told Stinson there was not going to be a barbecue, he'd have to hear about it every time they saw each other for the rest of his life. If he allowed the barbecue to happen, he'd have to accept that his wife had made a big decision on her own. That would set a precedent for their marriage he wasn't sure he wanted to accept.

Damned if he wasn't stuck between a rock and a hard place. The first week of his marriage was turning out to be a lot harder than he'd expected. His parents had made it look so easy to be married. He hadn't agreed with the way his father had kowtowed to his mother, but he couldn't argue the fact they had loved each other.

He wasn't in love with Hannah, but his body was damn sure in lust. Every time he saw the curve of her breast or watched her ass in the saddle, or even smelled her scent, his damn cock took over his brain.

The longer his mind whirled with thoughts, the more frustrated he got. He needed to talk to Hannah but he didn't know how. When the house was within sight, he pulled on the reins and stopped. It was time to do something.

"What's wrong?" Hannah pulled her horse to a stop with a bit more difficulty. She was still learning how to ride, but she'd come far after only a few days of practice.

"We need to go back and tell Stinson there is no barbecue."

Hannah rode over to him, her frown firmly in place. "Why would we do that?"

"I don't want him at my house."

She flapped her hand. "It's the perfect place to offer to buy his land. There will be lots of neighbors to witness it."

Matt wanted to argue with her, but dammit, she was right. Stinson loved to posture in front of people and if he was made to look like a greedy bastard, he might give in and accept the offer.

"You are the most aggravating wife I've ever had," he blurted out.

She flinched and then a mask seemed to fall over her expression. "I'm the only wife you've ever had."

At that moment, Matt saw only her; the rest of the world

fell away. His breathing sharpened and his heart raced. He leaned forward and grabbed the back of her neck. As his lips slammed down on hers, she gasped. His hand tangled in her curls, knocking her hat off.

Her untutored kisses made his blood run hot. He kissed her hard, a bruising kiss meant to intimidate and to punish. He needed to show her he was the man in their relationship, in charge of their marriage.

The kisses turned into much more than a lesson in power. The softness of her lips, her eagerness to return his ardor, drew him into a dark whirl of passion so sharp, it was his turn to gasp.

Her tongue rasped against his tentatively, then with more confidence. He forgot where they were. He forgot why he was angry. He wanted only to keep kissing her until his desire was quenched.

One of the horses hadn't shifted, pulling their mouths apart. Hannah looked dazed as she put her fingers to her swollen lips. She looked as sexy as any woman who had just been thoroughly kissed.

Matt was able to pull in a breath and almost cleared his head. What the hell was he doing? They were in the middle of nowhere and he might have taken her right there if the horses hadn't interrupted them.

"Dammit, Hannah, I-I don't know what just happened." His voice was shaking as much as his hands.

"I, uh, neither do I." She looked down and saw her hat on the dusty ground. It looked like the horse had stepped on it.

"I'm sorry." He jumped down and picked it up. The hat was probably older than she was, and the horse's hoof had put a final note on its usefulness. "I think we need to get you a new hat."

She looked stricken and he felt even worse. "It was my father's."

That explained a lot about why it was so beaten up. Matt hadn't wanted to make her feel bad by telling her the hat was pitiful. Now he had to replace it and without a lot of money, that might be difficult.

"We'll get you a new one." He didn't want his wife wearing her dead father's hat anyway. A woman should wear a female's hat. Somehow he'd find a way to get her a new one. After all, he had kissed her and distracted both of them.

"It's okay. I can wear Granny's old poke bonnet." She made a face. He'd seen that bonnet and it was as ugly as a dog's ass.

He made a silent vow to buy her a new hat. Although it seemed a minor problem, it was a promise he intended to keep.

The kiss, the hat, and the confusion diffused his anger. Matt had an abundance of pride, one of his major down-falls. He had to accept she was right about the barbecue and move on.

"Who gets to tell Eva about the barbecue?"

She smiled as the wind caressed the curls swaying back and forth against her cheeks. "I'll race you. Loser has to tell her."

With a whoop, she spurred her horse into action, leaving him standing there, a stupid grin on his face. He watched her ride, amazed by the natural seat she had. Then he noted she was getting farther away, leaving him with the chore of telling Eva she had to plan a barbecue.

"Shit!"

Matt threw himself into the saddle and chased after his wife. He didn't remember the last time he had smiled and laughed, but he did both as he raced Hannah home.

Hannah didn't recognize herself. She'd not only talked to the intimidating Mr. Stinson, but she'd also invited him to a nonexistent barbecue. Matt had been angry with her, and not because she'd made up the barbecue, but because she hadn't asked his permission before doing it.

That fact alone had made her angry enough to speak her mind. She hadn't even considered any consequences and amazingly enough, after yelling at her, he'd kissed her so deeply, it made her toes curl. There were definite advantages to being married. She could get used to the random kisses and the wildfires that erupted when their lips met. It was an amazing, thrilling experience.

As they took care of their horses, she kept sneaking peeks at him across the stalls. He was as handsome sweaty as he was clean. She'd never noticed men that way before. She wasn't sure if it was normal or not, but her body certainly recognized the attraction. As though the elemental connection they had drove them to be together again and again.

And hopefully again.

She finished with Buttercup and stepped outside the stall to rinse her hands in the water bucket. As she bent over to scoop up some water, a groan sounded from behind her.

"Woman, you're gonna kill me."

She glanced up at Matt. "I was just washing my hands."

His gaze landed on her behind. "I don't care if you're rubbing mud on your face, I wasn't looking at anything but your ass."

"Matthew!" Her cheeks heated at the bald statement.

"I can't help it, Hannah. After that kiss, I'm just not thinking straight." One large hand smacked her on the behind.

She yelped and straightened up, water flying every which way. He grinned and ran for the door.

"Remember, loser has to tell Eva."

"Cheater!" Hannah wiped her hands on her skirt and ran after him.

His long legs gave him a significant advantage. There was no way she could beat him to the house. So she decided to cheat, too.

Hannah threw herself to the ground. "Oh my ankle!"

He skidded to a stop and turned to look at her. "Are you hurt?"

"I think I wrenched my ankle, Matt." She touched it and moaned in pain.

Matt came back and knelt beside her. "Damn, Hannah, I seem to keep apologizing to you today. Let me help you up."

His solicitousness was sweet, but she was playing to win. As soon as she was standing, she kissed him hard.

"Race ya." She picked up her skirt and ran as fast as she could toward the house.

Matt cursed behind her and she heard his footsteps slamming on the hard-packed dirt. He was nearly on her so she dug deep for another burst of energy, reaching the door a split second before he did.

They slammed into the house, laughing and breathing hard. Joy suffused her, bubbled up inside as if it were a font. She'd never felt so happy in her life. How could a simple game of teasing with her husband bring such a gift? Hannah couldn't help the wide grin on her face as Eva and Granny looked up in surprise from a game of checkers at the table.

"Looks like they had a good visit." Granny cackled.

Hannah couldn't disagree, even though Matt was probably still annoyed with her about the barbecue.

"Hannah has some news." Matt's eyes dared her to challenge him.

"I got to the door first."

"No, you didn't. My boot hit the bottom of the door before your hand hit the handle." He crossed his arms over his chest. "Besides this was your idea, honey."

Honey?

She was momentarily nonplussed by the casual way he called her "honey." It was an endearment she'd heard a few times in her life, but never in regard to herself, of course.

"Oh, yes, the news."

Granny and Eva watched her expectantly. She smiled and decided it would be good for her and for the Grahams to celebrate.

"We're going to have a barbecue next Saturday."

Granny's brows went up toward her hairline. Eva nodded and gestured with her hand for Hannah to continue.

"I thought it would be good for two reasons. First, to celebrate the wedding and such. I want to meet the neighbors, too." She glanced at Matt. "I know there hasn't been much to celebrate this year, so I'm hoping we can change that."

Matt's gaze locked with hers and warmth seeped through her at what she saw. It wasn't love, but it was respect and definite affection. She fell deeper into his beautiful eyes and even swayed toward him.

"What's the second reason?" Eva's voice yanked Hannah back from the spell she had fallen under.

"Oh, the second reason. After I met Mr. Stinson, I decided he wouldn't be, ah, willing to sell the two-mile land belt. I thought at a barbecue with lots of folks around, he might be more willing." She saw Olivia standing in the hallway listening.

"*Sí, es la verdad.*" Eva nodded her head, then turned to Matt. "*Tue esposa es muy inteligente.*"

Hannah looked to Matt to translate. He grinned. "She said you are one smart lady."

Considering the amount of fussing Matt had done after she'd suggested the barbecue, it surprised her to see him smile. It was a small victory in the battle for her role in his life.

"I don't think it's smart at all." Olivia walked in, her arms crossed and the perpetual scowl on her face. "We have hardly any money and you let her plan to waste it on a party? What about Margaret?"

"Won't cost us nothing but a steer." Matt scowled at his sister. "Folks will bring food. Margaret can be a guest."

"He's right. They always do." Eva watched the two siblings carefully.

"Doesn't seem right throwing a party so soon after Ma and Pa were murdered." Olivia's words were laced with anger but also with anguish.

Hannah felt Olivia's pain in her own heart and understood now why her new sister-in-law was so resentful. As Matt's new wife, she represented moving on after losing their parents, a substitute mother for the young ones, and a new head of house. Olivia was angry at her loss, and she took it out on the likeliest target, Hannah.

"They would have been happy with Matt's choice," Eva said with a calm expression. "They wouldn't want you to grieve forever."

"You don't know what they would want, Eva. You're the goddamn housekeeper." A red-faced Olivia turned her wrath on Hannah. "And you're an ignorant orphan who dares to think she can walk in here and take over our family. You're an outsider and you always will be."

Hannah noted the tears on the other woman's face as Olivia fled the room. Her heart ached for everything the Graham family had gone through; they were now orphans, too.

"Don't feel sorry for her." Matt appeared at her side. "Livy was angry before our parents died and now it's worse. She can't allow herself to be happy and she doesn't want anyone else to be either."

"*Pobrecita.*" Eva rose to her feet. "I will go find her."

The joy and happiness she'd been feeling were now

gone, and her stomach twisted back up into a knot. Life as a Graham was proving to be a daily challenge.

"I'm going to get to work." Matt glanced at her lips and she couldn't help hoping he would kiss her, but he didn't. "I'll see you at dinner."

Hannah looked at her grandmother, who didn't appear worried at all.

"You've got yourself an interesting situation here, child."

It was an understatement of course. Hannah had a mountain to climb.

CHAPTER ELEVEN

Shuffling sounds pulled Hannah out of her slumber. She'd gone to bed early, exhausted, and was still alone in the bed. She cracked one eye and realized there was a small figure standing beside the bed.

"Catherine?"

The little girl leaned down to whisper in her ear. "We need you in our room, Hannah. Um, Rebecca needs help."

Hannah was on her feet in seconds, wiping the sleep from her eyes. "Is she okay?"

Catherine took her hand. "Yeah, she's okay. She just . . . needs help."

The two younger girls shared a small bedroom with two narrow cots. The two boys slept in a room at the end of the hall, while the two older girls had a room next to the master bedroom. Eva rounded out the house in the room across from the master. Matt's old bedroom stood empty.

When Hannah walked into the girls' room, she recognized the smell of urine immediately and understood why Rebecca needed help.

"I brought Hannah."

"Aw, Catherine, why'd you do that?" Rebecca sat on the edge of the bed, clutching her white nightdress.

"I can help." Hannah felt bad for the girl. Wetting the bed at the age of nine was embarrassing, especially when her seven-year-old sister knew about it. "I promise I won't tell anyone."

Rebecca fiddled with the fabric bunched in her hands for a few moments. "Okay. I'm not a baby though."

Hannah sat beside her. "No, I don't think you're a baby. You and your brothers and sisters had a bad thing happen to your family. Sometimes that makes people do things they normally don't."

"I don't wet the bed. Never." Rebecca sniffed.

Hannah squeezed her shoulder, remembering how it felt to wet the bed. The cold wetness and the stench were unforgettable.

"Then let's get you cleaned up so you can go back to sleep." She turned to Catherine. "Are there extra sheets?"

"Uh-huh. Eva keeps 'em in the chest in her room." Catherine seemed to know everything.

"Can you get in there without her knowing?" The last thing Hannah wanted to do was betray her promise to Rebecca.

Catherine nodded. "A'course. I'm good at sneaking."

"Not a big surprise." Hannah pointed her toward the door. "You get the sheets while I go get some warm water."

Catherine scampered out of the room, leaving Hannah alone with Rebecca. "I'm going to get some water to wash you up. Do you have another nightdress?"

Rebecca shook her head.

"I have something that will work. Stay here and I'll be right back." Hannah went into her own room first and found an old blouse that didn't fit her bosom any longer. She had planned on making handkerchiefs with it, but now she had another use.

There was a hot water reservoir in the big stove in the kitchen. Hannah quietly filled a bowl with water and took a bar of soap and a clean towel with her to the girls' room.

She had almost made it to the door when a big shadow appeared, scaring the life out of her. Part of the water spilled down the front of her own nightdress when she jumped. Matt's scent washed over her and she let out a shaky breath.

"Hell's bells, Matt, you scared the life out of me."

"What did you say?" He sounded more than surprised.

"I mean, you startled me." She now had the same problem as Rebecca with a wet nightdress. The cool night air immediately made her shiver.

"What are you doing up? And with a bowl of water?" He looked tired in the shaft of moonlight.

"I'm, um, the girls forgot to wash up before bed." It sounded like a lie, and it was.

"Oookay. . . . That's sort of odd." He touched her cheek. "Don't be long."

With that, he turned and went into their room. Hannah's body had tightened at the mere brush of his fingers. She wanted to follow him into the darkened room and feel his body pressed against hers, the rasp of his whiskers against her neck, her breasts. Lord, she wanted to touch him.

"Hannah?"

Catherine almost scared her into spilling the water a second time.

"I'm coming."

They crept back into the girls' room. Rebecca sat exactly where she'd been. Catherine set the sheets on her own bed and waited.

"Rebecca, we'll get you cleaned up. Catherine, you take the sheets off the bed while I help your sister." Hannah set the bowl on the floor and waited for the girl to remove her wet nightdress.

After an efficient wash and brisk dry, Rebecca was in the old shirt that hung to her knees. It would do for the night.

"Better?"

Rebecca nodded and hugged her quickly. The fresh

scent of soap and little girl enveloped her. She had grown to love these children; they were so easy to be with. They expected nothing but love in return.

The sheets were wet, but not soaked. It appeared that Rebecca had woken up when she started peeing. Hannah checked the straw-filled mattress and found it slightly damp. She used a corner of the towel with a little soap to wipe it down.

When she opened the clean sheet the girls stood on either side of her, holding up their little hands to help make the bed. It took twice as long to finish, but turned out to be a bonding experience between them. A secret to be shared.

Hannah bundled up the soiled sheet and nightdress. She would wash them out right away, to keep Rebecca's privacy. The girls climbed back into bed and watched her expectantly.

Hannah sat down on Catherine's bed first, tucking the blanket around her slim frame. As she bent down to kiss her forehead, Catherine squirmed out and hugged her neck.

"Thank you, Hannah. I knew you'd fix it up."

Hannah smiled and moved over to Rebecca's bed. She looked so small in the bed, her eyes wide in the lamplight. Hannah tucked her in too, and received another hug in return. She was glad to have helped Rebecca when she needed someone.

"You girls get back to sleep now. It's very late." They both nodded like little owls from their beds. "Goodnight."

Hannah took the soiled linens out of the room and closed the door as quietly as she could. She walked through the darkened house with a familiarity she hadn't had a week earlier. It was beginning to feel like home to her. She navigated her way into the kitchen and found a bucket.

"What are you doing?" Matthew's quiet question didn't startle her this time.

"Keeping a promise."

He sat at the table and watched her. Perhaps it was a dream because she wanted him there. The house was so quiet, every move she made seemed to echo. She filled the bucket with warm water, then submerged the nightdress, soaped it up, and rinsed it thoroughly. As she squeezed out the water, Matt made a strange noise.

Hannah peered at him through the darkened room and realized he was shirtless. Her stomach flipped and her core throbbed once, hard and fast. He watched her and groaned over what he saw. What did that mean?

She set the nightdress aside and cleaned the small area on the sheets that had been soiled. The soap was slippery in her hands as she worked. She also kept glancing at her husband out of the corner of her eye.

After rinsing off the sheet, she picked up the bucket and the clean laundry. "I'll be right back. I need to hang these on the line so they'll be dry by morning."

He simply nodded, a hazy figure in the gloom. She hurried outside and dumped the bucket, then hung up the nightdress and sheet on the line with shaking hands. The moon was bright, illuminating everything for her.

Something was going to happen; she just didn't know what it was. Hannah stepped back inside and waited for her eyes to adjust. Matt sat where she'd left him in the chair. Her heart thumped as she approached him, anticipation making her mouth dry and her body tingle.

He wore only a pair of drawers, his hand inside the front of them, moving up and down. She stared, fascinated by what he was doing. Her body seemed to recognize the motion because her pussy grew damp and her nipples hard.

"Come here." His husky whisper sent a shiver down her spine.

She moved closer, his scent filling her nose, ripening her need to kiss him, touch him, be part of whatever he was doing. He took her hand and kissed it, then tugged until she was right in front of him.

Hannah couldn't take her gaze off the movement in his drawers. He unbuttoned them completely and exposed his cock to her prying eyes. His hand moved up and down the shaft, squeezing and pulling.

"Ride me, honey."

Hannah had no idea what he meant. "Help me."

"Spread your legs and lift your nightdress."

She felt naughtier than she ever had in her life, but at the same time, more excited, too. It was that excitement that drove her to lift her nightdress and straddle him. The coolness of the night air felt good on the heat from her center. As she lowered herself, he took her hips and guided her toward his cock.

The head touched her entrance and they both groaned.

"We need to be quiet." His eyes glittered in the semi-darkness as she slid down on his shaft.

She gasped at the feeling of fullness, of rightness. He was deep within her and this time she was in control of their joining. Matt unbuttoned her nightdress as far as he could, then pulled it down to expose her left breast.

As soon as his hot mouth closed around her nipple, she clenched, everywhere.

"Oh God, do that again."

She used the foot railing on the chair to push herself up and down, while his mouth remained firmly latched on her breast, biting, licking, and sucking. Streaks of pure pleasure traveled from her nipple to her center, pulsing and tingling outward. She managed to find a rhythm; he pushed up and she pushed down.

It was so erotic, Hannah completely forgot where she was, only that she was with Matt and they were making love. She closed her eyes and reveled in it.

"I'm close, honey, so close." He pulled down the fabric to expose her other breast. "I need you to come, too."

She knew what he meant but she didn't know how to get there. One of his hands crept between them and started rubbing circles on her nubbin of pleasure. The other hand tweaked the now damp nipple. She clenched again hard as a wave began within her.

"Matt, I think I'm coming."

"That's it, honey, ride me." His movements became fiercer as she slammed up and down his shaft. His cock filled her, touched her womb, drove her to heights she never knew existed.

The storm of ecstasy slammed into her like a thunderbolt, stealing her breath, stopping her heart. She gripped the chair so hard, she heard it groan, right along with her. Hannah bit her lip to keep from crying out as her body convulsed with the most powerful pleasure it had ever felt.

Matt buried his head between her breasts, gripping her hips until his knuckles cracked. She felt his pleasure mingle with hers, his seed spill into her body. The heat between them could have melted iron.

She sucked in a shaky breath and opened her eyes. Matt stared at her, his expression unreadable in the moonlight. Before she could say a word, he got to his feet, arms firmly wrapped around her behind. He carried her to bed that way, his cock still hard, gently moving in and out of her.

When they got to the bed, she was disappointed when his cock slipped out of her. She wanted more.

To her surprise, he slid right back inside.

"Oh my." Hannah spread her legs, reveling in the slow, gentle glide. Their first joining had been fast and furious; now he took his time. She loved it.

If she wasn't careful, she might love him.

"Your hair. Spread out your hair for me." His husky words made her do as he bade.

To Hannah, they were making love. This was what she thought married people did. If her mind wasn't so scrambled, she might even admit she'd enjoyed the episode in the kitchen more. However without the frantic pace, he took his time touching her. He ran his hands up and down her thighs and stomach, up to her pouting nipples, then down to her thighs.

She watched him, the bright moonlight illuminating his every move as though he was bathed in silver. Matt appeared ethereal, not of the earth, a god of lore come to life. She threw her arms out and gloried in the amazing sensation of being with her husband.

Finally his pace quickened and his staff thrust harder, faster. His hand found her clit and flicked it as she was hoping he would. It didn't take long to recall her pleasure, to bring it forth again until she exploded into a thousand stars for her silver moonlight man.

He called her name softly as he found his own ultimate pleasure, his hands tightening on her thighs. She clenched around him, pulling him deeper into her core until he touched her womb. Hannah wanted his baby and she truly hoped his seed would find fertile ground.

Matt groaned and rolled over to lie on the bed beside her. The only sound in the room was their breathing and Hannah's heart thumping madly.

"Your hair. I'd never seen it unbound before, wild and free. It did something to me." His soft confession made her smile.

"Then I'll leave it down every night."

He rose and poured water into the basin, then used a soft rag to clean them both up. Hannah was boneless, completely drained of energy by two incredible rounds of lovemaking. By the time she crawled under the covers, she could hardly keep her eyes open. Matt lay beside her, spooning against her as had become his habit.

Hannah fell asleep almost immediately, more content than she'd ever been in her life.

The impending barbecue energized the ranch. Eva sent Javier and Lorenzo to the neighboring ranches with invitations. Within a few days, Eva told Hannah they expected at least seventy-five people to come.

It was an intimidating number, but Hannah was used to organizing meals for large groups at the boardinghouse. This was the biggest challenge she'd ever faced though. Fortunately she, Granny, and Eva worked together.

Hannah used all the scraps she could find to make a huge tablecloth while the boys put together a table from left over wood. Eva cleaned like a madwoman and Granny was put in charge of watching the three youngest Grahams. Together, the four of them made decorations out of whatever they could find.

Olivia was the only one not helping. She sulked most days, not bothering to talk to anyone. Hannah wanted to get her sister-in-law to talk, but didn't have much success.

It was Friday, the day before the barbecue. The tables were built, the patchwork tablecloth ready. Granny was outside with Eva supervising the hanging of the girls' decorations. The men were digging the pit and preparing the steer. Hannah worked on some mending to relax.

The time between dinner and supper was usually the quietest in the house. Hannah had a cup of coffee she sipped as she worked and hummed under her breath.

"Oh, I didn't know you were in here." Olivia stood at the entrance to the kitchen, nearly hidden in the shadows of the hallway.

"I'm just doing some mending. The room is big enough for both of us." Hannah offered a smile.

"This whole ranch isn't big enough for both of us." Olivia walked toward the stove. "What is Eva planning for supper?"

"I don't know. She's outside helping the girls with the decorations."

Olivia sighed and speared Hannah with an accusing glare. "This whole barbecue fiasco is your fault. You've turned everything upside down."

"I don't mean to." Hannah set the mending down and gestured to the chair across from her. "Will you sit and talk to me?"

"No."

Hannah threw her hands in the air. "I don't know what I did to make you hate me so much, Olivia. But Matt and I are well and truly married. Your anger isn't going to change that one bit."

"He was supposed to marry Margaret. Did you know that?"

Olivia had mentioned it before, but Hannah had ignored her revelation for fear of learning something she didn't want to hear.

"No, and it doesn't matter. He married me."

"Because your name was Hannah." Olivia might not have wanted to talk, but the words gushed from her mouth now.

"I know that. I knew that from the second he proposed." Hannah understood that the reason for her marriage was unconventional, but she had come to enjoy being married.

Olivia paced back and forth, her body fairly vibrating with energy. "You very nearly prostituted yourself for a husband."

That one stung. "There are many reasons why folks get married. I had no prospects for a husband and he needed a wife."

"No prospects? There isn't anyone out here to marry.

You took the most eligible bachelor in the county." Olivia's voice had risen. "Margaret was my ticket out of here. We were going to travel together. Maybe even go to New York. You took that from me."

Hannah's mouth dropped open. "I did no such thing."

"I had a beau once, sure I did. What girl didn't besides you? After some bastard killed my parents and Benjy disappeared, he didn't like my crying. My grief was too much for him." Her words were running into each other. "He ran off with that awful bitch Mary Walker. Then Margaret decided I wasn't good enough for her anymore. She expected us to fail without my parents. Last week was the first time she spoke to me in months."

Olivia shook her head, staring off into what Hannah could only assume was a gaping maw of grief. "I lost everything. *Everything.*"

Hannah's heart ached for what the Grahams had suffered. She had hoped the new land would bring them the fresh start they needed. However, Stinson had made sure their fresh start was soured before it truly began.

"I'm so sorry, Olivia. So very sorry." Hannah got to her feet and pulled her sister-in-law into a hug. At first Olivia was stiff and unyielding, but then she softened, shaking as she wept buckets of tears. Hannah just let her cry, wondering if the young woman had ever let herself grieve for what she'd lost. It likely had been bottled up inside her all this time.

After a few minutes, Olivia's sobs began to fade. She pulled away, accepting the handkerchief Hannah offered. The moment stretched out, sliding into an awkward silence.

"Would you like some coffee?"

Olivia nodded and sat down in her chair at the table with a sigh. "I don't like who I am anymore. I'm downright mean no matter how much I try to stop myself."

Hannah poured the coffee, then set the steaming mug in front of the other woman. She sat down and waited, hoping like hell Olivia would continue talking to her.

"Grief makes us do things we normally wouldn't." She sipped her own coffee. "I don't pretend to know how it feels to have gone through what you did but I can listen if you want to talk."

Olivia wiped her eyes with a corner of the handkerchief. She narrowed her watery gaze. "I've been nothing but a bitch to you. Why are you being so nice?"

Hannah shrugged, unwilling to blame Olivia for her anger. It wasn't truly directed at Hannah, but more at the world. "I take some blame for that, too."

Olivia seemed to accept the peace offering and turned her attention back to her coffee. The silence was comfortable as they both sipped. Hannah felt relieved they were talking and being civil.

"I feel like Matt set this whole ranch on its ear when he lied about having a wife." Olivia's gaze rose to meet hers. "He's spent so much time thinking about you, he forgot about us. Forgot about Mama and Pa, and about Benjy. I was angry with him and with God."

"Tell me about them." Hannah needed to know more about the elder Grahams and the youngest child, the boy who'd vanished like a puff of smoke.

Olivia was quiet for a few minutes; then, to Hannah's relief, she started talking.

"Benjamin was Matt's shadow. He was the spitting image of him, too. Walked like him, swagger and all." Olivia smiled. "Mama never worried about Benjy because wherever Matt was, he was always right behind him. Except for the day we were—"

The day the Grahams were killed and the barn burned. An unsolved murder in such a small town was bound to garner a lot of talk. Folks speculated it had been Indians, but there was no evidence of that. Others thought it was a couple of drifters or maybe Mexicans who were loyal to their country, trying to drive Texans off land that once belonged to them.

The oddest thing about the crime was the disappearance of the youngest sibling. There hadn't been a sign of Benjamin, dead or alive, since the Grahams had died. Hannah had heard the search had gone on for days, fanning out for miles. There had been no tracks, no trace.

"What about your parents? What were they like?" Hannah didn't want Olivia to bog down in her grief again.

"Pa loved Mama to distraction. Whatever she wanted, he made happen for her. They kissed and hugged a lot. He wasn't wishy-washy though. He was big like Matt, worked hard for everything he had. When Pa came back from the war, he was quieter than he had been. I remember when I was little, his laugh used to vibrate through my chest it was so loud. He wasn't like that anymore." Olivia paused to stare off into the distance again. "Mama kept us all together while he and Matt fought in the war. She was stronger than both of them put together. She managed eight children and this ranch and did a right fine job of it, too. Eva was here, but she was more of a housekeeper and cook than a mother figure. It was only after Mama was gone that Eva stepped in to help the young'uns."

Hannah digested all of the information, which answered quite a few questions she'd had. Matt was trying to be like his father, as most men would, but there was something else there she still hadn't pinned down. Later, she would try to find out what was driving him so hard, and what secrets he was hiding. She might not have any success but she had to try.

"I wish I had known them."

Olivia's gaze probed Hannah's until she finally nodded. "I think you mean that."

"I do. I lost my parents when I was seven. I don't remember much about them, just snatches of memories. Mama always smelled like roses and Papa like wood." Hannah had a hole where a girl's memories of a mother and father should have been. It didn't necessarily make her sad, but it sure made her lonely.

"No brothers or sisters?"

Hannah shook her head. "Nobody but Granny."

"She's your father's mother?" Olivia had begun to relax in earnest.

"No, my mother's mother. She and my grandfather took me in, but he died shortly after that. Granny has had more tragedy in her life than I have. I think she had two sons who died as children, too." Hannah stared into her coffee, realizing for the first time just how much her grandmother had been through.

"That why she opened the boardinghouse?"

"Yep. It was a big house and she had no money to speak of. I only did simple chores at first, but I grew up cleaning and cooking for large groups." Hannah smiled at her sister-in-law. "All along I was in training to join the Graham clan."

"I won't say congratulations. Some days I wish them all away. They're loud, pushy, greedy, and stomp on my last nerve." Olivia's gaze softened. "Then I think of life without all of them and know it doesn't matter how crazy they make me. They're my family."

Hannah ached for that kind of family and wished until her teeth ached that she would be accepted as part of theirs. Good, bad and ugly, the Grahams were everything she'd ever wanted. Matt had given her the gift of a family when he'd proposed to her. Hannah was marrying them as much as she was marrying their brother.

"I haven't made it very easy for you to join us." Olivia

ran her finger around the rim of the mug. "I was protecting me and mine, making sure no one would hurt us."

"And now?" Hannah held her breath, hoping to hear Olivia was finally past her anger.

"Now I can see we have a lot more in common than I thought. I knew you disappeared out of school, but didn't think anything of it." Olivia shook her head. "You know how Catherine feels because she's seven and she just lost her parents."

Hannah hadn't even recognized the truth right in front of her face. Olivia just put her finger on the very reason Hannah had found her place so easily with the two youngest Grahams. They reminded her of her own orphaned self thirteen years earlier. She was glad to be there for the girls, to brush their hair, mend their clothes, and even wash their sheets in the dead of night.

"Yes, I know how you all feel. It's not an easy thing to lose one parent, much less two." Hannah actually felt the connection between them blossoming. "I don't want to replace anyone, or even drive your brother to distraction. I just want to be part of your family, be a wife to Matt, and maybe one day, a mother to his children."

Olivia was silent for a few moments, then lifted her gaze to Hannah's. Her eyes were so much like Matt's, Hannah's heart did a little hiccup. She really was falling in love with her husband.

"I think that's a right fine idea." This time when Olivia smiled, it was genuine.

Hannah got to her feet at the same time as her sister-in-law. They hugged briefly, then sat back down.

"Would you show me how to sew?" Olivia pointed at the pile of mending. "With so many folks in the house, that pile has grown as big as Catherine. I always refused to learn, telling Mama I'd marry a rich man and never have to mend a thing. Too bad the one man I wanted to marry found a girl without tears in her eyes."

"Then he wasn't the man for you. I never even had a beau, so I knew Matt was the one for me. Yours is out there somewhere. He just hasn't found his way to the Circle Eight yet." Hannah patted the chair next to her. "Come on over and I'll teach you the basics."

Hannah spent the next hour with Olivia, showing her how to use a needle and thread. It was the most relaxing, enjoyable time she'd spent with her sister-in-law. By the time the hour was over, Olivia was mending a ripped seam in one of Caleb's shirts.

Catherine came running into the house, her pigtails flying. She stopped so suddenly she nearly fell over, pinwheeling her little arms to stop her fall. "Jehosophat! You're both smiling."

"It's been known to happen," Olivia said with a wink.

"You two were fighting like barn cats last I knew." Catherine put her fists on her hips. "About time you two became friends. I was tired of the bickering."

She sounded so much like Olivia in that moment, Hannah burst out laughing, earning identical, puzzled looks from both of them. Hannah waved her hand at them, trying to distract them from watching her embarrass herself.

"Did you need something, Cat?" Olivia asked.

"Oh, yep, I did. Strangers coming in a horse and buggy. Matt sent me to fetch you."

Strangers? Hannah's mirth disappeared in a blink. She looked at Olivia and they both got to their feet. Strangers on the ranch had been a deadly occurrence once before. The three of them left the house quickly and went outside to find out what was going on.

CHAPTER TWELVE

Matt had taken to wearing a pistol on his hip. It had been his Pa's from the war, now his, and he felt safer with it close by. Even though they were simply getting ready for the barbecue, he was armed. And with good reason apparently. A fancy horse and buggy was approaching the house.

He immediately sent Catherine inside, but she came right back out with Hannah and Olivia. Matt wanted to yell at all of them to get inside the house, but didn't want to be distracted by the inevitable bickering that would ensue. Instead he stood his ground, hand on his pistol.

Behind him, he knew Lorenzo, Nick, and Caleb had retrieved rifles and were standing there like a well-armed line of defense. He'd sent Javier into the barn to watch the horses. They'd lost half a dozen the last time strangers had come to the Circle Eight. Several had perished in the fire, and others had been taken by the murdering sons-of-bitches who had dared defile the ground with Graham blood.

The air crackled with anticipation as the buggy drew closer. It had fringe around the top like a fancy decoration in a rich man's house. He didn't recognize the rig or the horses and therefore wouldn't relax his guard.

He smelled Hannah's scent before she even spoke. She'd walked up directly behind him.

"Who is it?"

"I don't know. Now get back in the house with the girls."

He could almost hear her cursing him silently.

"I'll do no such thing. I'm your wife and I will stand by your side no matter what."

She reminded him of his mother, so strong and fierce. It surprised the hell out of him. Initially, Hannah had been so meek and soft-spoken. Two weeks of marriage had shown him she was merely hiding her lioness inside. While it made him proud to be married to such a woman, at the same time he wanted to spank her. She was distracting him just as he'd feared.

"Step back now," he growled under his breath.

To his shock, she appeared beside him, holding a rifle. His mouth dropped open.

"Before you ask, I know how to shoot it. Don't order me around anymore, Matthew Graham." She gripped the rifle in the right places, her hands so tight the knuckles were white. "I will protect this family with you."

Matt's brain was spinning. Hannah probably didn't even realize just how much she had turned him on his ear. Was there a day that she wouldn't surprise him?

He was going to yell at her again to get inside but the buggy had arrived, and he had no time to spend on chastising his wife. Not that she would listen to him anyway.

A man and a woman rode in the buggy. They were unfamiliar and Matt cursed under his breath to have all the children out in plain view.

The buggy stopped in front of them and the man hopped out. He was dressed in black trousers and a black coat, white shirt with a silver string tie. His face marked with a jagged scar on his jaw and a pair of cold blue eyes Matt could see fifteen feet away. On the man's head sat a flat brimmed black hat to match the black, dusty boots on his feet. The shirt and his eyes were the only break in the darkness of the stranger. His gaze flickered to the pistol in Matt's hand.

He stepped around to the other side of the buggy and helped the woman down. She was older than the man, probably around Eva's age, with her salt and pepper hair in a tight bun beneath a straw hat. Her clothing was of good quality, a gray traveling suit with shiny brass buttons.

When her gaze found Matt's, a tremor shook him from head to foot. Something told him the woman was the bearer of bad news and he didn't want to hear it.

"Good afternoon." The woman's voice was tense. Her syllables were as sharp as her gaze. "I'm looking for Matthew Graham."

"That'd be me." Matt didn't move his hand from the pistol.

"I'm Mrs. Leticia Markum. I've been asked to investigate a claim of fraud by the land claim office."

His gut twisted and the taste of bile coated his throat. Fraud? Hannah sucked in an audible breath beside him.

"Fraud with regard to what?" Hannah sounded so much smarter than he was.

"And you are?" Mrs. Markum speared Hannah with her fierce gaze.

"I'm Hannah Graham, Matthew's wife."

Mrs. Markum's grin was not at all friendly. "Fraud with regard to being married as he purported to be on the land claim form."

"I assure you, Mrs. Markum, we are well and truly married." Hannah nodded to the buggy. "There's no reason for any investigation."

"We received a letter stating you had not been truthful on your land claim." Mrs. Markum remained as stiff as a board. "I must investigate."

"And your driver?" Matt watched the man. He didn't

appear to be armed, but he could have a weapon hidden anywhere on him.

"Ranger Brody Armstrong. He's here for my protection and to ensure my investigation proceeds as it should." Mrs. Markum nodded to the man.

Matt wondered why a Texas Ranger was minding this bitch when he could have been fighting at the frontier. It wasn't a wise move to ask, but he sure as hell wanted to. He had noticed a hitch in the man's step, so perhaps he'd been wounded in the war.

"What do you want, Mrs. Markum?" Matt asked impatiently.

"I need to verify that your marriage is legal and valid. This is a formal investigation, Mr. Graham. While the government of the Republic of Texas is in its infancy, we will follow the laws or slide into anarchy." She somehow straightened her already impossibly straight shoulders. "My husband serves in the government and I assist him in this capacity. Wives often do that for their husbands."

It was damn odd to have a woman investigator, but maybe her husband was one of Sam Houston's friends. Mrs. Markum liked to push people around, that was obvious. Matt recognized the look of annoyance on the ranger's face and his opinion of the man went up.

"What exactly does that entail?" Hannah hadn't relaxed her stance either. She was definitely not the meek girl he thought he'd married.

"I need to see your marriage certificate, examine your sleeping quarters, and question others on your supposed marriage." Mrs. Markum gestured to the house. "With your permission, we can begin in the house."

Matt's teeth ground together. "There's no way I'm letting you in my house, lady. I don't even know who you are or what you really want, but it ain't happening."

"Mr. Graham, if you do not cooperate, I can only report

that the claim of fraud is true." Her teeth shone like a wolf's in the bright sunlight.

"First of all, we need proof you are who you say you are," Hannah challenged. "This ranch has suffered at the hands of strangers."

Matt should have realized he was reacting with his heart instead of his head. Hannah was absolutely right. They didn't trust strangers, and for good reason.

"Is that so?" Mrs. Markum frowned.

"Yes, it's so. My parents were murdered and my brother disappeared this spring." Matt almost spat the words, his jaw beginning to ache from clenching it so hard.

"I assume this was reported to the authorities?"

Matt almost leapt at her, but the ranger must've seen something in his gaze because he spoke up quickly.

"It's true, ma'am. I read the report myself." Armstrong's voice was deep and dark.

"I see. Well, I have no nefarious intentions."

"That remains to be seen." Hannah sounded as angry as he felt. "Do you have any kind of verification of your investigation?"

Matt watched as Mrs. Markum's steely expression faltered. "Verification?"

"Yes, ma'am. Papers that prove you are who you say you are. You must have something." As Hannah kept after the other woman, Matt wanted to cheer for her.

"Of course I do. In my reticule. Mr. Armstrong, will you fetch it for me from the buggy?"

Ranger Armstrong shook his head and a chuckle threatened to pop out of Matt's mouth. "Ma'am, I'm not an errand boy. I'm a Texas Ranger."

Mrs. Markum huffed an impatient breath and walked back to the buggy herself. She fiddled around inside for a few minutes, then emerged with a sheaf of papers. Matt's heart lodged in his throat.

"Here is the verification. I have a letter alleging the fraud and the original deed signed last week for the land grant." Mrs. Markum shook the papers in the air.

"I will read them before we go any further." Hannah stepped toward her. Matt wanted to yank her back but didn't. His wife was a match for the other woman, and he was proud of her, even if it scared him to death to watch her walk toward the strangers.

Hannah took the papers in one hand, the rifle still in the other. She tucked the rifle under her arm, the barrel pointed at Mrs. Markum's chest. After Hannah read through the documents, she handed them back.

"That's my signature on that deed and my husband's. I don't know who wrote that letter, but it's a pack of lies." Hannah walked backward until she was beside Matt again.

"Then let me complete my investigation and I can be on my way."

Matt wanted to tell the woman no and get her off the ranch right away. Yet his gut told him to finish this so the woman could get back to whatever hole she'd crawled out of.

"Then let's get this done."

Hannah led Mrs. Markum into the house while the ranger stayed outside by the buggy. Matt decided to remain with the man rather than follow the women. Something told him it would be a good idea for him to talk to Ranger Armstrong. For once his brothers and sisters were quiet and watchful.

"I don't cotton to what Mrs. Markum is doing, but the Republic has to act like a government." Armstrong lit up a cheroot. "That means making sure folks are following the law."

"She's a bitch." Matt ignored the gasps behind him. His little sisters had heard worse, but no doubt Catherine and Olivia would chastise him later for his language.

"That she is." The ranger puffed on his cheroot. "This your family?"

"Yep."

"Look like a good group of folks." Armstrong gestured to Matt. "I wanted to talk to you about something."

Matt hesitated, not willing to be close enough to give the ranger room to outmaneuver him.

Armstrong held up his hands. "I'm unarmed. Left my weapons in the buggy."

"Okay then, let's talk." Matt stepped toward him and they walked toward the back of the buggy.

"I wasn't lying when I said I saw the report about your parents." Armstrong's eyes were a startling blue up close. "I think I can help."

Hannah led the woman through the house, showing her each room and telling her who slept where. When they entered the master bedroom, she showed the woman her clothes hanging on the nails as well as the drawers in the chest with her meager possessions.

"How long have you lived here?"

"We've been married two weeks, but engaged for longer. I moved in here after we were officially married." Hannah knew Matt had started the land grant claim before he had proposed. A little white lie about being engaged wouldn't hurt.

"Do you have your marriage certificate?" Mrs. Markum's gaze settled on Hannah's ring.

"Yes, of course." Hannah retrieved it from the small chest she kept her most prized possessions in. Her parents' marriage certificate, her own hastily scribbled birth certificate, and the letter she'd written to God at age seven. Someday she would read it again and perhaps even share it with Matt. Today she just wanted this nasty woman out of her life.

Mrs. Markum perused the document, then handed it

back to Hannah. "You were married after Mr. Graham filed for the land grant."

Hannah folded the paper carefully. "Yes, but we were planning on getting married. I didn't have any family to speak of, but his was still recovering from their parents' murder. We were going to wait, but we didn't want to lose the land grant."

She hoped she sounded truthful. Her fantasies around the man she would one day marry had become so real in her dreams, she almost believed her own white lies.

"I see. Legally the grant was not signed until after the marriage, which means you either are telling me the truth or a spinster like you saw a chance to marry a handsome rancher about to become land rich." Mrs. Markum's gaze was more disconcerting than her words.

"Is your investigation complete?" Hannah kept the angry words she wanted to say behind her teeth but oh, how they wanted to escape.

Mrs. Markum stared at her for a few beats before she nodded tightly. "Yes, I believe the land grant is valid, however sideways your marriage came to be. The letter, however, will remain with the grant along with my report on what I found."

Hannah gestured to the door and walked behind the officious woman, towering over her tiny stature. "Who wrote the letter?"

"Excuse me?" Mrs. Markum paused with her hand on the knob.

"Who wrote the letter claiming Matt had committed fraud?" Hannah didn't recognize the handwriting and it wasn't signed. However, it was written in a distinctly feminine hand.

"I don't know, Mrs. Graham, and frankly I don't care." Mrs. Markum left the house without a backward glance.

Hannah took a moment to catch her breath before she

followed. She had to find out who had been so vicious as to claim Matt had come by the land through fraud. The letter was a cruel ploy written by a coward who lurked in the shadows.

She promised herself to find out who had done it and protect her new husband and her new family.

When Hannah emerged from the house, Matt was deep in conversation with the ranger. Mrs. Markum had climbed into the buggy and was currently shooting daggers with her eyes at her escort.

To Hannah's surprise, Matt shook the ranger's hand. After turning the buggy around, the two strangers left the Circle Eight. Everyone seemed to breathe a collective sigh of relief.

The three younger girls crowded around her, all chattering at once like a flock of magpies. She wanted to go ask Matt what he and the ranger had been discussing, but couldn't. He'd gone over to Caleb, Nick, and Lorenzo, and the four of them had disappeared into the barn.

Granny walked over with Eva and they both looked at her expectantly. Olivia watched from the newly created table. Hannah extricated herself from the girls and held up her hands.

"Okay, everyone. I showed her the house, the marriage certificate, and answered her questions. She said the land grant was valid and the investigation was over."

"*Dios mio,* that woman was a *bruja.*" Eva made a strange sign with her hands at the retreating buggy.

"You did good, Hannah." Granny grinned. "I thought you were going to take a swing at her."

The younger girls all looked confused while Eva chuckled. Hannah felt her cheeks heat, but decided she had to be honest. This was her family after all.

"I thought about it, but I didn't want to give her any reason to stay a second longer."

This time everyone laughed and Hannah felt an enormous sense of relief. She gazed around and realized that she finally felt like a Graham.

"Let's get ready for the barbecue."

Matt could hardly focus on the pit. His mind whirled with the events of the day, particularly with what Ranger Armstrong had told him. He hadn't shared the information with anyone yet, so it was his burden to carry until he decided to tell someone.

Lorenzo and Javier were butchering the steer, which left the three Graham boys to finish the pit. They had to get the coals hot enough so the steer would cook the entire day. If they didn't put it in on time, it wouldn't be tender as he liked it.

Eva would appear with the rub any minute, so they picked up the pace. The heat made his skin feel tight and his eyes dry. It had been years since they had attended a barbecue, and they'd never hosted one. His parents had been more concerned with keeping the family safe and fed.

Eva had been the one to tell him what he needed to do to cook the steer. Any barbecue was a big event in itself, but this was also the first time the Grahams would welcome their neighbors to the Circle Eight. They would show everyone they were not only surviving their parents' deaths, but celebrating their new beginning with his marriage.

It sounded stupid to him, but Eva insisted that was what they had to do. That left him and his brothers sweating over a pit big enough to hold the steer. Lorenzo and Javier brought half the butchered steer. The brothers obviously had experience with this sort of thing and Matt deferred to their knowledge, learning as he helped them get everything done.

He looked up to find Hannah watching him. Her gaze

was questioning and he could guess what she wanted to know. Matt shook his head, unwilling to talk to her, and turned his attention back to the pit. Her frustration was probably hotter than the coals he was currently stoking. Matt didn't want to talk to her and there was no way he'd let her push him into it.

A wife was important to a man, but Hannah had to understand no matter what, he was the head of the house. The bedroom was their private domain. What happened there did not give her license to tell him what to do elsewhere.

By the time they had covered the pit and decided on a shift to watch it, Matt was exhausted. The sun had set, and his body was covered with sweat, dirt, and soot. The barbecue was the next day, which meant his rest would be short because there was so much to do. Hannah had been wrong, it wasn't just a simple matter of nailing a few tables together and cooking a steer. There was a hell of a lot of work involved in feeding seventy-five people, even if there wasn't a lot of money spent.

Matt walked in to find Hannah sitting in the kitchen with a cup of steaming liquid in her hand. She wore a shawl over her white nightdress. The memory of exactly what had happened the last time she wore that nightdress made his body stir to life.

"Hungry?" Her voice sounded as tired as he felt.

"Yes, but I think I'm too tired to eat." He sat down heavily in the chair across from her. "More than anything, I want to get clean."

She smiled. "I heated water for a bath."

Matt couldn't help smiling back. Somehow she knew exactly what he needed before he did. He should be scared by that fact, but he didn't want to think about it. In fact, he didn't want to think at all.

Hannah pulled the tub in from the back porch and filled

it with three buckets of hot water, then added two buckets of cold. She already had soap and a towel waiting for him along with a clean pair of drawers.

"Need help getting clean?"

Her question shocked him. She had been such a quiet, soft-spoken woman, even shy, and now she was a seductress. He couldn't quite reconcile the two and trying to do so made his head hurt. Matt didn't answer her and after a few moments of watching him undress, she sat down and picked up her mug again.

He climbed into the tub, trying to ignore the fact he was naked and his wife was five feet away. At least his cock appeared to be as tired as he was. As he sank into the water, which was the perfect temperature, he sighed with relief.

"You spent some time with that ranger." It wasn't a question, but she was fishing for information.

Matt closed his eyes and leaned his head against the back of the tub. "I don't want to talk about it right now."

"Then I won't tell you what Mrs. Markum said."

Matt sighed. "Fine." He really didn't want to think about the conversation anymore but Hannah hadn't given him a choice. "Armstrong read the report on the murders and Benjy's disappearance. He told me there had been ten other ranches within a hundred miles that had been attacked, folks killed and children taken."

She gasped. "Ten?"

"Ten. Armstrong didn't give me much but I do know he's investigating five of them himself." Matt tried not to picture what happened to the other ranchers, wives, or children. He could hardly get the image of his parents' bodies out of his head.

"Did he have any information on what happened here?" Her voice had softened.

"He knows as much as I do." Matt planned on meeting up with Armstrong next week to talk to the man more.

The ranger was tight-lipped and hid secrets behind his cold blue eyes.

"It's good that a ranger is working on it, right? I've heard they are very tough lawmen."

"I hear the same thing. Whether or not he comes through remains to be seen." Matt didn't expect her touch, but it didn't startle him either. She dipped a rag in the water, wrung it out then soaped it up. As Hannah washed the grime from his body, he felt he'd died and gone to heaven, her touch was nearly perfect.

"Mrs. Markum told me someone wrote a letter accusing you of fraud, that you lied about the land grant." Hannah started soaping up his hair.

"Who?" He managed to keep his calm although the idea that someone would accuse him of anything illegal made him want to punch something.

"She said the letter was unsigned. I showed her the house and our marriage certificate." Hannah scrubbed his scalp, her strong fingernails earning a moan from his throat. "I did tell a white lie though."

Matt's eyes popped open. "What did you lie about?"

"I told her we were engaged before you went to file for the land grant the first time." She sighed, and he hated the fact that she'd been put in the position to have to lie to save him. "I don't have much family, so I told her we were waiting for the grieving to pass before we got married. Then with the land grant requiring you to be married, we went ahead and tied the knot."

She sounded so matter of fact, as if she hadn't lied to a government person. *For him.* Matt had done it for his family, for his father, but she had done it for *him.*

Hannah had showed him with her simple gesture just what it meant to be first in someone else's heart. Matt's stomach thumped so hard against his ribs, it vibrated his bones. Could her heart be involved already? They'd known

each other only two weeks. Matt didn't pretend to understand how women thought and he sure as hell wasn't going to ask. He wasn't ready to hear the answer.

"Thank you for that, Hannah. I didn't mean for you
to tell any kind of lie for me." He dunked his head and
rinsed the soap from his hair. When he emerged, she sat
beside the tub watching him. Her gaze was pensive.

"Mrs. Markum said she was keeping the letter with the
land grant." Hannah shook her head. "I don't know that
we've seen the last of her. I think she's some important
man's wife."

"I don't care who she is. She's a bitch." Matt was re-
warded with a chuckle from Hannah, although most
women would have chastised him for cussing.

"I won't argue that. I didn't like her at all." Hannah
reached out and touched his cheek.

He wanted to melt into her, pull her into his arms, and
make love to her until neither one of them could see
straight. Matt was teetering on the edge of falling in love
with his wife and it scared him witless. He didn't want to
be a man who was led around by a woman. He needed to
stop his feelings from going any further.

"Can I have a towel?"

"Oh, I'm sorry." Hannah got to her feet, her large breasts
at eye level for a moment, which made his traitorous cock
jump. Thank God the water hid the movement.

She held the towel open, waiting for him to step from
the tub. His gaze held hers and he was torn between his
head and his urges. If he got out of the water and stepped
into her arms, he'd tussle in the sheets with her. If he took
the towel from her, there would be no sex that night.

Matt took the towel with a weak smile. Her expression
looked shocked for a moment and then she turned away,
leaving him in the tub alone.

Damn.

★ ★ ★

Hannah shouldn't have been disappointed. Matt was exhausted from preparing the barbecue pit and she had no right to expect him to make love. But after the intimate moments they'd shared while he bathed, she'd thought maybe they would.

He had relaxed under her hands and she had completely enjoyed bathing him. But as soon as she'd finished, his gaze became shuttered again, leaving her with nothing but an ache between her legs and hardened nipples.

She washed up for bed and climbed in before she had time to think about being naked. Married people didn't need to make love every night, did they? She fussed around under the covers without really getting comfortable. Matt came to bed within ten minutes and she pretended to be asleep. The truth was she was awake a lot longer than she should have been. As she fell into a fitful sleep, Hannah ached to touch her husband.

CHAPTER THIRTEEN

The day of the barbecue Hannah was up before the sun, her heart and body still aching. She dressed quietly, leaving Matt still sleeping. If she had more courage, she might have woken him up, but she couldn't quite make herself do it.

No one else was awake so the house was quiet as she went out to milk the cow. Catherine had shown her how and now Hannah felt confident she could do it herself. The gray light of dawn colored the yard as she made her way to the barn with just a bucket.

She stepped into the barn, and paused at the darkness inside. She hadn't brought a lamp, hadn't thought of it really, so she either needed to go back to the house to get one or go into the gloom of the barn without one. Hannah decided to just get the cow milked and not worry about needing to see. She could leave the door open to shed light into the interior.

The cow lowed at her as she went into the stall. She sat on the stool and placed the bucket strategically to catch the milk. The cow's warm udder felt good in the coolness of the predawn morning. Hannah leaned her forehead against the cow as she milked her, finding the experience relaxing. The soft sounds of the animals, the sound of the milk hitting the pail, they were becoming familiar to her, comfortable. Hannah knew she would be happy here.

It never occurred to her to be afraid or to take precautions to protect herself. She was at home and safe on Graham land. When a pair of strong arms grabbed her, she was so surprised, she didn't make a sound. Her attacker wrapped one arm around her waist, the other around her throat.

Adrenaline surged through her. Her heart had never beat so hard in her life. Who was this and what did he want? The man smelled of sweat, tobacco, and something rancid. She struggled to get free, although her brain told her not to, until his arm tightened so much on her throat she was barely getting any air.

"Let me go." Her shout was only a whisper.

"You listening to me, girlie?"

Hannah managed to make a noise that sounded like a yes.

"That husband of yours needs to stop talking to Armstrong." He tightened his arm again, cutting off her air supply completely. "If'n he don't, I'll come back here and he won't never find your body or that pretty little blonde. You understand me, girlie?"

Hannah tried to nod but his arm was so tight, she couldn't. She scratched at his arm, desperate for air. The only thought in her mind was she didn't want to die before she'd really had a chance to live. He had threatened Catherine, and she had to protect her young sister-in-law.

Black dots swam in front of her eyes, and she mustered up the courage to fight him one last time. She was a Graham now and she would do the name proud. She kicked out hard with her old boot, connecting with his shin. He loosened his grip enough for her to get some air.

"You fucking bitch."

Next she brought her elbow back into his stomach, but

it was padded with so much fat, her blow didn't accomplish anything. She tried to kick him again, but he was ready for it. He replaced his arm with his hand and really started choking her with fingers like talons.

Hannah was angry enough not to care what he did. This stranger had dared to hurt and threaten her and her family. She started fighting him for all she was worth, scratching and kicking. As the black dots became a roar of blackness in her mind, her last thought was of Matthew.

She should have woken him up that morning and told him she loved him.

Matt awoke as the sun crept in through the lace curtains. He knew he was alone the second he opened his eyes. To his surprise, he was disappointed Hannah wasn't there, and not just because his cock was painfully hard. He wouldn't admit it to anyone, but he enjoyed spooning with her, feeling the heat from her body mix with his. Other than riding Winston, it was about the only time Matt felt at peace.

Today there would be no spooning and no ride. The neighbors could start arriving at any time and his shift at the pit started at eight. Judging by the position of the sun, it was just past six, so he had time to eat some breakfast.

When the door to his room burst open, he was just climbing out of bed. He was about to yell at whomever it was, but Catherine started yelling first.

"Mattie, come quick! Somebody hurt Hannah!"

Matt didn't remember putting his pants or boots on but he was wearing them as he ran across the hard-packed dirt to the barn. Hurt Hannah? Who would hurt her? His gut clenched as he stepped into the barn. She lay on the straw-covered ground, as still as could be.

He dropped to his knees next to her. When he took her hand, he realized his own were shaking. What kind of cruel God would take so much from him? She was warm, and through the haze of confusion and grief, he recognized she was also breathing.

A whoosh of pure relief zinged through him. He slid his arms under her and picked her up. She moaned and her head lolled back. Anger replaced all his emotions when he saw fingerprints on her neck.

Somebody had choked her.

"Is she okay?" Catherine practically danced beside him. "I came to milk the cow but she already done it cause I showed her how, and she was lying there like a doll on the floor."

"You did good, sprite." He didn't want to scare his sister with his fury, so he kept it contained. "Get the door open for me."

Matt brought Hannah into the house, past a surprised Eva, and into their bedroom. As he laid her on the bed, her eyes fluttered open. She gazed at him for a few beats before she smiled.

"Love you, Matt."

Then she was out again. Matt thought he had been shaking before, but now his damn knees were knocking together. First he'd found out that someone had tried to kill her, and now she'd told him she loved him.

Matt wanted to cry.

"¿Que pasa, hijo?" Eva was right on his heels, pushing him out of the way. Mrs. Dolan knocked him aside, too.

"Somebody choked the hell out of her." Matt stared at the marks on her neck. He was torn between staying at her side and tearing off after the bastard who had done this to her.

"¿Porqué?" Eva unbuttoned Hannah's blouse, exposing the entire length of her neck. Mrs. Dolan gasped and to his surprise, cursed under her breath.

"Damn." Matt couldn't help cussing himself.

Eva pushed Hannah's hair out of the way and examined

the back of her neck. "I think whoever the *bandejo* was, he only bruised her. I don't think there is permanent damage."

"I don't care if it's permanent or not, I want to rip his arms off." Matt ignored Catherine's gasp behind him. "How dare he hurt my wife?"

Eva turned to him. "Stop complaining and help me. I need water, as cold as you can get it. Martha, I need rags, too."

Mrs. Dolan went to get the rags. Matt didn't want to leave the room, but he did because he knew cold water was for the swelling. If they could keep the swelling down, Hannah would fare better. He grabbed a bucket from the kitchen, then stomped out to the well and pumped it until the water gushed good and cold.

When he returned with the bucket, at least three of his sisters had woken up and were currently crowded in his bedroom doorway.

"Move."

They scattered like feathers in the wind, lucky for them. Matt was in no mood to be patient with anyone. He set down the bucket and Eva immediately dipped a rag in the water. Mrs. Dolan stood at the foot of the bed, watching. As Eva wrung it out, she gestured to Hannah.

Matt looked down, surprised to see his wife's eyes open. "Hannah." He took her hand and squeezed it gently. "You don't get to milk the cow anymore. You spilled half the milk."

She tried to laugh, but winced at the attempt.

"It's okay, honey." His damn knees shook so, he sat down on the edge of the bed, watching Eva press the cold rags against Hannah's neck. "Do you know who did this?"

She shook her head.

"Did you see him?"

She shook her head again. "Message." Her rusty whisper made him want to roar at the heavens.

"A message to me?"

Hannah nodded. "No Armstrong."

Matt's blood ran cold. "Somebody choked you to give me a message to stop talking to Armstrong?"

Her gaze looked scared and angry at the same time, but she nodded.

He pressed her hand between his as he struggled with the rage that poured through him. Not only did the message have the opposite effect from what the son of a bitch wanted, but Matt would personally hunt him down and use his balls for coyote bait.

"Don't do anything stupid, Mateo." Eva changed the cold compress and speared him with one of her *"bruja"* glares. "Today is the barbecue and your wife needs you here."

"Shit." He'd completely forgotten about the barbecue and his shift at the pit. The last thing he needed was to be polite to his neighbors. For all he knew, Stinson was the one who had sent the mongrel to choke Hannah. "We need to cancel the barbecue."

A chorus of nos came from outside the room. It seemed that every one of his siblings was out there.

"It's too late. The meat will go to waste if we don't have it." Olivia spoke up from the doorway.

Matt turned to see them all looking between him and Hannah; their identical expressions of worry almost made him forget how angry he was.

"Besides we need to show whoever it is we're not scared of them," Caleb offered. "Maybe they'll expect us to tell everybody to go home."

"We need to show them what Grahams are made of." Nick stuck out his jaw just like Pa used to do.

"Yeah, we're no cowards." Elizabeth was generally the quiet one, but even she looked fierce.

"We'll find out who hurt Hannah so we can hurt them back." Catherine climbed into the bed and snuggled up against Hannah.

"I like your kin, Matthew." Mrs. Dolan grinned. "I think we need to stand together."

His family had all gathered around his wife as if she had been part of the Graham clan forever. The sight dampened his fury so much that he could see the logic for not canceling the barbecue.

Whoever was behind the attack on Hannah would expect them to cancel. His brothers and sisters were right. They might just flush out the person responsible for not only Hannah's injuries but for his parents' death and Benjy's disappearance. The hunt was on. And he'd make damn sure everyone there knew he'd been talking to Ranger Armstrong.

The Grahams were going to war.

Hannah's throat hurt, especially when she talked, but she was well enough to get out of bed an hour after she woke up in it for the second time that morning. Matt kept hovering, along with Granny and Eva. None of them would let her move.

"I need to help." Her voice was raspy but she managed to be heard without too much pain.

"Pshaw, child. There ain't nothing that important for you to do." Granny sat like a sentry in a chair next to the bed.

"Everyone else is working." Hannah gestured to her throat. "I don't need this to help."

"Wait until folks start arriving, then you can get up. In the meantime, rest." Granny gestured to Eva, who stood in the doorway. "Do you have a scarf she can wear?"

"*Sí*, I have a pretty one *mi mama* made when I got married." Eva disappeared, leaving Granny and Hannah alone.

"That husband of yours was white as a sheet when he brought you in."

Hannah stared at her grandmother. "He was scared?"

"Oh, scared and angrier than I've ever seen anyone. He would have torn apart the man who hurt you, but he was too busy fussing over you." Granny chuckled. "I do believe your husband is falling in love with you, child."

Hannah managed not to let her mouth drop open. Granny was a smart lady and a good judge of people. Hannah had to believe she was right about Matt, but he surely didn't act it around her. The man was still bossy and cold outside the bedroom.

"Good thing, too, because you done told him you loved him."

This time, Hannah's mouth did drop open. "I did no such thing."

"Oh, yes you did. Plain as day. Me, Eva, and him heard it." This time Granny's cackle made Hannah panic.

"I couldn't have. I mean, I don't remember." She searched her memory and the last thing she could recall was the man choking her in the barn. When she woke up in the bedroom, she could hardly talk much less confess her love. What if Granny was right and she had told Matt she loved him?

Was it such a bad thing?

Yes, if he didn't feel the same. And in such a short time? Two weeks was hardly long enough to fall in love, but she was well on her way.

"He must know I was out of my head." Hannah pushed the thought out of her mind. She had other things to worry about. If Matt had heard her, then he could darn well ask her about it.

Eva appeared with a beautiful scarf in her hand. The colors were so vibrant, it looked like a sunset, with gold, red, green and orange, even pink and purple. They all blended together to form the most beautiful thing she'd ever seen.

"Eva, I can't use this." She knew she'd either rip it or stain it with the food she'd be serving.

"Of course you can." Eva helped her sit up. "Hold up your hair, *hija*."

Hannah wanted to protest some more, but as soon as the scarf touched her bruised neck, she closed her eyes at the sensation. It was magnificent, the most wonderful fabric she'd ever had the privilege of touching. Eva tied the scarf to cover the bruises, then stepped back.

"*¡Que bonita, hija!*" The housekeeper clapped her hands. "The color was made for you."

Hannah wondered how Eva could possibly think she was beautiful, when plain was all she'd ever be. She got out of the bed, grateful to be on her feet. No one protested, so she walked over to the small mirror on the wall and peered at her reflection.

Her hair was a cloud of curls, forming a halo of brown. The scarf stood out as if someone had painted an explosion of color on her neck. Even her mud brown eyes looked different because of the scarf.

"Wow."

"*Sí, hija, muy bonita.*" Eva picked up the brush and worked on the snarls in Hannah's hair. "Now let's get you ready to meet the neighbors."

Hannah endured ten minutes of discomfort until her hair was neatly contained, as much as possible anyway, in a braid. Eva stepped back to admire her handiwork, then turned to Granny.

"What do you think, Martha?"

"She's a beauty, just like her mother was." To Hannah's surprise, tears appeared in her Granny's eyes. "I can't believe you're all growed up and a married woman."

Hannah took her grandmother's hand. "I'm still the same girl."

Granny held up Hannah's hand, the silver band winking in the sunlight. "No, child, you're not. And it's a good thing."

"A wagon is coming over the rise. We need to get ready." Matt put one foot in the room, barked his orders, then turned and left.

Hannah wanted to kick him.

"Don't worry about him. He's deeper than he thinks he is." Granny winked at her. "Now help me up so we can get cracking."

The three women went outside together, prepared as best they could be for the day. Hannah's throat hurt, but the scarf actually made her skin feel better.

"Wait, what if people ask me about the scarf?" Hannah kept her gaze on the very full wagon headed toward the house. Her stomach did a jig at the sight.

"No one will ask you why you are wearing it. If anything they will be jealous of how beautiful you look in it." Eva smiled and took her arm.

Granny took her other arm. "Eva's got the right of it. Just keep smiling."

Hannah took a deep breath and got ready to face the second half of the hardest day of her life.

Matt was still seething inside. Nothing was going to quench that fire until he found who had hurt Hannah. Some lowdown snake thought a Graham would fold like a deck of cards. That fool was going to have the entire family on his ass, with blood in their eyes.

He managed to act polite for his neighbors, but he scrutinized every one of them for guilt. Throughout the next few hours, he also kept Hannah in his line of sight. Always.

At first he had trouble finding her until he realized she was the striking woman wearing a bright scarf. He'd never thought of her as beautiful, but the colors in the scarf made her shine like a vibrant flower in the sunlight.

He told himself he wasn't staring at her because he was struck dumb by how pretty she looked. Hannah was his wife, so he didn't need to be fussing about her looks. He watched her only out of concern for her safety.

Nick and Caleb, however, thought his fascination with his wife was hilarious. They kept coming up behind him and talking in a falsetto voice.

"Oh, Mattie, don't I look pretty?"

"Mattie, will you kiss me?"

He punched them both at least once; then they got smart and moved out of the way before he could reach them. Of course that made them laugh harder. Matt found himself feeling angrier by the second, and wishing the entire barbecue would just be over.

Wishing it so did not make it happen, of course. Matt had to endure the teasing, be polite to the neighbors, and mind the pit. He kept his eye on Hannah while he searched the crowd for Ranger Armstrong. That man had a lot of questions to answer, starting with why someone would almost kill his wife to stop the two of them from talking.

Lorenzo and Javier pronounced the meat ready around four in the afternoon. With Nick and Caleb, the four of them managed to move the meat to the tables, already groaning with the food the neighbors had brought. Matt supervised, unwilling to leave his position where he could see just about everyone. The only neighbors who had not arrived were the Stinsons. He didn't know if he should read anything into their absence. Guilt, perhaps?

"Looking for me?" Armstrong appeared beside him, much to Matt's consternation. Still dressed in black from head to foot, the ranger was like a living shadow.

"Dammit, man, are you part Indian or something?"

Armstrong turned his cold blue gaze on Matt, but didn't answer. Perhaps he was part Indian and Matt had just insulted him. It didn't matter one way or the other. He wasn't interested in the man's feelings, just what he knew.

"I was looking for you." Matt glanced at Hannah. "You see that scarf my wife is wearing?"

One dark eyebrow went up. "You wanted to show me your wife's scarf?"

"No, I wanted to show you the bruises on her neck where some bastard almost choked the life out of her this morning." The fury he'd felt came rushing back at him like a black cloud. Matt had to clench his fists and teeth to keep from howling.

Armstrong pulled him back toward the side of the barn before he spoke. "Tell me."

"He gave her a message for me. Said to stop talking to you. He used your name, Armstrong." Matt glanced at Hannah and a wave of worry for her hit him. She smiled and chatted with the neighbors as if she hadn't been nearly killed eight hours earlier.

"What exactly did he say?" Armstrong's jaw had a tic.

"I don't know. I wasn't there." He gestured to Hannah. "I can go get her and she can tell you herself."

"Fine then. Go get her." Armstrong was as bossy as he could be, but right about then, Matt didn't care. He just wanted his family to be safe.

He walked over to where Hannah was chatting with young Maggie McRae, the fifteen-year-old daughter of the neighboring rancher. Matt took Hannah's elbow and whispered in her ear.

"I need you." He hadn't meant to say it that way, but that's what came out of his mouth. Of course, what he meant was he needed her to talk to Armstrong. Her reaction told him she read a lot more into his statement than intended. Hell, he didn't know his ass from his head right about then. "The ranger is here."

Her smile faded and she nodded. "Excuse me, Maggie. I'll be right back."

They walked over to where the ranger waited. Hannah didn't take his arm or his hand, and he told himself he was not disappointed. Armstrong stood where Matt had left him. The lawman seemed as tough as leather the way he was so still, so unyielding.

"Ma'am." He tipped his hat to Hannah. "Name's Armstrong."

"Mr. Armstrong. Pleased to meet you. I'm Hannah Fol—I mean Hannah Graham." Her cheeks pinkened as she stumbled over her married name. Matt wasn't bothered by it. Hell, he wasn't used to introducing her as his wife.

"Your husband tells me someone gave you a message." He gestured to the scarf. "One that left marks."

Her gaze narrowed and the shyness disappeared. Hannah looked as angry as he felt. Her rusty voice was a testament to what she'd endured that morning. "Yes, some lowdown snake hid in the barn and choked me until I blacked out." She glanced at Matt. "He told me my husband needed to stop talking to Armstrong or he'd never find my body or Catherine's."

Hannah's words were like a slap. Matt reeled back, unhappy she hadn't shared the entire message with him before now.

"What? Why didn't you tell me that before now?"

"I told you." Hannah frowned. "The important thing was Armstrong's name."

Matt took her arms and yanked her against him until they were nose to nose. "The important thing was that he threatened your life again, and the life of my sister. I don't give a shit about Armstrong if you are in danger because I'm talking to him."

Her gaze searched his. "Matthew." The husky whisper was enough to drive him over the edge.

Before he realized what he was doing, his lips slammed into hers and he kissed her with all the pent-up fury and emotions churning inside him. Her mouth opened beneath his as his body hardened, inch by inch.

"Ahem, Graham, this isn't really the place to do that." Armstrong's voice broke the haze of pure passion Matt had fallen into.

He stepped back from Hannah and took a shaky breath. Her lips were reddened and moist from his kisses. Damned if her nipples weren't hard beneath her blouse, too. What the hell was wrong with him?

"Sorry. I, uh, let's get back to the stranger." His body throbbed with lust for his wife, but Matt managed to tear his gaze away from Hannah to look at Armstrong. "And why he would warn me away from you."

Armstrong frowned. "There aren't many who know I'm here, and if they do, they don't know why I'm here."

"Somebody does. I want to find out who." Matt knew something dark was going on in their little corner of Texas and he wanted to know who was behind it.

"Not any more than I do. I'm supposed to be a ghost around here." Armstrong glanced at Hannah. "Is there someplace private we can talk?"

"I'm going to hear what you have to say, Mr. Armstrong. Don't think for a minute I'll simply walk away." Hannah surprised Matt again with the vehemence in her voice.

"Fine, but I don't care if you're a woman or not. If you repeat anything I tell you, I will take action." Armstrong didn't need to say what he would do, but Matt understood just the same.

"You don't need to threaten my wife."

"I'm not threatening her. I'm warning her and you." Armstrong's jaw clenched so tight, the scar on his face whitened. "I don't share information, ever, but since you two are already involved, I reckon I need to tell you. Otherwise you might just keep being a thorn in my paw."

"Then start talking." Matt couldn't imagine what the ranger was doing in their neck of the woods that was so secret, but he knew it was the key to what had happened to his parents, his brother, and his wife.

Armstrong looked hard at both of them for a few moments before speaking. "Sam Houston himself asked me to investigate what's been happening. I told you about the other ranches. Word of the violence got to Sam's ear and he wanted to find out who was behind killing the citizens of Texas."

Matt was impressed. Sam Houston? Ranger Armstrong was rubbing elbows with some big men.

"What does that have to do with Hannah?"

"Someone saw me here talking to you yesterday. That means that person knows why I'm here." Armstrong glanced at the crowd of people eating and talking. "More than likely one of those folks right there."

Matt turned and realized he didn't know whom to trust. His family, the people he loved, had a murderer in their midst. The thought made his blood run cold.

"How can we help?" Hannah pulled their attention back from the barbecue.

"I can't ask you to do that. Just know that I'll be around looking into things." Armstrong frowned. "I don't need you fiddling with my investigation."

"I refuse to do nothing." Hannah put her hands on her hips. "I was attacked and that vermin threatened my little sister."

"Mrs. Graham, I can't let you—"

"You won't *let* me do anything." Hannah poked one finger into the ranger's chest. "I decide, not you."

Armstrong stared down at her, his scowl deeper than the pit they'd dug for the barbecue.

"You're bossy, if you don't mind my saying so."

"So are you." Hannah looked like a rabbit facing the big, bad wolf.

Matt didn't know whether to spank her or kiss her, but Hannah seemed to change the ranger's mind. He relaxed his stance and nodded.

"Fine, but if I tell you to get out of my way, you do it."

"Agreed." Hannah touched the scarf. "I don't want to ever feel afraid again. I find myself ready to shoot the man who made me feel that way."

Matt swore the ranger nearly cracked a smile.

"You're quite a woman, Mrs. Graham. Too bad you're married." Armstrong pushed his hat back a smidge, staring at Hannah.

Matt found himself fighting a pang of jealousy. He needed to get the ranger's attention back on the problem. "Can you tell us what you know?"

Armstrong's gaze moved back to the crowd. "The attacks come when the ranch hands are out on the range, so it's someone who knows the comings and goings of the ranchers. They kill women, take at least one if not two children, and burn what they can."

"Why?" Hannah frowned so hard her eyebrows touched.

"I don't know. That's what I'm here to find out. If I can figure out what they're after, I can stop them." Armstrong's expression was one of frustration.

"What happened to the other ranches after the attack?" Hannah's voice had dropped.

"Five of the ranchers lit out of Texas completely. Two of them hunkered down and now carry guns." Armstrong hesitated.

Matt knew there were ten total and realized there were other ranches not accounted for. "And the other three?"

Armstrong shook his head. "All dead or missing."

Hannah stepped away, her arms wrapped around her

belly. She stared out into the open range, her gaze shining in the mid-afternoon sun. Matt wondered if she was thinking about her brush with death or his own parents' murders. Either way, her thoughts were heavy enough to make her fight for control.

Matt hadn't realized there was a pattern to the attacks, that there were other people who had lost loved ones, had suffered fear and grief. Hannah was right. They had to help stop this mayhem so others didn't have to endure the dark hell left behind by these bastards.

"Do they leave anything behind? Anything that might point to who they are?" Matt hadn't found a thing.

"No, but there is a pattern." Armstrong's gaze flickered to the fancy wagon heading toward them. "Someone has been buying the land either left behind by the dead or sold by the ones who ran."

Matt knew who it was before Armstrong even said his name. And at that moment, the Stinsons' buggy rolled onto his ranch. His hands clenched into fists.

"Stinson has a lot of money and a lot of land. He's got a lot more now, and I hear he's building a big herd of cattle, too." Armstrong stepped back into the shadows. "Be careful, Graham. You, too, Mrs. Graham."

With that, the ranger disappeared from view. The words Matt forced back down his throat threatened to explode when Stinson stopped the buggy. Margaret smiled at him while Jeb waved.

All Matt could think was *murdering bastard*.

Chapter Fourteen

Hannah could hardly keep a smile on her face. Anger and fear churned in her stomach at all she'd learned from the ranger. How could anyone murder innocent people just to get more land? Was dirt worth more than someone's life? If Stinson was capable of killing their neighbors, there was likely nothing he wouldn't do in the name of greed.

She carefully avoided talking to any of the Stinsons, moving away each time they grew near. Let Eva and Granny be polite to them. Right about then, Hannah might have spit in their faces.

The only good thing about what she'd heard from Armstrong was that he was investigating the crimes. At least the murders wouldn't go unpunished, not if she could help it. Hannah would help the taciturn ranger no matter how much he warned her away. This was her family now and they'd been hurt, not to mention her own brush with death. She would not go down easy.

The barbecue was in full swing when Lorenzo and Javier pulled out a guitar and fiddle. To her surprise, they could both not only play but also had lovely singing voices. Their neighbors, relaxed with food and good cheer, started dancing.

Hannah had never been to a barbecue or a dance, and found her foot tapping along with the beat. The smiles and laughter abounded as the ranchers danced under the waning daylight. She wanted to join in but had no idea what to do, and her husband didn't seem the type to dance.

"Why are you hiding over here, Mrs. Graham?" Frederick Stinson's voice scraped along her skin. She barely stopped herself from flinching.

"I'm not hiding, Mr. Stinson. I'm making sure folks enjoy themselves." She started to walk away but he took her elbow.

"Whoa there, little filly. How about you take a turn around the dance floor with me?" Stinson didn't give her a chance to respond. He simply took her out to the dance floor and started dancing.

Her anger overrode her fear, but she knew if she pulled away from him, there would most definitely be a scene. She gritted her teeth and hoped it looked like she was smiling. To her surprise, Frederick Stinson was a graceful dancer and moved fluidly, regardless of her own clumsiness.

Hannah tried to keep quiet, she truly did, but her mouth started moving and she was hopeless to stop. "Have you met Ranger Armstrong, Mr. Stinson?"

He stumbled but regained his balance almost immediately. "No, I haven't had that pleasure."

"You really should. He is a very nice man." Hannah could hardly stand to touch Stinson. His hands were softer than hers, with no calluses to speak of, and his palms were damp. She needed to get away from him. "Very smart, too."

This time when he stumbled, she broke away from him. He reached for her again but she sidestepped him.

"Thank you for the dance, Mr. Stinson." She managed to make her way through the dancers, and away from him.

Matt stood at the edge of the dancing with a deep scowl on his face. She turned left and avoided her husband's wrath. Hannah could hardly believe what she was doing, and how alive she felt doing it.

Granny sat in a rocking chair on the front porch and she beckoned Hannah closer. With a quick look behind her, Hannah darted onto the porch and sat beside her grandmother in the empty rocking chair.

"What are you up to, child?"

"Hiding from the men out there."

Granny's eyebrows went up. "Hiding from the men? Has someone hurt you again?"

"No, I'm just, I don't know how to describe it." She rocked back and forth, the cool early evening breeze exactly what she needed. "I'm too full of things right now."

"Too much food?"

"No, I haven't eaten anything yet. There's just so much happening at once, I don't know which end is up." She took a deep breath and blew it out slowly.

"I reckon I know what you mean." Granny nodded. "Sit here a spell and get your wits about you."

Hannah took Granny's advice and stayed put. She saw Stinson walking through the crowd, chatting with people, smiling and acting as if he were the host. She was disgusted that she'd even touched him, much less danced with him.

"You're going to strike sparks with that fiery look," Granny mused. "Who is he?"

"Frederick Stinson."

"The neighbor who snatched that land between the Circle Eight and the new land?" Granny peered through the crowd.

"Among other things."

"He's very handsome."

"Granny! The man is a snake." Hannah saw Jeb Stinson heading toward the porch and told herself not to get up and run again. Jeb likely had no idea what his father was up to.

"You best stay clear of the man then."

Easier said than done, of course, but there were so many things she knew about and could not ignore. That included the Stinsons and the threat to the Graham family.

"Good evening, Mrs. Dolan. Mrs. Graham, may I call you Hannah?" Jeb smiled, his pearly white teeth shining in the setting sunlight.

"No, you may not. It's Mrs. Graham and it's going to stay that way." Matt stepped up beside him. "She's married, Jeb, so quit flirting."

"Hey, I can't help if it I see a pretty lady and I just feel the need to make her smile." Jeb chuckled, earning a surprised smile from Hannah. "You see, it worked!"

Matt's scowl returned. "I need to talk to my wife if you don't mind."

"Oh, but I do mind. I heard my father danced with the hostess. What kind of man would I be if I didn't dance with her too?" Jeb ignored Matt's protests, as well as Hannah's, and led her out to the dancing couples.

It was a lively song with a lot of foot stomping and swirling. Hannah couldn't catch her breath as Jeb twirled her around and around. She found herself smiling at his good-natured silliness and enjoyed herself for a few moments.

Then her scarf fell off.

Jeb's eyes widened and he snatched up the scarf, leading her into the shadow of the house quicker than she'd thought possible.

"Hannah, what happened to you?" He reached out toward her neck and she reared back.

"Please don't touch me. I'm fine." She took the scarf and tried to remember how Eva had wrapped it earlier.

"Like hell you're fine. Someone tried to choke you." Jeb's voice grew angry. "I can't believe Graham would do that to you. I'm going to—"

"Matthew did nothing to hurt me, Jeb. I appreciate your concern, but this is none of your business." Hannah touched his rock hard arm. "Please forget you saw my neck and enjoy yourself."

"I can't do that." He moved closer and she suddenly felt very small next to his large body. "You are a good woman and deserve better than a rancher without two nickels to rub together."

Hannah tamped down her panic and told herself to be strong. Jeb wouldn't hurt her. He was just worried about her.

"I love my husband. He is a good man and that's that." She turned to walk away from Jeb, but he took her arm again.

"Please, Hannah, don't run away yet." His fingers twined with hers and she yanked her hand away.

"I did not give you permission to call me by my first name, Mr. Stinson. Don't touch me and don't ever think you can bad mouth my husband." Her anger returned and with it the courage she needed. "I suggest you get your sister and father and head home."

This time he didn't try to stop her, which was good because she would have kicked him. She ran right into a wall, which turned out to be her husband.

"Matthew." She sounded out of breath even to her own ears. "My scarf fell off and I had to fix it. How does it look?"

The orange glow of the sun gave him a fiery look as he reached out to adjust the scarf. His hand grazed her jaw as his gaze locked with hers. Hannah's body came to life as though he'd cast a spell over her. She nearly fell into the pool of his blue-green eyes.

"Jeb try anything with you?"

"Yes, but I told him you were a good man." She swayed toward him, eager to touch him, to feel him. Her core throbbed with an ache that needed to be satisfied.

"That's not all you told him."

Oh dear Lord, he'd heard her tell Jeb she loved her husband. If he hadn't heard her before when she was out of her head, apparently he'd heard her this time.

Matt moved closer and everything around him fell away. As his lips touched hers, Hannah was able to shake off all the darkness riding her back. She moaned into his mouth as the kiss deepened.

"I guess you weren't kidding, Mrs. Graham." Jeb walked past them in a huff.

Both Hannah and Matt laughed as they moved back a step, taking up where they'd left off.

"Did you mean it?" His softly worded question made her heart hiccup.

Hannah closed her eyes and looked down at her feet. "Yes."

His thumb pressed her chin back up. "Good. You're mine." After a hard kiss, he tucked her arm in his and walked her back to the barbecue.

She didn't quite understand what "you're mine" meant, but it was probably the closest thing to "I love you too" she'd get.

Matt's gut was on fire. At the sight of Jeb dancing with his wife, jealousy had eaten him up like a dragon from a storybook. He'd stomped after them, eager to kick Jeb's ass from one end of the Republic to the other. But when he'd paused to listen, he'd heard Hannah defend him, put Jeb in his place, then confess she loved him.

He'd thought perhaps he'd heard her wrong earlier in the day or maybe she had been out of her mind. This time, however, she was lucid and completely clear when she told Jeb she loved Matt. He had to ask her, he just had to, and she willingly confirmed what she'd said.

His wife loved him.

It had been the strangest, craziest day of his life, but at the end of it, his wife loved him. Matt wasn't about to admit to his own feelings for her, but armed with her love, he felt a little invincible.

Matt walked toward Frederick Stinson with determination in his step and Hannah on his arm. He found the rancher at the bowl of beans, talking to Olivia. In the door of the barn, he spotted Armstrong, who was also watching Stinson with Olivia. What in the hell was going on?

"Stinson." Matt kept his voice even, although inside he wanted to tear the man's arms off for not only touching his wife but obviously sizing up his sister.

"Graham. I was looking for you earlier, but I couldn't find you. I spent the time talking to your lovely sister. How is it this pretty young gal isn't married yet?" Stinson leaned toward her and Matt could swear the other man was looking at his sister's breasts.

He almost lunged for the man, but Hannah caught his arm. Damn, the woman was stronger than she looked.

"Mr. Stinson, we'd like to discuss a business matter with you." Her voice was high and tight.

"Ladies ought not to talk about business. That's a man's job, little missy." Stinson rocked back on his heels. "You let your women run amuck, Graham. I saw your wife with no less than three men tonight."

Hannah held his arm tighter. "It is my business because it involves my family." Her smile looked forced.

"We got our land grant, Stinson, but I'm thinking you might know that," Matt began. "We want to offer you a deal to buy that little patch of dirt between this ranch and our new property." There, that sounded reasonable.

Stinson rubbed his chin. "That's a mighty tempting offer, but I don't know that I want to sell any of my land."

The music faded as Lorenzo and Javier turned their attention to what was happening between Matt and Stinson. Conversation around them also seemed to stop.

"I'll have to go near fifty miles out of my way to get from this ranch to the new land." Matt kept his tone as light as he could. "It would be right neighborly if we could either buy that patch of land or work out an arrangement to cross it with our animals."

Stinson shook his head, and then his gaze flicked to a spot over Matt's shoulder. Matt had a feeling Hannah's plan to call the rancher out in front of everyone was working. The last thing Stinson wanted was to be thought badly of. He had a reputation as a smart but tough man; however most folks respected him. Until his parents' deaths, Matt had been one of them.

Now he knew better.

"I didn't know my owning that strip landed you in such a situation, Graham. I would think the land grant office would be more logical." Stinson shook his head as though he hadn't masterminded the entire thing.

"Seems you had already claimed that skinny piece of land, so there wasn't anything they could do." Matt squeezed Hannah's arm. "I want to build a bigger ranch for my future children and my brothers and sisters. I'm sure you understand that."

Margaret appeared at her father's side. "Daddy, this barbecue is boring. Can we leave now?" She turned a pouty gaze on Matt, and damned if she didn't wink at him.

"Not right yet, pumpkin. Daddy is finishing up some business." Stinson patted her head as though she were a pet, rather than his nineteen-year-old daughter.

"I know the strip of land also borders McRae's ranch." He turned to find red-haired Angus McRae in the crowd. "He probably needs to get across it, too."

Angus nodded his shaggy head. "Aye, that's true."

"What do you say, Stinson?" Matt asked, forcing his own smile.

"For my neighbors, yes, I'll let you use the land. I need to see a map, of course, to make sure I know the patch of land you're referring to." Stinson's smile was as fake as Matt's.

That's when he became certain Stinson was behind everything. Armstrong was right about all of it. Son of a bitch! Why couldn't he have seen before now just how evil men could be? His father had been such an honorable, strong man, it had never occurred to Matt that others could be so different.

Matt gestured to the house. "I have the map the land grant office gave me. I can show it to you now."

Stinson tutted. "No need to stop the fun because of a business deal. We can talk tomorrow and let folks enjoy the rest of the evening."

"Why don't we meet tomorrow at Angus's ranch at nine? We can make our arrangements then." Matt didn't want Stinson on his land any more than necessary. He figured by putting the meeting on another rancher's property, Stinson might actually agree to it.

"That sounds fine, young Graham. Now why don't you have your Mexican boys start playing again so folks can dance." Stinson's leering gaze landed on Hannah and Matt couldn't stop the growl in his throat.

Javier and Lorenzo must've sensed the tension was about ready to bust wide open because guitar music floated through the air again. Hannah's fingers dug into his arm and he recognized just how close he was to losing control. He was actually vibrating with anger.

"Come dance with me." Her whisper tickled his ear, pulling him from the edge.

"I can't dance."

"Me neither, so we'll make fools of ourselves together." She tugged on his arm. "C'mon, cowboy."

Matt didn't want to dance, but he didn't want to commit murder in front of half the county either. He let Hannah lead him toward the open area folks had been dancing in. Javier starting singing a Mexican ballad.

Hannah managed to wrap her arms around him and took his hand. "Now dance."

They swung back and forth like a bell, neither one of them had a lick of rhythm. Somehow just touching her, breathing in her air as she let it out, calmed him. She had some kind of magic in her and he was glad for at least the dozenth time that day that she was his wife.

Other guests joined them and soon ten couples were swaying to Javier's beautiful ballad. By the time the last notes fell away, Matt felt better. He didn't want Hannah to know how close he'd come to accusing Stinson of murder. It would've jeopardized Armstrong's investigation and any chance of actually catching the bastard.

To his surprise, he spotted Armstrong talking to Olivia on the side of the porch. He assumed the ranger was just pursuing his investigation but Matt would have to keep his eye on the other man just the same.

"Better?" Hannah took his hand and looked at him inquiringly.

"Yeah. I won't shoot anybody. Yet." He blew out a frustrated breath. "Why don't you go check on Eva and I'll go talk to Armstrong?"

Hannah frowned but she squeezed his hand and walked away, leaving him to his own choices. He could kick Stinson's ass but that wouldn't get him anything. Instead he went toward Armstrong, and to his consternation, Olivia walked the other way as soon as he got close.

"What are you doing with my sister, Armstrong?"

"Just talking. Can't investigate without talking to folks."
Armstrong nodded. "Nice work getting Stinson out of his
house tomorrow. I can be in and out while he's gone. I expect the son to go with the father to McRae's house. He
follows his Pa around like a puppy."

Matt hadn't thought of it before, but it was true Whenever he saw Frederick Stinson, Jeb was two steps behind
him. It wasn't strange for a son to want to be like his father,
but by the time he was sixteen, Matt had been working the
ranch and not following his father around. Jeb was nice
enough, but the man didn't have any skills beyond smiling
and flirting.

"Now we need to make sure the girl is gone, too. I asked
your sister to invite her for tea or something." Armstrong
frowned at Olivia's retreating back. "She's got quite a
mouth on her for a young lady."

Matt didn't really care if Olivia cussed at the ranger, but
he felt better somehow knowing she didn't have romantic
notions about the man.

"Good idea. Livy and Margaret are friends." Matt didn't
want his sister to feel obligated to help, but knowing her,
she heard a lot more than she ought to about what was going on. "Then what do we do?"

"*We* don't do anything. I go in and snoop around." Armstrong's gaze dared Matt to contradict him.

"You can't get in there and out without someone noticing you. Stinson has fifty people working for him. You're
not a ghost, Armstrong." Matt folded his arms across his
chest. "You have someone you trust to be your lookout?"

Armstrong stared off into the distance for a few moments before his cool gaze met Matt's. "No, but I don't
need one."

"I don't necessarily believe you, but I'm trusting that
you will do what you can to find what you need."

"I'll be leaving now. Make sure you get on over to

McRae's by nine. I'm counting on you." Armstrong melted into the deepening darkness behind him, leaving Matt to wonder if he was trusting the right person.

He had to be because if he wasn't, the future of the Graham ranch might never happen.

Hannah washed the dishes with a feeling of relief. She absolutely hated washing dishes, but the normalcy of the chore somehow calmed her frayed nerves. The entire day had been like a dream, perhaps more of a nightmare.

Eva left her in the kitchen, seeming to understand that Hannah needed to be alone. The low hum of conversation outside centered around the bonfire the boys had built just beyond the barn. Peace had settled over the Graham ranch, and the guests were nearly gone.

Matt was nowhere to be found; perhaps he was hiding someplace, too. After all they'd found out today, she wouldn't blame him a bit. His neighbor was probably behind his parents' murders and his brother's disappearance. Missing children were generally thought of as dead, but the ranger's information made it sound as if the children had been taken, not killed.

There were so many reasons why people chose evil, but when the life of a child was involved, she just couldn't understand how anyone could commit such a crime. They were innocent, untouched by the ugliness of the world. Now Benjamin Graham was gone, subjected to who knew what. He would never regain the innocence snatched from him, but she prayed he was still alive.

Her heart hurt for the Graham family. She hoped that by helping Ranger Armstrong, they could put the ugly past behind them and really start living again. Oh, they ate, slept, and breathed each day, but Matt had just proven to her that he wasn't living. He just existed from day to day.

Hannah knew he would never truly fall in love with her until he banished the demons that haunted his every moment. He had nightmares in his sleep, often moaning out loud. She hadn't told him about it, for fear she'd embarrass him, but the unsolved crimes were slowly eating away at him, bite by bite.

She rinsed the last plate in the cool water in the bucket and set it on the pile. The barbecue had been a success, albeit one of the strangest days she could remember. Life at the boardinghouse had been so boring and mundane. Her new life on the Circle Eight was nothing if not unpredictable. She was up for the challenge though. Hannah was so glad she had accepted Matt's proposal even if someone had tried to kill her because of it.

The memory brought jitters to her whole body, and she knew she had to sit down. The chair was blessedly solid beneath her.

"*Hija,* are you okay?" Eva poked her head in the kitchen from the hallway.

"Yes, no, I don't know." Hannah leaned forward and cradled her head with her arms.

Eva rubbed her back. "Ah, *hija,* you need sleep. In the morning, you will feel better." She touched the scarf. "Let me check your throat."

Hannah sat back up and untied the scarf. "Thank you for letting me use this. It's the most beautiful thing I've ever worn."

"It is the person who makes a thing beautiful, not the other way around." Eva smiled as her fingers gently explored Hannah's neck. "There will be bruises so you keep the scarf. *Mi mama* would be happy for you to wear it."

Hannah nodded, her throat tight with the generosity of this woman who barely knew her. "Thank you again."

Eva kissed her forehead. "Anything for *mi hija.*" Eva turned to leave.

"Wait, I need to ask you—" Hannah's eyes pricked with unshed tears. "Why?"

Eva frowned in confusion. "Why what?"

"Why did you welcome me into your home? Why do you treat me like one of your *hijas*? I'm not your daughter and you don't even know me." Hannah struggled not to burst into tears. "Why?"

Eva folded her into a hug. "You love with all your heart and soul, Hannah. I knew as soon as I met you that you were someone to trust, someone who will love Mateo with everything she has. Catherine loved you right away, too. She knows, just like me, you are one of us."

Hannah had never realized what she'd been missing in a family. Granny had done her best, but she was old when Hannah came to live with her. Without brothers and sisters, without a mother and a father, Hannah had always been lonely. The Graham family had taken her in immediately, filling the hole in her heart.

"Thank you, Eva."

"How about some tea before bed?" Eva stoked the fire in the stove to heat a pot of water. "I have some herbal tea I make myself."

"Tea would be really nice." Hannah was torn between being sad and being absurdly happy. She had everything she wanted, now she just had to find a way to keep it.

Tomorrow Matt would be at the McRae ranch for a while. Perhaps if she went over to the Stinsons, she might find something to help Armstrong with his case against the rancher. When she'd been at the ranch several days earlier, she had passed by what appeared to be Stinson's office. If she went by for a visit, she might just get lost and end up there for a look around.

Hannah would help her husband whether or not he liked it.

★   ★   ★

Matt made sure the bonfire was completely out before he headed back to the house. Everything was dark except for a solitary light in the kitchen. Eva always left one burning if one of them wasn't home when she went to bed. It kept everyone from getting bruised shins and it was a welcoming sight after a long day.

He made his way into the house and blew out the lantern. The night before, Hannah had bathed him, shown him how much she loved him without words. He grew hard at the memory, felt the rush of heat he'd experienced several times that day for Hannah.

It was late, nearly midnight, and she'd be long since asleep. She'd started the day by nearly getting killed, then played hostess to the biggest party they'd ever had at the Circle Eight without letting on once she had been attacked. Hannah had surprised him more than once that day, proving to him he'd found the right woman to be his wife. Even if it had been because of some turnips.

When he opened the bedroom door, he was surprised to see her standing at the window. She turned to face him and the moonlight turned her into an ethereal being. His body hardened almost painfully as he closed the door behind him.

"Hannah." His voice was a rusty whisper in the stillness of the room.

"I'm yours."

He shed his clothes quickly, almost falling while taking off his boots. As he approached her barefoot, his cock was like a divining rod pointing straight toward exactly what it wanted.

She opened her arms and he pulled her against him, his mouth slamming onto hers with a ferocity that he had never known before. Her softness cradled his hardness as his blood rushed around his body, pounding past his ears.

"I need to feel your skin."

To his delight, she pulled off her nightdress to reveal nothing but what God had given her. He ran his hands down her shoulders, back to her round buttocks. She moaned low and soft in her throat when his touch moved to the front of her body. He cupped her breasts, loving the weight of them in his hands.

Matt dropped to his knees and took a nipple in his mouth. She trembled as he lapped, nibbled, and sucked at her. He moved his hand between her thighs, gently parting the incredibly soft skin until he found what he wanted. She was wet and welcoming, making his cock thump against his belly.

"I need you, Matt."

He would have responded in kind but he couldn't find his voice. So he scooped her up and brought her to the bed instead. When she lay there looking up at him, her brown eyes like liquid heat in the silver moonlight, he paused to stare at her. His wife was a gift and he wanted to be sure she knew that.

Although he didn't have a lot of experience with women, he knew enough to make Hannah feel good. Together they could learn everything they needed to know about keeping each other happy.

He dropped to his knees again and parted her thighs. Her glistening cleft waited, its pink folds enticing him to taste, touch, pleasure. He kissed her nether lips, earning a surprised gasp from Hannah. When his tongue found her clit, the gasp turned into a full-fledged moan. Her tangy taste coated his tongue, exciting him to the point he found his hand sliding up and down his shaft.

Lick. Tug. Lick. Tug.

As her thighs quivered against his cheeks, he lapped and sucked at her. When he pushed two fingers into her, she clenched around him so tight, he knew he wouldn't last long if he entered her too soon. He needed to make sure she came first.

His fingers thrust into her as he increased his tongue's rhythm. She made a funny, kittenish sound in her throat, which turned into a low keening moan as she grew closer to her peak. When he started sucking on her clit, she grabbed the quilt and dug in her heels.

"Maaaaattthheeeewwww—" She drew out his name as she came, her juices becoming sweeter, her channel tighter.

He couldn't wait a second longer. Matt stood and plunged into her welcoming core. He came almost immediately, filling her with his seed as her own orgasm shuddered around his staff. Stars swam behind his eyes as he experienced the most powerful ecstasy of his life. He held onto her hips, plunging in with each wave of pleasure. When he was wrung dry, he collapsed beside her, shaking with the force of what he'd just experienced.

Whether he would admit it to her or not, Matt knew he was in uncharted territory. Nothing had ever felt like that with any other woman. It was she who made the difference. For the first time in his life, he was afraid he couldn't stop himself. Matt was falling in love with Hannah.

After he caught his breath, he tucked them both under the covers, naked as the day they were born. When they spooned together, their body heat mixed to form a cocoon around them. It felt safe, comfortable. As he listened to his wife breathing softly, Matt promised himself he would find a way to control himself around Hannah. If he didn't, he might never be the same.

Chapter Fifteen

M att kissed Hannah before he left for the McRaes', leaving a stupid smile on her face. The girls made silly kissing noises in imitation while the boys make disgusted sounds. To Hannah, the embrace meant the world to her. Perhaps he was starting to feel things for her. The possibility lit a glimmer of hope in her heart that there was a fighting chance for the love she needed from him.

As soon as he was out of sight, she ran into the house and changed into her riding skirt. Olivia appeared wearing one as well and looked at Hannah in surprise.

"Are you going somewhere?"

"I just needed a little time to myself. Yesterday was so busy." Hannah's smile was forced but she hoped her sister-in-law didn't notice.

"Matt would have our hides if we let you ride off by yourself. Take Caleb or Javier with you." Olivia pulled on her gloves with a frown. "I'm going to the Stinson ranch for tea with Margaret."

Inspiration hit Hannah like a knock to the head. "May I come?"

Olivia's brows went up. "You want to have tea with Margaret?"

"No, I mean yes. I just want to get away from the ranch

for a little while." This was a perfect opportunity to get into the Stinson ranch without having to sneak.

"She's bound to be catty to you." Olivia looked guilty. "I know she's not the nicest person in the world, but she's my friend."

"It's okay. I won't mind, really. It will be my first real tea." Hannah shrugged. "Not much opportunity for lady-like teas at a boardinghouse."

"Or on a ranch for that matter." Olivia smiled. "You should put on the scarf first. We don't want to give Margaret any more reason to be, ah, difficult."

Hannah was delighted to put on the scarf and go out to the barn with her sister-in-law. She didn't know what she would have done without the escort to the Stinson property. Now she had the perfect excuse to be there.

Javier saddled their horses for them, frowning the whole time. "Matt will not like this."

"He's not my boss so he has no say in what I do, or what Hannah does for that matter." Olivia got up on her horse with more agility than Hannah could ever hope to have.

After using a mounting block to awkwardly mount Buttermilk, Hannah was ready to face the lioness in her den. With a grim smile, she nodded to the worried-looking Javier and the two women started riding toward the Stinson ranch.

She would show Matt just what she could do for him.

Matt rode up to Angus McRae's ranch with a knot in his gut. He wasn't surprised to see Stinson's prize stallion already there, tied to the hitching post in front of the sprawling ranch house.

He dismounted and retrieved the map from his saddlebags. This was the moment he would have to stand firm against Stinson and his greed. He sure as hell hoped his father was somewhere nearby, giving him strength to face the challenge and not lose his temper in the process. Strength and logic would win the day, not anger and passion.

Matt knocked on the door and Maggie opened it. The redheaded younger daughter blushed when she saw Matt. The fifteen-year-old had always followed him around from the time she could toddle. But he was almost ten years older than she and certainly didn't want her pining after him.

"Good morning, Maggie. I'm here to see your father."

She stammered a response and led him into the house. The men were seated in Angus's office in the front corner of the house. He had put in a large picture window so he could watch his five daughters whenever they were outside. With no sons to take over the ranch, McRae knew there would come a time when too many young men would be sniffing around his land and his daughters.

The big red-haired man sat behind his desk while Stinson leaned on the corner of it, as if he owned the room. Matt considered accidently pushing him off his perch, but decided it would be a bad start to the meeting.

"Did you bring the map, Graham?" Stinson didn't seem the least bit concerned he was about to be exposed as a thieving murderer.

Matt laid the map out on the desk and the three of them stared at it. "Right here is my ranch and here is yours, Angus." He traced the outline with his finger. "Here is my new land grant and here is the two-mile gap between them."

There was a moment of silence before Stinson laughed. "That little wiggly line? What is it?"

"It's your property." Matt wanted to punch the laughing jackass.

"No, it's not. Why in the hell would I buy a piece of property like that?" Stinson straightened up. "You got your facts wrong, Graham. Maybe next time a grown-up ought to come with you." His cocky grin made Matt's temper almost bubble over.

Then a sudden thought struck him, snatching the anger as quick as a hawk. "What do you mean it's not yours?"

"Just what I said. There ain't no money to be made on such a small tract of land." Stinson frowned at Matt. "What makes you think it's mine?"

Matt's stomach fell to his knees. "I saw the deed. It's in your name, along with another half dozen pieces of land west of here."

This time it was Frederick's turn to look surprised. "What the hell are you talking about?"

"It's not you, is it?" Matt was suddenly very afraid for his sister. "It's Jeb."

"What's Jeb? Graham, would you start making sense?" Stinson was a jackass, but he was a straight shooter who would tell a man to his face what he thought of him. This whole situation with the land, the murders, the missing children, didn't point to him.

It pointed to his son. The twenty-five-year-old with nothing but a big smile who waited to inherit his father's ranch. Impatiently.

"I think Jeb has decided to snatch up as much land as possible, perhaps even arrange for you to have a riding accident." Matt ignored the confused anger on Frederick's face. "Armstrong was right. It was a Stinson all along, but not the one he suspected."

"Graham, I think you have gone loco." Stinson folded his arms across his chest but Matt saw a glimmer of uncertainty in his gaze.

"Someone wants as much land as he can get no matter what the cost. My parents, Benjy, and half a dozen other families are all gone, either dead or disappeared. Their properties were purchased by you."

"The hell you say. I didn't kill nobody and I haven't bought any property." Stinson glanced at the map. "You saw the deed with my name on it?"

"Yes, I did, and so did Hannah. I'm guessing if we travel to Houston, we'd find quite a few deeds with your name on them." Matt couldn't believe the affable Jeb was behind it all. "Where is Jeb?"

"At home like always. He said Margaret was having company so he stayed to flirt with 'em." Stinson's gaze didn't leave the map.

"At home? Oh my God, Olivia is the company. She was going to have tea." Matt knew he had to get to Stinson's ranch immediately. "Angus, go to town and get the sheriff. Meet us at the Stinson place." He turned to Frederick. "You ready to find out the truth?"

Stinson's eyes met his and Matt saw confusion and anger swirling in their depths. "I don't believe a word of what you said but if someone is buying land in my name, I want to find out who and why. You're going to have some apologizing to do when we get to my ranch." He slammed his hat on his head. "Let's go."

The two of them left Angus's office in a hurry. As they untied the horses from the hitching post, Matt hoped Winston was ready to fly.

After Olivia knocked on the door, Hannah waited beside her on the ornate front porch of the Stinson ranch. She was trying to figure out how to get into the office without anyone noticing. It was imperative she find some scrap of evidence that Stinson was up to no good.

When the door opened, she knew Olivia was as surprised as she was to see Jeb in the doorway. He smiled and bowed at Olivia.

"Welcome, Miss Graham. I'm so glad to—" He spotted Hannah standing a few feet away. "I didn't expect to see you though, Mrs. Graham. What a lovely surprise." His grin was unsettling and made her warning bells ring loudly. "Margaret is expecting us for tea." Olivia glanced at Hannah. "Well, just me really, but I convinced Hannah to join me."

"Please come in. Both of you." Jeb opened the door and gestured with his arm for them to enter.

As Hannah walked in, she swore she felt Jeb's breath on her neck, and she hurried to catch up to her sister-in-law. She took Olivia's arm.

"Something's wrong," Hannah whispered.

Olivia frowned at her, then turned back to look at Jeb. "Where is Margaret?"

"She's feeling poorly this morning after the barbecue." Jeb put his arm around their waists and led them through the house. "However, our housekeeper had the tea and sandwiches all ready. Margaret asked me to host in her place."

Hannah stared at the handsome, charming Jeb, wondering just what it was that set her on edge. He seemed so friendly and sincere, but she didn't quite feel comfortable with just the three of them. What if Hannah hadn't accompanied Olivia? Her sister-in-law would have been alone, unchaperoned with Jeb.

That could have been exactly what he wanted. Jeb Stinson was hunting for a wife, if Hannah wasn't mistaken, and could ruin Olivia just by being with her alone. Possibly even take it a step further and rape her.

Hannah was doubly glad she'd come. Now she could stop the snake from defiling her sister-in-law and find evidence his father was swindling, murdering and kidnapping folks. Her smile was genuine if a little self-satisfied.

"Poor Margaret. Does she need a poultice or some of Eva's special tea?" Olivia turned to go toward what Hannah assumed was Margaret's bedroom, but Jeb stopped her.

"Oh, she wouldn't want you to see her like this. She's been, ah, vomiting all night. Probably some bad beans or something." Jeb ushered them back toward the terrace, toward the garden that had seemed so lovely a week earlier. Now with the clouds hiding the sun, it seemed almost sinister and the bright flowers had lost their vibrancy.

On a small table were a teapot with two cups and a plate of tiny sandwiches. There were also only two chairs and Hannah knew she'd been right about Jeb's nefarious motives. Maybe Margaret wasn't even sick. Perhaps he'd done something to his sister so he could get Olivia alone. The possibilities were endless.

"I think we'll need another cup and chair, Jeb." Olivia frowned at him.

"Of course. I shall be right back. Why don't you two lovely ladies enjoy some refreshments while I go rustle up what we need?" He disappeared back into the house, shutting the glass paned door behind him.

"That snake." Olivia snatched up a sandwich. "He was going to have tea with me alone."

"I thought so, too. Olivia I don't trust him. I think he's trying to find himself a wife and he's zeroed in on you." Hannah glanced around the beautiful garden. "There isn't a soul around, which means he could do whatever he wanted to you."

"Matt would kill him." Olivia's flat tone said what Hannah was already thinking.

"I believe you're right. I need to get into the house for a few moments but I don't want to leave you here alone." Hannah had to bring her sister-in-law into her confidence. "I want to look in Mr. Stinson's office for evidence."

"What kind of evidence?"

"I can't give you all the details, but Ranger Armstrong is investigating him. I want to help as much as I can, maybe even help solve your parents' murder."

It was what Hannah didn't say that Olivia heard. Her gaze narrowed and her eyes hardened. "That bastard."

"I want to see what I can find. Will you help me?"

"Damn straight I'll help you. I knew that Armstrong was up to something when he convinced me to have tea with Margaret." Olivia huffed out a breath. "Gave me some humbug story about possibly courting Margaret and wanting my help. Ha!"

Hannah hadn't realized Armstrong was such a good liar, but perhaps as a lawman, he sometimes needed to be untruthful to get what he needed. After all, she was a normal woman who had been about to commit a crime by breaking into her neighbor's house. She couldn't cast any stones against the man.

"He's just trying to help find out who's behind the crimes." Hannah took her hand. "Are you ready? If Jeb catches us, we'll be in hot water."

"I hope he does. I want to call him on this attempted seduction anyway." Olivia tightened her grip. "Let's go find out what Stinson is up to."

When they walked into the house, Jeb was coming right toward them.

"Stay here. I'll distract him," Olivia whispered, then turned a full smile on the younger Stinson. "There you are. I was hoping you'd come back soon. Take me to the kitchen please. I brought some special tea to share with Margaret, but now I can share it with you."

Hannah stayed in the shadows until they disappeared from view. Heart pounding, she tiptoed down the hallway to the room she thought was the office. As she slipped through the door, she held her breath until the snick of the lock sounded.

It was definitely the older Stinson's office. The weak light from the cloudy day filtered through the large picture window. A huge wooden desk dominated the room, covered with papers, a few old cups of coffee, and a dark lantern. She sat down in the chair, which squeaked like a giant mouse. Hannah froze in mid-motion, waiting for someone to discover what she was doing.

Minutes later, which felt more like hours, she sucked in a shaky breath and started searching. There were plenty of papers: feed receipts, bills of sale, and letters from people like Sam Houston. None of it seemed to be illegal, and some of it was even impressive.

Frustrated, Hannah moved to the drawers, and after more fruitless searching, decided Mr. Stinson must not keep his illegal activities mixed with the legal. The bottom drawer was locked so she used a letter opener to pry it open. He would know someone had been there, but if he was in jail, it wouldn't matter a whit.

Expecting to find a pile of evidence, Hannah was disappointed to find a bottle of whiskey and two glasses. Why would he keep the liquor locked up in his desk? Perhaps one of the staff or even Jeb or Margaret had a problem with drinking too much?

It didn't matter why; there was nothing here. *Nothing* to help the case against Frederick Stinson. She put everything back the way she'd found it and crept out of the room.

"Why, there she is!" Jeb's loud voice made Hannah jump a foot in the air. "I think she must've gotten lost in this big house."

She turned to find Olivia with a panicked expression, her arm in Jeb's punishing grip. "Run," she mouthed.

Hannah shook her head, unwilling to let her sister-in-law face whatever consequences she had brought on both of them. "Not lost, just being nosy." Hannah managed a silly laugh. "I admit I wanted to snoop a bit. Sorry, Jeb." Her grin felt brittle but she offered him one anyway.

"Oh, Hannah, now you know that's not the truth," he

said in a startlingly cold voice. "It'll be a sad day for the Grahams when you two go missing, or maybe even turn up dead. You shouldn't have taken that shortcut through the ravine. The coyotes can be mighty hungry when they find a wounded animal." Jeb, who had appeared so sweet and vapid, was finally showing his true colors, and they were as black as pitch. He didn't appear to be loco, far from it. His gaze was clear and calculating.

Hannah had assumed Frederick Stinson was behind the attacks, as had everyone else. They'd been dead wrong.

She ran at him, ready to do what she had to to get Olivia free. To her surprise, Jeb was strong as an ox. He grabbed her braid and twisted it so hard, the pain radiated down her head to her feet. Olivia tried to push him and he retaliated by pulling her hair until she fell to her knees with a loud crack. She cried out in agony and there was nothing Hannah could do to help her.

"I can't let you get in my way, ladies. I had hopes one of you could be the next Mrs. Stinson, but now you will simply be the dead Graham girls." Jeb dragged them both down the hallway by their hair.

Hannah met Olivia's gaze, her face wet with tears and covered with stark terror. She had to do something. Hannah would not be the Graham who let her family down, not when they needed her most.

Jeb dragged them to a dark room under the house. He threw Olivia against the wall and she landed in a soundless heap. Horrified, Hannah was too slow to act. Jeb backhanded her so hard, blood filled her mouth. She spat on the floor, and he kicked her in the stomach with a boot that felt more like a boulder.

"Don't mess up the floor, Hannah. You know how hard it is to get blood stains out?" He pushed her to her back, then pressed his boot into her chest. "I could crush you right now and not have to worry about you anymore. I knew you were the smart one. Somehow Matt found you, hidden treasure that you are."

Blackness crept around Hannah's vision and for the second time in as many days, she faced death.

"Fuck you, Jeb."

His face registered surprise before he threw back his head and laughed. "I knew I liked you for a reason." His foot eased up. "I just may keep you for myself after all."

Dazed and lightheaded, Hannah could only watch as he tied her up and gagged her, forcing blood down her throat from her mouth. She nearly choked on it before she was able to roll to her side and let it slide out of her mouth. After tying the motionless Olivia up too, Jeb leaned down and cupped Hannah's cheek.

"Be a good girl now." With that, he left them alone in the cold, dark room under the house. There was not a peep of light and the only sound was a scurrying in the corner. Hannah had to find a way to get free, or both she and Olivia could be dead by the time Jeb came back.

Hannah managed to get into a sitting position, and although her head swam for a moment, she stayed that way. Pride and determination coursed through her. She would make her husband proud and be a true Graham, no matter what.

Matt rode like the hounds of hell were chasing him. To his surprise, Stinson kept up with him. The horses were equally matched, although the older rancher bragged about his prize stallion to anyone who would listen. Appeared as though a gelding could give him a run for his money. Matt didn't want to waste time stopping at his ranch, but knew he needed reinforcements if they were to gain victory. He rode into the yard in a cloud of dust.

"To the Graham!" It was an expression his father always used when he wanted all the children to come to him immediately. He explained that back in the day, it was a battlecry for the Graham clan.

It still worked and everyone came running, including Eva. The one Graham missing was Hannah.

"Javier, Lorenzo, Nick and Caleb. Saddle up and follow us to the Stinson ranch." He speared Eva with a worried gaze. "Is Hannah feeling poorly?"

"No, she felt fine this morning. She went to tea with Olivia at the Stinsons. *¿Que pasa, hijo?*" Eva stepped toward him but before she even started talking, Matt had turned his lathered gelding east and kneed him into a gallop.

Hannah was there, at the Stinsons' ranch. What was she thinking? She didn't even like Margaret, so why would she have tea with her? Granted, it was safer to travel in pairs, but there was no reasonable explanation for Hannah to go with Olivia.

"Matt!" Caleb shouted from behind him, but there was no way in hell he was going to slow down.

His wife and his sister were in danger. Matt couldn't lose the woman he loved or the sister he cherished because of his own lack of forethought. He leaned low and spoke into his horse's ear.

"I can't let her die, Winston. Help me save her so I can tell her I love her." Matt's heart thumped against his ribs, and cold fear crept into his bones with each passing minute.

Armstrong was supposed to be at Stinson's house. Maybe he was there and would help the women stay out of trouble. This was Hannah and Olivia though, both of them stubborn and strong-willed as mules.

Matt hung on as his horse's hooves ate up the miles. He knew his family and Stinson were behind him, but he had to arrive first. There wasn't any other option.

* ★ *

Armstrong had been in the office reviewing every scrap of paper he could find when he heard a female voice in the house. It had to be Olivia, the outspoken woman had tried to get information from him last night. When he'd refused to give it to her, she'd warned him she wasn't done with him.

Yet here she was in the Stinsons' house, as he'd asked. Truth was, she was probably the most beautiful woman he'd ever met. Instead of talking to her like a gentleman, he'd been short and almost rude. But rather than wilting like a flower, she'd snapped to attention like a warrior.

Even though he told himself to focus on business, he found his dreams full of Olivia Graham. In the morning, he'd woken in his bedroll with a hard on. He'd shaken off the remnants of his erotic thoughts of her and gotten busy.

Now she was in the Stinsons' house and he had to hope she would follow through on what he'd asked. When the door handle rattled, he disappeared out the large window and ducked into the bushes.

After a few minutes, he'd realized what he'd heard was someone else rifling through Stinson's office. Damn Olivia! She was supposed to keep her hosts busy, not take it upon herself to snoop around.

As he rose to give her a talking to, he heard footsteps leaving the room and the door closing. Jeb Stinson's voice was overly loud, enough so Armstrong heard him quite clearly.

Girls? What girls? Was the man doing something to his own sister and Olivia? A woman's cry of pain was followed by another and then a horrendous cracking sound. Armstrong had climbed back through the window, unwilling to allow Olivia to be hurt helping him. When he'd made it through the narrow window, he'd eased the office door open and peered out.

The hallway was empty. The only sign someone had been there was the bright scarf lying on the floor. He'd seen Hannah Graham wearing it the night before. Armstrong's heart had slammed into his throat. Quickly, he'd searched the house but now he still had found no other sign of them.

Where were they?

Hannah worked at the gag with her teeth and tongue, fighting the pain until she managed to get it to her chin. She swallowed, almost choking on the blood. Jeb's slap had loosened a few teeth and she'd cut her tongue. She spit out as much blood as she could before she scooted over to where she thought Olivia had landed.

"Olivia?" She moved to her right and sighed with relief when she bumped into a warm body. "Can you hear me?" Hannah heard a small groan and blew out a shaky breath of relief. "I'm going to try to get us loose."

Lucky for her, Jeb had tied her hands and feet together in front, so she could lean down and gnaw at the knots. Her lips grew raw from rubbing against the rope but she finally managed to loosen the knots and slip one hand out.

She wiped the blood from her chin on her sleeve, then finished untying herself. Hannah reached for Olivia, who hadn't made another sound. With shaking hands, she untied her sister-in-law, then reached for her face.

"Liv? Please wake up. I don't think I can carry you out of here." Hannah's whisper sounded as desperate as she felt. "I don't know when Jeb is coming back. We need to get out."

"Hannah?" Olivia's voice was slurred but it sounded like an angel's singing to Hannah.

"Yes, come on. We have to get out of here." Somehow she helped Olivia to her feet and the two of them hobbled to the door.

When Hannah tried to turn the knob, she realized the door was locked. She pressed her forehead against the wood, fighting the panic that clawed at her. There had to be another way out, there just had to be.

She guided Olivia back to the wall and helped her sit. "The door is locked."

"Mm." Olivia didn't sound like she would last long. Jeb had thrown her so hard against the wall, her head was probably broken open. Hannah had never been around someone with such a serious injury, but she heard both Eva and Granny in her head, telling her to stay calm. She felt Olivia's head and her hand came away sticky with blood.

Hannah ripped part of her skirt to make a bandage and wrapped Olivia's head as tightly as she dared. It would have to do until they could get her real help.

"Stay here. I'm going to see if I can get us out of here." She felt around the small room, finding vegetables, jars full of what was probably preserves, and a few baskets. Nothing helpful.

Hannah searched around the door and got nothing but a few splinters. There had to be something she could use to get out.

"Call for help." Olivia's weak suggestion surprised Hannah.

"I can't do that." Hannah had found an inner well of strength and she wasn't going to abandon it just yet. She continued her journey to the right of the door and found a metal bar. With a triumphant grin, she went back to the door. Using all her strength, she pried the metal bar against the door until it splintered.

A shaft of light blinded her temporarily. She tucked the metal bar into her waistband and peered out the door. There didn't seem to be anyone about, but that didn't mean Jeb wouldn't come back any second.

Hannah returned for Olivia and together they crept out of the small cellar room and started toward the stairs.

Matt leapt off his horse the moment he neared the Stinson ranch. There were no horses tied up outside, but that didn't mean no one was home. Without waiting for anyone to open the door, he crashed through it, shouting Hannah's name.

He scared the housekeeper and a cat, but he didn't care enough to even apologize. Shouting his wife's name, he stalked through the house until he reached the veranda doors. He slammed through them too and found Jeb sitting at a table.

The surprise on Jeb's face looked genuine. He set a sandwich down and picked up a mug of what looked like tea.

"Matthew Graham, I never thought you were the rude sort. What are you doing here howling like a fool?" Jeb was either a fantastic thespian or a complete lunatic.

"Where are they?" Matt growled.

"Who? I'm here alone. Margaret went to town with your sister. My father was supposed to be with you." Jeb took a sip of the tea. "I'd offer you a drink but I'm certain you'd refuse. Something sure has put a bee in your bonnet."

Matt stalked over to Jeb and grabbed him by the shirt. They were similar in size, but Matt's daily labors and his fury made him twice as strong.

"I will snatch the life right out of you if you've hurt them."

Jeb's eyes widened and Matt saw a dollop of fear in his blue gaze. "I haven't hurt anyone."

"You killed my parents." Matt's voice was raw with pain and rage. The thought of giving this murderer his friendship made him sick. It didn't matter a bit if he'd been as fooled as everyone else.

"Matt, I don't know what you're talking about."

Matt shook him, his arms shaking with the effort of not killing Jeb outright. "I will not give you another piece of my life. I'm going to ask you one more time, where are my wife and sister?"

Jeb's gaze moved past him. "Hannah, tell your husband you're okay."

Matt turned, hope making him blind to the danger Jeb presented. Too late, he realized his mistake. Jeb brought the cast iron teapot down on Matt's head with a resounding thud. His teeth slammed together and the ground slapped him in the face.

Armstrong couldn't find the women. He knew they were in the house, but damned if Jeb hadn't stashed them someplace good. He'd looked in at every door in the entire house. To his surprise, he'd found nothing. Where were they?

The scarf hadn't appeared out of nowhere and he knew exactly why Hannah was wearing it. She wouldn't willingly give it up. Someone had done something to both women, and it was up to Armstrong to find out just what it was.

A commotion in the back of the house brought him running as quietly as he could. He peered out the window in the office and saw Matt shaking Jeb like a dog. Armstrong didn't know what the hell Graham was up to, but he needed to put a stop to it.

Armstrong checked his pistol before he stepped cautiously outside. When Jeb slammed the teapot against Matt's head, Armstrong realized he'd been investigating the wrong Stinson. Matt had obviously figured it out, and the ranger was embarrassed to be so slow to recognize the truth.

Now he had to save Graham, as well as the man's sister and wife. Armstrong wasn't prepared for Jeb to pull out a gun and point it at him.

"You know, I was wondering when you would make an appearance." Jeb cocked the pistol. "I was watching you last night, making cow eyes at my intended bride."

"I wasn't making cow eyes at anyone. Mr. Graham invited me to the barbecue when we met last week. I was much obliged for the invite." Armstrong held up his hands. "I followed him over here because he was talking crazy."

"Damn right he was talking crazy. He tried to kill me." Jeb set the pot down on the table. "I never saw such a thing."

Armstrong wondered whether Stinson's innocuous behavior was all an act or whether he was facing one of the smartest killers he'd ever met.

"Why don't you put that pistol away so I can arrest Graham for attacking you?" Armstrong kept his voice even, calm, although his gut was churning like a twister.

"Oh, no, I can't do that. Matt threatened my life. I won't put the gun down in his presence again." Jeb turned the pistol on Matt's inert form. "I have to protect myself."

Two things happened so fast Armstrong had to blink to be sure he wasn't seeing things. First, Hannah appeared behind Jeb, covered in blood, her hair a wild cloud both blood-streaked and dirty. Then Olivia ran past him, also bloody and bruised, screaming like a banshee from a tale his granny used to tell.

"Don't you hurt my brother!" She threw herself at Jeb just as Hannah conked the man on the head with some kind of metal bar.

The younger Stinson fell to the ground beneath a heap of female anger. Armstrong was there in a blink, pulling both women up and out of harm's way. Of course they didn't seem to care for his assistance and scratched and bit at him.

"Olivia! Hannah! Stop. It's me, Brody Armstrong!" He

managed to pull them off Jeb, who looked as though he'd been tossed down a ravine.

"Your first name is Brody?" Olivia had dried blood all over her hair and forehead. He'd never been so glad to see a woman alive.

"Don't remind me. My mother was a true Irish woman and thought I should have a strong Irish name." He pulled both women to their feet. "Now what the hell happened here?"

Hannah was breathing hard as she pushed her hair out of her eyes, then spat a bloody wad on the ground. Armstrong thought he had seen everything, but these two had just proved him wrong.

"Jeb tried to kill us. We stopped him." Her grin was positively feral and liberally sprinkled with blood.

Truthfully the women were making Armstrong nervous. "Your husband was hurt. You might want to tend to him."

"Matt!" Hannah ran to him and knelt down, pulling his head into her lap. She touched the gash on his forehead with such tenderness, he had to look away.

Olivia had found Jeb's gun and was currently pointing it at him. "I should kill him now."

"Let the law handle him, Miss Graham."

She snorted. "You should call me Olivia. I think we're on a first name basis by now."

Just then Frederick Stinson, Javier, Lorenzo, Nick, Caleb, and Angus McRae all barreled through the door. When they caught sight of the women, Jeb, and Matt, their expressions were almost comical.

"What in the name of God happened here?" The elder Stinson looked as though he might explode.

"I'm placing your son under arrest for murder, fraud, and kidnapping." Armstrong pulled a length of leather from his pocket. "You can visit him in the jail."

Hannah and Olivia threw their heads back and let loose a battle cry that had all of the men taking a step back. Armstrong could just imagine what kind of children Hannah and Matt would have. Too bad he couldn't stick around to find out.

Chapter Sixteen

Matt woke slowly, his head pounding as though it had been split open by an axe. He cracked one eye open and recognized his bedroom at the ranch. Confusion was replaced by panic when he remembered what had happened.

He sat up so fast, his stomach came right up with him. Matt bent over the side of the bed and a bucket appeared below him. As he vomited, a soft hand touched the back of his neck and he knew without looking it was Hannah.

When he had stopped making a fool of himself, he lay back on the bed and was finally able to look at Hannah. Her face was bruised an ugly shade of purple and green on one side, her lip split and swollen, and one eye was black, as though she'd been in a brawl. His mouth dropped open when she smiled.

"I'm so glad to see you awake. It's been two days, Matt." She took his hand and kissed the back of it. "You scared me."

"*You're* scaring *me,* Hannah. What the hell happened to you?" He didn't dare touch her for fear he'd hurt her healing wounds.

"I'm fine. Just a bit bruised. You were really hurt." She moved closer and touched the side of his head. "The doctor said Jeb might have cracked your skull. I wanted to beat him all over again when I heard that. Are you in pain?"

"My head does pain me something fierce." Matt reached up, surprised to find a bandage wrapped around his head. The left side was particularly sore. He felt plenty of whiskers on his face. Matt hoped there wasn't a mirror nearby because he didn't want to see what he looked like.

He tried to remember what had happened. Images of blood and screaming women ran through his mind. He wondered if he'd dreamed it or if Hannah had really rescued him instead of the other way around. It shouldn't surprise him. After all, his entire life had been turned on its head since they'd married.

"Did you and my sister attack Jeb?"

She blushed. "Kind of. He'd locked us in the root cellar and we got free. Then I saw he'd hurt you and I didn't hesitate to defend you."

Her brown gaze was so guileless, so completely full of love, he had to look away. His throat had tightened up, and he swallowed three times before he could speak.

"Thank you, Hannah. I, uh, ain't so good with words." He took her hand, embarrassed to see his own trembling. "When I asked you to marry me, I didn't know what was in store for us. Now I can't imagine my life without you."

She blinked a few times and then nodded. "Neither can I."

"Is it okay if you kiss me?" He really wanted to make slow, sweet love but that would likely have to wait at least until he could sit up without help.

Hannah smiled. "I think I can arrange it with your caretaker."

She rose and leaned toward him, and her breath puffed against his lips. He closed his eyes and she kissed him so lightly, she could have been a butterfly.

"You need to sleep and get better. Don't worry; we're taking care of everything."

Sleep crept over him like a warm blanket. The last thing he saw was Hannah's eyes. The last thing he heard was her quiet whisper.

The next morning, Hannah was up before the dawn again. Doing chores helped her to focus, to forget all the horrible things that had happened on the Stinson property. The relief she felt when Matt had opened his eyes had sent her outside to cry after he'd gone back to sleep. She wept for the love she'd thought she'd lost before ever really experiencing it. Hannah had sobbed until her throat was raw and she didn't have a tear left to shed.

When she crawled into bed, she slept for the first time since Matt had been injured. He couldn't spoon up behind her yet but his body warmth and even the sound of his breathing were enough for her. Now he was sleeping deeply and no longer unconscious. Hannah woke feeling refreshed and ready to get back to normal.

The sun was just peeking over the horizon when Granny came into the kitchen. Hannah was surprised to see her up so early.

"Mornin'." From experience, Hannah didn't engage in conversation with her grandmother just yet. Instead she poured a cup of hot coffee and set it down on the table.

"These old bones can't get comfortable no more." Granny sat down with a groan and snatched up the cup. She sniffed in the hot brew before taking a noisy slurp. "Your man wake up?"

"Yes, thank God." Hannah started rolling out the biscuit dough. "He doesn't remember much."

"Good thing. He'd probably pitch a fit if he knew what you'd done." Granny shook her head at her. "Not many women could do what you did."

"What did she do?" Matt's voice made Hannah slip and she nearly dropped the glass she was using to cut out the biscuits.

"She saved your life and captured the bastard who tried to kill you." Granny slurped again.

Matt shuffled into the kitchen, his clothes messy but his eyes clear. His hair stuck up every which way on top of his head, pushed up by the bandages. He was pale and a little shaky, but Hannah thought he'd never looked so handsome and *alive*.

He sat down and she gestured to her own cup. "Go ahead and drink it. I just poured it."

With a grateful sigh, he wrapped his hands around the hot mug and sipped the coffee. "Now tell me what exactly you did to save my life."

"She saved me, too." Olivia didn't look much better than her brother, but she had only been knocked out. The doctor said her skull was hard enough to survive the hit against the wall. Her knees were bruised and she winced when she walked. It would be a while before she could run, but she could get around just fine.

Matt frowned at Hannah. "I think I need to hear more starting with why you were at Stinson's ranch in the first place."

Hannah started putting biscuits in the pan without answering. Olivia poured herself a cup of coffee and sat down beside her brother.

"She asked me if she could go with me. When we got there, Margaret wasn't home. Jeb invited us in and we realized he was the one who was behind the attacks, not his father." Olivia met Hannah's gaze; the bond between them had deepened now. "Jeb hit us, tied us up, and locked us in a root cellar of some kind. Hannah managed to untie us and get us out."

Matt's eyes widened. "How the hell did you do that?"

Hannah finished putting the biscuits in the oven and started cleaning up the mess she'd left behind. "My teeth, my willpower, my brain." She shrugged. "Anybody could have done it."

"Like hell." Granny smacked the table with her open hand. "About time you stopped apologizing for being strong and smart."

Hannah jumped at her grandmother's loud pronouncement. "I'm not apologizing."

"Damn right, you are. Tell your husband how you lost two teeth because Jeb hit you so hard. Tell him how you lost skin on your lips gnawing on the rope to get yourself free and how you used a metal bar to pry the door open. How you about carried Olivia upstairs." Granny got to her feet. "Or tell him how you used that metal bar to knock some sense into Jeb's stupid head."

Matt's mouth dropped open and Hannah couldn't help squirming under his gaze. This was what she didn't want, to have what she did laid out for everyone to talk about again. Never mind that Matt hadn't heard it the first time; she still could hardly believe it was true and she'd lived it.

"You did all that?" Matt got to his feet and took her wrists, turning so he could see the chafing from the ropes. He kissed the inside of one wrist and a shiver ran down her arm.

"Yes."

Matt wiped away her tear with his thumb. "I've got to be the luckiest man in Texas."

Hannah's heart thumped hard as she raised her gaze to meet his. "You lost so much."

He shook his head. "I lost my parents and my brother, but that's part of life. What I gained—Hannah, I can't think of a man who would do what you did. You humble me."

Hannah gave him a small smile. "I'm a Graham. I did what I had to."

Matt pulled her into a hug. "My mother would have loved you, too."

It was the closest she'd come to a confession of love from her husband, and she held onto it and tucked it away. Perhaps one day he might find the words. For now she could be content with what he'd given her because she loved him.

Matt sat on the porch with Armstrong in the afternoon. He felt so much better being out of bed that he ignored Eva and Hannah's clucking and remained outside. The ranger had been staying in the tack room at the barn while everyone healed up.

"Where is he?"

Armstrong didn't ask who; he didn't have to. "Sheriff locked him up but I was supposed to take him to Houston yesterday."

"I appreciate your waiting." Matt knew the ranger was accountable to Sam Houston himself. "Will you get in trouble for not bringing him in?"

"Nah. I sent Sam a wire. I plan on leaving in the morning. I get itchy when I'm in one place for too long." Armstrong took a drag off his cigarillo.

"Two weeks is too long?" Matt shook his head. "I can't imagine being anywhere else."

"I love to wander." Armstrong's gaze flicked to the door as it opened. Olivia shuffled out and the ranger sat up straighter.

"Matt, your wife and Eva are about to come out here and haul you back to bed." Her gaze skittered past the ranger and she looked out at the horizon.

Matt watched her as if she'd changed overnight. The one thing he could count on from his sister was her directness. Now she was acting shy with Armstrong. What else had happened while he'd been unconscious?

"I ain't going back to bed." Matt stretched out in the

rocking chair, leaning back until his head just touched the back. "Me and the ranger are talking."

"I can see that." Olivia stepped out and shuffled to the other rocking chair beside Matt.

He didn't know what to think of her behavior, so he ignored her. There was obviously something she wanted to know from Armstrong.

"Did you interrogate him?"

"Yes, but he didn't tell me anything. Claimed he was attacked by your wife and sister." Armstrong took another drag and blew it out before he spoke again. "Says he doesn't know shit about your parents or brother, or about the other ranches. I'm still looking for evidence at the ranch."

A slight breeze tickled Matt's skin, cooling the sweat on his forehead. "What happens now?"

"We keep investigating him. His Pa is giving me free rein to search everything." Armstrong glanced at Olivia. "I found the room where the girls were tied up."

Matt's hands tightened on the arms of the chair. "And?"

"Blood, rope, a couple teeth and a torn up door handle. Just like your wife said."

"Jesus Christ." Matt had heard what everyone had said, but to hear the ranger tell it so bluntly made his gut twist.

"We've got Jeb for the crimes against them. In the meantime, we keep digging until we find what we're after."

"That's not good enough." Matt choked on the frustration building inside him. "I want him to swing for my parents' murder, and I want to know where Benjy is." His voice rose until he was shouting, making his head throb in tune with his heart.

"I know, but right now you gotta be patient." Armstrong rose to his feet. "I won't be back before I leave."

"No, you're not leaving with him. Not until I talk to him." Matt struggled to stand. "That bastard is going to have to answer to me."

Armstrong put one arm on Matt's shoulder. "Ain't nothing you can do if you fall off a horse and break the other side of your head. Besides, your wife would likely shoot me if I let you."

Matt's fury had started to grow the more he thought about never finding out what he had to know. "I have to talk to him, Armstrong. I have to."

The cool-eyed ranger stared down at him. "I'll come by with him first thing on my way out of town. You get a few minutes but no more. I shouldn't even let you have that. I could get my ass chapped for doing it. I got to follow the law."

Matt wanted to say the hell with the law and kill Jeb himself. If he did he'd never find out what had happened, but he might not find out anyway. Armstrong was doing him a favor and he did appreciate it, even if he was angry enough to bite through steel.

"I guess I'll see you in the morning then," Matt said through clenched teeth.

"You're welcome." Armstrong's mouth kicked up in some semblance of a grin. "See you in the morning."

"Good-bye, Brody." Olivia's voice made the ranger almost miss a step.

"Damn." It was a soft curse but the breeze carried it to Matt's ears.

Olivia grinned. Matt shook his head. The ranger kept walking.

The predawn light turned the prairie into a gray world of shadows. Matt paced back and forth on the porch, watching the horizon for Armstrong to appear. He knew the ranger would be on his way early, and Matt had to talk to Jeb before he was taken to Houston.

It was Matt's only chance to talk to the man who had been his friend, who had apparently betrayed him com-

pletely. Jeb had become a monster. Matt needed to understand why. The question had danced around in his brain all
night long and he had to ask it.

More than likely, Jeb wouldn't give him what he
needed. He had to try anyway. There were so many questions Matt needed to ask. The most important one would
come first; then he would ask where Benjy was. There was
a break in their circle of eight, and although his wife was
amazing, he wanted his little brother back.

Hannah stepped out on the porch wearing a shawl. Her
braid sat on one shoulder, curls sticking out as if she'd done
it up in a hurry. As she walked toward him, he held up his
right arm and she tucked herself underneath it. Her warmth
seeped into his bones and he felt better almost immediately.

"You took your bandage off."

He kissed the top of her head. "It was making me itch."

"It was keeping your wounds clean so you can heal." She
put one arm around his waist and leaned into him. "You
need a bath."

Matt barked a laugh. "I need a shave, too. I'm sure I'd
scare small children and dogs looking like this."

"Your smell would, too."

When they'd met, he hadn't realized she had a sense of
humor or how outspoken she was. Hell, the woman had
practically run from him when he'd spotted her across the
turnips. She'd proven to be a treasure beyond his imaginings.

Now he understood what his parents had had, why his
father would give up everything for his mother. Matt had
thought him less of a man for it, but the truth was, Hannah made him feel more of a man. His heart ached with
the overflowing feelings his voice couldn't express.

The bald truth of what had happened at the Stinson
ranch, how she had saved him, should have shamed him. It
didn't. He was proud of her and how much grit she had.

Most women would have simply given in, but she'd dug in and fought.

He loved her.

Matt's vision went a little gray around the edges as the realization hit him. *He loved her.* He'd never believed it would happen to him, fought against it from the second he suspected he had feelings for Hannah. It had taken a brush with death for him to realize what he had was love.

As he was trying to figure out a way to tell her without sounding like a fool, he heard the sound of horses approaching. His romantic notions tucked away, Matt waited, vibrating with a kettle full of dark thoughts. When the men finally appeared, he stepped away from Hannah and waited on the steps to meet them.

Armstrong held the reins of both horses. Jeb had been tied to the saddle horn and his feet tied to the stirrups. It gave Matt an evil pleasure to know if Stinson did try to escape, he couldn't even get off the saddle.

"Here we are, Graham. Say what you gotta say and we'll be on our way." Armstrong tipped his hat to Hannah. "Mornin', ma'am."

"Morning, Ranger Armstrong." Her head was high although her face was a rainbow of bruises. Matt swelled with pride at the way she stood her ground, shoulders back and chin up. Hannah was a hell of a woman.

"Isn't anybody going to say good morning to me?" Jeb's smile bore only a slight resemblance to a real one.

"I've got things to say to you, but they sure as hell ain't good morning." Matt put his hands on his hips and stared at his former friend. There were so many reasons why Jeb could have chosen the right path, now was the time to find out why he'd chosen the wrong one. "Let's start with why. Why the hell did you do it, Jeb?"

"Do what, Matthew?" His pretended innocence made Matt want to rip his arms off.

"You killed my parents." Saying it out loud made Matt's stomach almost meet up with his throat. "And you took Benjy. Why?"

Hannah reached for his hand and he held onto her, grateful for her strength.

"Matthew. Are you asking me why men do the evil things they do?" Jeb shook his head. "I don't have an answer for you."

"You son of a bitch." Matt's hand tightened on Hannah's as rage coursed through him unabated. If he'd had a gun, he would have ended Jeb right then and there.

"Most assuredly, that I am. Can't you see that greed is what drives most? You and your happy clan have little and aspire to nothing. You're less than a man, Graham, and it's you I pity." Jeb made a tsking sound with his tongue. "Stuck with a cow for a wife, and a tiny little plot of land. No future, no money. Nothing."

Matt's anger gave way to a bitter acceptance. Jeb would never tell him what he needed to know, likely took pleasure in playing games over it. "Armstrong, I appreciate your bringing him by. Hope you have a safe trip to Houston."

Armstrong tipped his hat to Matt and Hannah, then kneed his horse into action. As they started to move away, Jeb squawked.

"Wait, what? I haven't answered your questions." Stinson fought at his bindings. "Don't leave yet. I-I'm not done."

"Oh yeah, you're done." Armstrong's grin was feral and colder than his blue eyes. "Now shut up or I'll gag you."

They rode off into the grayness, leaving Matt with a hollow feeling inside. No matter what happened, he sure as hell would never understand why. Jeb was a greedy piece of shit who simply took what he wanted, no matter what the cost. That was the truth Matt had to accept.

He'd likely never find Benjy. That was a truth that would be excruciating to accept. Somewhere deep inside, he'd always hoped Benjy had been given to some farm couple to raise, as a last act of cruelty to the Grahams. Now he had to face the possibility Benjy was dead or worse.

It was a dark day for everyone.

The day after the ranger took Jeb to Houston, Hannah was teaching the girls how to sew when a knock came at the door. Matt wasn't allowed to ride or work yet so he was sitting in the kitchen with them. He met her gaze with a frown.

Matt walked to the door while the Graham women watched him. He opened it at the second knock and looked surprised to see Frederick Stinson there. Hannah stood to greet the rancher and was as surprised as Matt by the older man's appearance. He'd aged twenty years in only a week, with sunken cheeks, larger patches of gray in his hair, and pain-filled eyes. Even his shoulders slumped in defeat.

"Please come in, Mr. Stinson." Hannah gestured to the girls to go. Rebecca, Catherine, and Elizabeth listened and took the sewing down the hallway. Olivia remained with them, sitting at the table since walking was still difficult for her to do without pain in her knees.

Mr. Stinson walked in and took off his hat. "I wondered if you would slam the door in my face, Graham. I probably would have."

"It's not your crime. I'm not going to make you pay for it." Matt gestured to the table. "Sit down. Coffee?"

"I'd be much obliged. It was a dusty ride." Stinson sat and looked at both Hannah and Olivia. "I needed to come by and apologize to the two of you."

After everything that had happened, Hannah had contemplated going to see Mr. Stinson but Eva had told her not to. "He is a hard man, *hija*. When he is ready, he will come to us." Since the housekeeper seemed to know people well, Hannah took her advice. Judging by Mr. Stinson's appearance, she was glad she had.

Hannah poured him a cup of coffee and returned to the table. As she set it down in front of the man, she was surprised to see his hand shaking.

"I don't know why Jeb turned bad or why he would hurt our neighbors. I taught him nothing but good things." He shook his graying head. "He wouldn't tell me what happened. Wouldn't even talk about what happened to Margaret." His chin wobbled and his normally steely eyes filled with tears.

"What about Margaret?" Olivia finally spoke although her face was as hard as the table.

"Nobody's seen her since the day Jeb did what he done." He ran his hands down his face, the scrape of the whiskers on his hand loud in the quiet room. "I looked for her everywhere, but she's disappeared."

Hannah saw the shock on Matt's face. No one would ever have suspected Jeb would do something to his own sister. She covered Mr. Stinson's hand with her own.

"I'm so sorry. Is there anything we can do to help?"

"No, but I thank you for the offer." He looked at Matt. "I didn't know what you went through. Now I've lost everything I had."

Matt finally sat down and his shoulders relaxed. "No, you haven't lost everything. You've still got neighbors."

Hannah's chest swelled with pride in her husband. Given how much pain Jeb had caused the Grahams, it took a big man to still offer his father friendship.

"I appreciate that. I surely do." Frederick wiped his eyes with the heels of his palms. "You folks don't owe me a thing."

"That's the good part about being a neighbor. You never

worry about owing." Matt's gaze reflected his own pain. She knew he'd been pacing at night, unable to sleep.

Stinson pulled a folded paper from his shirt pocket. "I asked Elliot Barnum in town to take a look at the map. He told me it's all legal."

Matt frowned. "I didn't lie to you, Stinson."

"I know that now. I'm gonna sign over that two-mile patch of land to you and Angus."

Hannah gasped along with Olivia.

Matt's frown deepened. "Why would you do that?"

"I don't have any use for it. And after everything Jeb did to your family, I couldn't keep it." Stinson got to his feet. "I've taken up enough of your time."

He shook Matt's hand and nodded to Olivia and Hannah. With a shuffle that appeared to be that of an old man rather than a forty-five-year-old, he left the house.

The three of them stared at each other in silence for a few moments after Stinson left. Hannah noted his untouched coffee on the table. The legacy of what Jeb had done would affect the Grahams, the Stinsons, and all the other families he'd attacked. Frederick Stinson would live with that burden the rest of his life, and more than likely, die a lonely old man. She truly hoped he would find Margaret. If not, the man had lost his entire family in one day.

"Poor man." Olivia shook her head.

"He was a hard man. He gave his children everything they ever wanted and look what that brought him." Matt stared at the closed door. "I hear his wife died giving birth to Margaret and his second wife left him. Now he is completely alone."

"You were kind to him." Hannah had seen a new side of her husband today.

"He didn't do anything beyond being a lousy father. I meant what I said. Jeb will answer for what he did but his father shouldn't have to." Matt got to his feet and kissed Hannah's forehead. "I'm going to the barn to check on Winston."

He left the two women alone and shut the door gently behind him.

"My brother can be stubborn," Olivia offered.

"I've noticed that." If they were going to move past the tragedies the Grahams had suffered, Hannah had to find a way to break through the walls her husband had erected around himself. She loved him, but she needed to help him.

Matt woke before dawn after a fitful night's sleep. He was going to go riding, come hell or high water. There was no reason he shouldn't—he certainly felt well enough. He missed his early morning rides, that time to himself when he could think.

Three weeks married and he hadn't made love to his wife in a week. She'd been nearly killed because he couldn't protect her, same as his parents and his brother. Matt had failed her, as he'd failed his family. For that, he couldn't forgive himself.

He stepped outside and took a deep breath. The warm air felt good as he walked to the barn. The smell of new wood was still strong, another gift from the neighbors after the old barn had been burned. There had been gifts in his life he would never forget. Hannah was the best of all. He didn't deserve her if he couldn't take care of her.

Winston whinnied the moment Matt got near his stall. The gelding had obviously missed him as much as he had missed the horse. The morning rides were special for both of them.

After he'd saddled the horse, he led him out of the barn and stopped in his tracks. Hannah stood on the porch wearing a white nightdress, her hair unbound.

His body tightened up like a bow string at the sight. She was incredible, so sexy and tempting, he almost turned around and brought Winston back into the barn. As she walked toward him, the wind picked up her hair and it fluttered behind her. He'd never seen anything more beautiful, and damned if his eyes didn't prick with tears. She'd turned him into a fool, but it didn't matter.

He loved her.

Matt knew he needed to tell her, too. As she got closer, her nightdress billowed in the warm breeze, making her laugh. Her smile made his heart skip a beat.

"Going for a ride?" She kept her voice low.

"I go in the morning before anyone else is up. Well, I guess you are now." He thought about all those early morning rides alone. Then he realized this time he didn't want to be by himself. "Come with me."

Her eyebrows went up. "You want me to ride with you?"

Matt pulled her close, until he was close enough to touch her, put his hands in her glorious hair, and kiss her until he had to come up for air.

"Yes, ride with me, honey. I need you to ride with me." He forced himself to step back, to let go of his warm, tempting wife.

She scrutinized his face for a few moments before she smiled again. "I'll be back in five minutes." Hannah reached up and kissed him hard, then ran for the house.

The wind still kicked up, making her hair and her nightdress billow around her. She had to put her arms out for balance when a strong gust came through. Matt was hit between the eyes with the image of Hannah dressed as she was. She looked like an angel, his angel.

He took off his hat and dropped to his knees, disregarding the horse's curious stare. His heart swelled with the idea she had been sent to love him, to watch over him, to heal him. Perhaps his mother had whispered in God's ear to send a woman to do just that.

Matt squeezed his eyes shut and said a prayer of thanks for finding Hannah. He was a simple rancher's son with too much responsibility to bear, the weight of the world on his shoulders. Matt had been floundering until Hannah came into his life.

She'd given everything to him, including her heart, her blood, and her love. He felt humbled by all of it, sure someone had made a mistake and given him exactly what he needed. Now he had so much, and although he'd lost people he loved, he had gained a partner, a soul mate to stand by his side.

He didn't realize five minutes had passed until her boots appeared in front of him. Matt glanced up to find her braiding her hair, with a hat tucked under her left arm and a curious look on her lovely face.

"Are you praying?"

He jumped to his feet and took her face in his hands. Before he could stop himself, he told her what was in his heart. "Hannah Graham, I love you."

Her eyes widened and then a beautiful smile spread across her face. "Matthew Graham, I love you, too."

Matt whooped, regardless of the sleeping people on the ranch, picked her up and swirled her around until she begged him to stop. She slid slowly down his body. Their ragged breaths mingled and he kissed her softly. Matt knew a moment of pure joy and his heart was healed.

"Let's ride."

Hannah nodded and they went back in the barn to saddle Buttermilk.

Hannah could hardly keep the smile off her face. Matt had told her that he loved her. *Loved her!* It was enough to keep her happy for the rest of her life. Their marriage hadn't been a traditional one by anybody's standards, but whatever forces had brought them together had done a good job.

She knew he liked early morning rides. Although he probably shouldn't be on a horse yet, his invitation to accompany him was marvelous. Hannah didn't have a great seat yet on a horse, but she was getting better. The sway of gentle Buttermilk was even becoming familiar to her.

He led her to the edge of the property, to an enclave of cottonwood trees with a small pond in the center. It was idyllic, a perfect spot to stop and rest.

Matt dismounted and came over to her, holding up his arms. She shook her head. "I'm too heavy for you."

"That's not true. I'll catch you. Trust me, Hannah." He stared up at her, his beautiful blue-green eyes so full of love, she couldn't help falling into his arms.

To her surprise, he helped her down without so much as a grunt. Hannah was not a small girl, but he surely made her feel like one. He laid out a blanket from his saddle and they both sat, side by side, watching the water. Hannah hadn't felt this relaxed for a month. She'd never expected to feel that way with a man, even her dream man. Of course, her dream man was now her husband and only he would fill her nighttime thoughts.

"I come out here by myself a lot. Winston and me, we don't always like everybody's noise." Matt pulled up a blade of grass and twirled it in his fingers. "I kept this spot a secret until now."

Hannah lay back and put her hands under her head. "Thank you for showing me. I like it. A lot."

He tickled her nose with the grass. "I like you a lot, too."

She took his hand and tugged until he lay on his side, looking down at her. "I was worried about us."

His smile disappeared. "Life ain't been easy if you're a Graham. I keep hoping each bad thing will be the last."

"You haven't given up on finding Benjy or who killed

your parents, and I don't think you should." She reached up and touched his cheek. "But I think you need to start the rest of your life."

"I am. I got the land grant, didn't I?" He scowled. "And I married you. What else can I do?"

"You think about them every day. You even dream about them."

His face registered surprise. "I do?"

"Yes, you call for them in your sleep. You even cry sometimes." She turned to face him. "I don't think you've said good-bye to your parents yet."

"I don't know what that means." He got to his feet and walked a few feet off. His expression was wary and she knew he was pulling away from her. This was the moment that decided how close they would be, how successful their marriage would be.

Hannah rose and walked toward him. "They wouldn't want you to put your own life aside to fuss about them each and every day. Your parents are proud of you, and you have to be the one to let them go."

He stared at her, his eyes wide. She didn't think he would respond and her heart began to sink.

"I can't." His voice was barely above a whisper.

She took his hands. "You can and I can help you. Where are they buried?"

His face paled a little. "By that big tree near the corner of the house. Liv thought they'd like to be in the shade but close enough to keep an eye on us."

"Let's go then." She picked up the blanket.

"Go where?"

"To the graves. You need to say good-bye and that's the best place to do it." Hannah remembered very clearly standing at her mother's grave with its crude cross and crying her eyes out. It was a chance for her to say good-bye, one forced on her by Granny. Now it was her turn to do the same for the man she loved.

"I don't want to."

"Too bad. You're going anyway." She took Buttermilk's reins and tried to get back in the saddle, unsuccessfully, until Matt's big hands pushed her rear end up. Looking down at his handsome face, she gave him a sad smile. "Let's ride, cowboy. We need to bring this one home."

"I wanted to make love to you here."

"And you will. But today we need to put the ghosts to rest and get the grieving done." Hannah was taking her Granny's advice and holding on with both hands. Matt was hers; now she needed to keep him.

He didn't say a word but he stood there for a few minutes, staring into the water. She held her breath while her heart did a funny pittypat, until he hopped on Winston and kneed the horse into action. The ride home was somber but Hannah was determined to make this step.

When they got to the tree, she wasn't surprised to see two bunches of wildflowers on the simple graves. The brothers and sisters obviously took care of them, kept them well swept and let their parents know they loved them and missed them.

Hannah dismounted with less grace than Matt, but on her own this time. She knelt down between the graves. "Hello, Mr. and Mrs. Graham. You don't know me but I'm Matt's wife. I'm sorry I didn't know you, but I feel like I do through your children. Thank you for raising such a bunch of amazing folks. I promise to always love Matt and give him my heart and soul. You can tell God I said thank you for bringing him to me."

She rose and glanced up at Matt, who still sat in the saddle. "You're going to have to get down here to make it work."

"I can't." His jaw was tight enough to make his skin twitch.

"You can and you will." She held up her arms. "I'll catch you. Trust me."

The corner of his mouth went up a smidge. "You're a stubborn woman, Hannah Graham."

"I'm trying." She waited, hoping against hope he would do what he needed to.

Matt finally dismounted and took her hand. She didn't comment on the fact it was shaking or that his palm was clammy. She just walked him over to the graves and knelt next to him.

It took another few minutes and quite a few deep breaths before Matt started talking.

"Ma, Pa, I feel kind of silly doing this. I know you didn't want to leave us, but the man responsible is in the law's hands now. I won't give up on finding Benjy though. I promise." He let out another loud breath. "I miss you and I hope you can be proud of what I've done, what I'll do, and I sure hope you like Hannah. We'll name your grandchildren after both of you." Matt's voice cracked and she tightened her grip on his hand.

His breathing became ragged and she just held on, waiting. Out of the corner of her eye, she saw tears sliding down his cheeks, so she turned and pulled him into her arms. The dam within him must have finally burst as Matt buried his face in her neck. Safe in her embrace, Matt wept and finally grieved for those he'd lost.

It was after midnight when Hannah went in search of her husband. Once he had let his feelings out, he'd returned to the graves twice already, telling his parents this and that. It was good for him, but he needed rest. And she needed him.

Hannah spotted a light in the barn and walked over.

When she walked through the open door, she found Matt hanging up some tack on the nails on the wall. His expression was full of guilt.

"Is it late?"

"Very." She leaned against the door. "You missed supper."

"I needed to work." He pushed back his hat and squeezed his nose. "I didn't mean to be so late though."

"It's all right. You must be hungry." She wrapped her arms around his waist and pressed her forehead against his chest. "You certainly smell like you've been working."

He chuckled and pulled her close. "I can always count on you to tell me I smell."

"I'm sorry." Her voice was muffled against his shirt.

"I know somewhere I can get clean and we can, ah, get close."

She looked up at him with a grin, her heart already starting to pick up. "The pond?"

"The pond."

"It's awful dark out. Won't it be dangerous?" The last thing they needed was another injury. Both of them were still recovering from the last ones.

"We'll ride Winston at a nice slow walk. The moon is bright and I know the way like the back of my hand." He kissed her hard. "Trust me."

"I do." She reached out and cupped his cock.

He groaned and hardened within seconds. "I can't ride with that thing in my trousers."

"Then it should ride in my trousers." Hannah couldn't believe she'd said that, but now that she had, she laughed at her own bawdiness.

"I don't know if I can make it to the pond either." Matt took the lantern and turned the wick down until it was just a glimmer of light. "I have a blanket and a clean stall."

"I'd go anywhere with you, Matt." Hannah meant every word. She had started out a lonely woman and was now a woman loved by her husband, with a family she could love in return.

He took her hand and led her to the back of the barn, to the stall with all the hay bales stacked in it. Hannah watched as he shut the door behind them and hung the lantern on the hook. Matt's eyes glowed in the meager light.

"Now what?"

"Now we get naughty." He reached for her buttons at the same time she reached for his. The rest of their clothes disappeared quickly. Soon they were both naked and their discarded clothing made a nice blanket on the hay.

She sat down on the pile closest to her and found Matt's cock directly in front of her. Without thinking about what she was doing, Hannah took him in her mouth. He was hot, hard, and salty in her mouth.

"Oh God." His breathing became irregular. "What are you doing?"

"Making you feel good." She licked at him as she would a sweet treat, finding her own body warming up quickly by giving him pleasure.

"You've got quite a tongue."

She would have thanked him but her tongue was busy sliding up and down his staff. Hannah had no idea what she was doing but it had felt good when he had licked her so she was just following her instincts. His cock pulsed in her hand, the base of it so thick she couldn't wrap her fingers completely around it.

A rush of power went through her as she made a grown man tremble at her touch. She tasted him with each pass of her mouth. He tasted of man, of love, and of passion. Hannah could definitely get used to pleasuring him with her mouth. The throbbing began low and deep inside her, as she felt his excitement build. His thighs grew taut and he thrust into her mouth.

"You need to stop, Hannah." He tugged gently on her hair. "I don't want to finish before you even start."

She wanted to continue licking him, but she was also anxious to be joined with him. This would be their first time since he'd told her he loved her. Their joining would be a consummation of that love.

With one last suck and a lick at his tip, she let him go. He let out a shaky breath and leaned over her.

"Lie back, woman." Although he didn't usually talk to her like that, Hannah found herself liking it.

She found a comfortable spot and did as he bade, the hay crinkling beneath her. The soft sounds of the horses, the chirping of the night creatures, were the only things around them. They were in their own paradise, their little piece of heaven on earth.

Her heart swelled with love as he nudged her entrance. She held his gaze as he pushed inside her, inch by inch. The love in his eyes made her breath catch. When he was fully sheathed inside her, he stopped and took a breath.

"What's wrong?"

He chuckled painfully. "I didn't want to come the second I was inside you."

She reached for his hand and placed it on one breast. "Then keep yourself occupied."

This time he didn't laugh. He smiled, then bent down to take the other breast into his mouth. His tongue swirled around the turgid peak, lapping at one nipple while his hand tweaked the other. She grabbed his behind and pulled until he got the message and started moving.

His was a slow pace, one meant to savor the joining, prolong the pleasure. She closed her eyes and reveled in it, contracting around his cock, pulling him in deeper with each thrust.

He bit her nipple and she gasped, her muscles tightening, so he did it again. It was a trigger, one that sent them both careening toward their peak. Hannah felt it in her toes, traveling upward, and in her breasts, traveling down. The tingles and zings of pleasure moved through her until they all coalesced between her legs.

His mouth found hers in a bruising kiss, one that mimicked what his body was already doing with hers. Her tongue slid against his, warm and slippery.

She scratched at his back, urging him to go faster, harder. He didn't need encouragement as his pace had quickened along with the pulsing inside her. She held on when the explosion began deep within her. Her silent scream of pleasure was meant for him, for her love.

She clenched around him, becoming one with him. He bit her again, this time as he found his own peak. Hannah was transported to the stars, her husband by her side. Her heart stopped as the perfect moment made the world around them pause. Exquisite ecstasy showered down around them.

Hannah trembled with the power of what they'd shared. She had always enjoyed making love with Matt, but this was different. This transcended all of those experiences, and crossed into a sharing of souls. She had found the other half of herself.

"Love you, Matt."

"Love you, Hannah."

They snuggled together, using his shirt as a cover, and slept. Matt and Hannah had found what they'd been searching for all their lives. Love.

Have you tried Emma Lang's other books?

Ruthless Heart

He led her astray, and she never wanted to go back . . .

Sheltered all her life, Eliza Hunter never imagined herself alone in the vast Utah plains, much less trailing a mysterious, rugged man hired to hunt down her beautiful younger sister. Unable to reveal the truth about her pursuit of him, Eliza plays student to his teacher, transforming herself in the process. And when she finds herself sharing the warmth of Grady's campfire, wrapped in his arms, hypnotized by his power, soon she is a naive spinster no more . . .

Grady Wolfe is more than a loner, he's a man forever on the run. With a body and soul finely honed from living off the land, Grady knows he should leave the irresistible woman alone, but she stirs something in him he hasn't felt before. Now he's lost in the woods for the first time in his life—with a dangerous job to do. And no one—not even the luscious Eliza—is going to stop him.

Grady had never met a woman like Eliza, if that was even really her name. She talked like a professor, rode around with twenty pounds of books, and could build a campfire like nobody's business. Yet she was as innocent as a child, had a sad story about a dead husband he didn't believe for a second, and seemed to be waiting for him to invite her along for his hunt.

He snorted at the thought. Grady worked alone, always and for good. There sure as hell was no room for anyone, much less a woman like Eliza.

He had damn well tried his best to shake the woman, but the blue-eyed raven-haired fool wouldn't budge. Truth be told, he was impressed by her bravado, but disgusted by his inability to shake her off his tail the night before. Rather than risk having her do the same thing again, he decided to ride like hell and leave her behind. He should have felt guilty, but he'd left that emotion behind, along with most every other, a long time ago. Grady had a job to complete and that was all that mattered to him.

The only thing he was concerned about was finding the wayward wife he'd been hired to hunt and making sure she regretted leaving her husband, at least for the five seconds she lived after he found her.

Grady learned as a young man just how much he

couldn't trust the fairer sex. His mother had been his teacher, and he'd been a very astute pupil. No doubt if she hadn't drank herself to death, she'd still be out there somewhere taking advantage of and using men as she saw fit.

The cool morning air gave way to warm sunshine within a few hours. He refused to think about what the schoolmarm was doing, or if anything had been done to her. If she could take care of her horse and build a fire, she could take care of herself. Food could be gotten at any small town, but then again maybe she could hunt and fish, too.

Somehow it wouldn't surprise him if she did. The woman seemed to have a library in her head. Against his will, the sight of her unbound hair popped into his head. It had been long, past her waist to brush against the nicely curved backside. Grady preferred his women with some meat on their bones, better to hang on to when he had one beneath him, or riding him. He shifted in the saddle as his dick woke up at the thought of Eliza's dark curtain of hair brushing his bare skin.

Jesus Christ, he sure didn't need to be thinking about fucking the wayward Miss Eliza. If she was a widow, no doubt she'd had experience in bed with a man. It wasn't Grady's business of course, so he needed to stop his brain from getting into her bloomers, or any parts of her anatomy.

As the morning wore on, Grady's mind returned to the contents of her bags. The woman didn't have a lick of common sense and fell asleep, vulnerable and unprotected. Good thing he didn't have any bad thoughts on his mind or she wouldn't have been sleeping. She even snored a little, something he found highly amusing as he'd rifled through her things.

Her smaller bag had contained a hodgepodge of clothes, each uglier and frumpier than the last, a hairbrush, half a dozen biscuits in a tattered napkin, and some hairpins. A measly collection of a woman's life, and quite pitiful if that was all she had. Perhaps she'd been at least partially truthful about taking everything she owned and hitting the trail. Her husband must have been a poor excuse for a provider if this collection of rags was all she had.

The bag of books was just that, a bag stuffed full of scientific texts ranging from medical topics to some titles he couldn't even pronounce. In the bottom of the bag was a battered copy of *Wuthering Heights*. He didn't know what it was, but it was much smaller than the other books, likely a novel. She obviously put the spectacles to good use judging by the two dozen tomes she had in her bag. He wondered how she'd gotten it up on the saddle in the first place.

"Fool." He had to stop thinking about Eliza and what she was doing and why. Grady would never see her again.

As a child, Grady learned very early not to care or ask questions. It only bought him a cuff on the ear or a boot in the ass. A boy could only take so much of that before he kept his mouth shut and simply snuck around to find out what he needed to know.

As a young man, it served him well and garnered the attention of the man who taught him how to hunt and kill people in the quickest, most efficient way. Grady had learned his lesson well, even better than his mentor expected. When the job was put before him to hunt and kill the very man who had taught him those skills, Grady hesitated only a minute before he said yes.

The devil rode on his back, a constant companion he'd come to accept. He didn't need a woman riding there, too.

Restless Heart

He craved her like the earth craved the rain . . .

Sam Carver had the kind of body that turned a woman's head, and the kind of eyes that had seen more than his share of trouble. But he couldn't get enough of the mysterious, ethereal beauty who had showed up in his little Wyoming town, working at the Blue Plate, keeping to herself.

He knew Angeline Hunter was running scared, pursued by a fanatic who threatened her life. But no matter what it took, Sam would convince his angel to put her trust in him, to put the painful past behind her and learn just how pleasurable the present could be. . . .

"Your beau is here."

Angeline stopped in mid-motion. "Excuse me?"

"Your beau is here. Samuel Carver is here for dinner and I would swear he's spiffed up for it." Alice grinned widely. "He's ordered the ham and potatoes, with apple pie. Do you want to serve him?"

"No, I do not." Angeline felt her nervousness returning and silently cursed Alice for her silly enthusiasm.

"Oh, why not? He asked for you." She waggled her eyebrows. "He might not be rich, but he sure is sweet." With a cheeky grin, she took the plate and left the kitchen.

"You might as well talk to him. Don't listen to Alice prattle on about him being a half-breed. He's a good boy, no matter who his mother was." Marta put ham on another plate. This time it was for Samuel Carver. "If you hide in here, it will make it worse."

Angeline knew she was right. The longer she hemmed and hawed about the gift and the man, the worse it would be. She needed to tell him there could be no future between them.

With a firm spine, she put potatoes on the plate to accompany the ham and nodded to Marta. "I'll be right back."

Angeline stepped into the restaurant and looked around.

There were a number of people at tables, but she had no idea what the man looked like. Alice's silly description meant nothing except that he was a man. As if she'd conjured the waitress, Alice appeared next to a man sitting in front of the bay window. She pointed and winked at Angeline.

Now she really was uncomfortable, because Alice had no tact or consideration for other people. The man looked up and saw Angeline standing there.

The ground shifted beneath her.

His hair was the color of midnight, so dark it was nearly blue-black. It hung straight to his shoulders, too long to be fashionable. The ends curled up slightly as if a breeze had come through and ruffled it. His shoulders were wide, but not overly so.

He had an intense stare that made goose bumps crawl over her skin. His eyes were also darker than pitch, black pools that seemed to be bottomless. To her surprise, his skin was lightly tanned, with tiny laugh lines around his eyes and mouth. He could be any age, but she knew him to be twenty-nine. He had the demeanor of a man who had seen too much in his short life.

The bright blue of his shirt contrasted so much with the rest of him, she had to blink to absorb it all. He was a striking man, not classically handsome but fascinating.

Angeline did not ever remember seeing him before, which wasn't surprising because she worked in the kitchen most days.

She managed to swallow, somehow, before she stepped toward his table with her heart firmly lodged in her throat. He watched her with wide eyes, unsmiling and unthreatening. She couldn't have explained it to anyone, but Marta had been right—Samuel Carver was no threat to her.

"Good afternoon, Miss Hunter." His voice had a lilt to

it, one she'd never heard before. It was like warm honey on a piece of toast.

Angeline thought perhaps she would be embarrassed by her reaction, but she wasn't. "Good afternoon, Mr. Carver." At least she set the plate down on the table without dropping it.

He smiled. "I hope you're enjoying the book."

She licked her lips and managed a small smile. "I've never had a new book before. I-I wanted to say thank you, but it's much too extravagant for me to accept.?

There, that sounded reasonable and intelligent. He, however, shook his head.

"I can't take it back."

"Please, it must have cost you a lot of money." She put her hands in her apron pockets and clenched them into fists, her right hand pressed up against the book. "It's not appropriate for me to accept it."

He hadn't even glanced at the plate. His gaze was locked on hers. "I know it was forward of me, but I saw you reading on the back steps one day. You seemed to be at peace with a book in your hands."

Angeline unwillingly nodded. "Yes, that's exactly it. It's almost as if the books give me peace."

This time when he smiled, she found herself smiling back. The situation had gotten complicated in less than five minutes.

"I feel the same way about books. So please accept the gift from a fellow reader. It's nothing more."

She was torn between what she had to do and what she wanted to do. Angeline could not become attached or involved with any man, regardless of her silly heart's reaction to him. It didn't make it any easier to conjure up every other reason why she needed to keep her distance from him.